SLIPPERS AND THIEVES
SPECIAL EDITION

BOOK 4 OF THE FAIRY TALES OF THE MAGICORUM

CHRISTINA BAUER

COPYRIGHT

Monster House Books
Newton, MA 02464
ISBN 9781945723872
Second Edition

CONTENTS

DEDICATION

**For All Those Who Kick Ass, Take Names,
and Read Books**

COLLECTED WORKS

Fairy Tales of the Magicorum
Modern fairy tales with sass, action, and romance
1. Wolves and Roses
2. Moonlight and Midtown
3. Shifters and Glyphs
4. Slippers and Thieves
5. Bandits and Ball Gowns
6. Fire and Cinder
7. Fairies and Frosting
8. Towers and Tithes
9. Mirrors and Mysteries

Angelbound Origins
About a quasi (part demon and part human) girl who loves kicking butt in Purgatory's Arena
1. Angelbound
2. Scala
3. Acca
4. Thrax
5. The Dark Lands
6. The Brutal Time
7. Armageddon
8. Quasi Redux

9. Clockwork Igni
10. Lady Reaper
11. Angry Gods
12. Phantom Corsair

Angelbound Lincoln

The Angelbound experience as told by Prince Lincoln
1. Duty Bound
2. Lincoln
3. Trickster
4. Baculum
5. Angelfire
6. Rixa
7. Mordred

Angelbound Offspring

The next generation takes on Heaven, Hell, and everything in between
1. Maxon
2. Portia
3. Zinnia
4. Rhodes
5. Kaps
6. Mack
7. Huntress
8. Gage
* This is a completed series.

Angelbound Xavier

Xavier's story
1. Archenemy
2. Archnemesis
3. Archangel

Pixieland Diaries

Sassy pixie Calla loves elf prince Dare. Too bad he hasn't noticed her. Yet.
1. Pixieland Diaries

2. Calla

3. Dare

4. Winter Prince

5. Ley Queen

This is a completed series.

Dimension Drift

Dystopian adventures with science, snark, and hot aliens

1. Scythe

2. Umbra

3. Alien Minds

4. ECHO Academy

This is a completed series.

Beholder

Where a medieval farm girl discovers necromancy and true love

1. Cursed

2. Concealed

3. Cherished

4. Crowned

5. Cradled

This is a completed series.

SLIPPERS AND THIEVES

SLIPPERS AND THIEVES

FAIRY TALES OF THE MAGICORUM • BOOK 4

CHRISTINA BAUER

Years Ago

1. CHAPTER ONE

ELLE - AGE FIFTEEN

*F*irst, homework.
Then, jewel heist.
Oh, yeah.

Rubbing my eyes, I refocus on my computer screen. A final study question appears.

> *SUN is to BRIGHTNESS as MAGIC is to...*
> *a) casting*
> *b) eternity*
> *c) fading*

I click on *c) fading.* A green checkmark appears on screen.
Nailed it. Yay, me!

Not that my final question was super-tough to answer or anything. Everyone's aware that magic is disappearing from the world. Shifters, fairies, and casters—folks called the Magicorum— are basically an endangered species. I should know. I'm one of them. In my case, my father's a caster while my mother's a fairy.

A knock sounds on the door. "Elle, may I come in?" That's Mom.
"Sure."

The door swings open; Mom steps inside. She's willowy and petite with large blue eyes and long blonde hair. My heart sinks.

Mom's shoulder bones jut out against the straps of her yellow sundress. She's getting more skeleton-like by the day. Meanwhile, I'm a younger and healthier version of her. I can't help feeling a little guilty about that.

"How are you?" My voice wobbles as I ask the question.

"Better and better." Mom waves me off. "Is your homework done?"

Once again, Mom veers the conversation away from her illness. In Mom's mind, if you don't talk about being sick, then it isn't happening. And today, like most days, I don't have the heart to bust up her system. If Mom says she's better, then I won't push it. After all, we've tried tons of healers. Plus, we live in New York City, home of the best cancer treatment centers ever. Nothing has made a difference.

I plaster on a fake smile. "Almost finished here."

Mom closes the door behind her. I frown. *Closed-door chats* are never good.

"I wanted to talk alone," says Mom. "You see, Marchesa's daughters are the same age as you." She twists her fingers together at her waistline. "Both Agatha and Ivy love their high school. They're meeting all sorts of new people."

In this case, Marchesa refers to my mother's lifelong *frenemy*, Lady Marchesa Oakwood. Lately, Marchesa has been sharing *supposedly* helpful tidbits about her daughters. Sadly, the stories only make Mom feel like she's failing me. A protective urge runs up my spine. Marchesa's supposed to run our family store, not load Mom with worry.

"Agatha and Ivy aren't me." I tap my chest. "Here's one girl who likes online stuff."

"But this is your parents' office." Mom frowns. "It's not a regular classroom."

"Come on. This is a seriously cool spot." *And I mean it.* The office is small with red brick walls. There's even a great view of Second Avenue.

Mom still looks concerned, so I go on. "Hey, I get the deal."

There's no need to explain more.

In this case, *the deal* is the fact that I'm the warden of all fae magic.

It means I'm super-powered, which is certainly nice. But fae aren't like other Magicorum. While shifters and casters worship their wardens, the fae kill theirs. That's why I take online classes and generally avoid new people. My full-time job is pretending to be a *blah* fairy.

Mom's face brightens. "I'm glad you understand the, uh, deal."

I raise my pointer finger. "Now I must tell you—"

"If it's about Marchesa, please don't say a word. She's a good friend."

"Who upsets you all the time." I raise my hands, palms forward. "Just saying."

"Marchesa's heart is in the right place. Don't forget how her husband, Marshall, ran off right after Agatha was born."

A nasty part of me thinks, *maybe Marshall escaped because Marchesa is a horror show? Or because his daughter just got named Agatha?* But I keep that bit to myself.

Mom sighs. "Then Marshall died in Amsterdam."

Saying it that way, and it doesn't sound too bad. But in reality? Marshall was a kind of caster called a *potion master*. He enjoyed poisoning his imagined enemies until, one day, he drank his own toxic brew by mistake. Hard to feel sorry for a guy like that.

"At least we never got on his bad side," I state.

Mom shoots me a serious look, but it doesn't last long. "True." She smiles. "And you're absolutely fine with online classes?"

"Do you *really* think I'd keep my yap shut otherwise?"

Mom chuckles. "No, I don't."

"Then we're both good, right?" In my heart, I want *everything* to be good, not just conversations about online classes. That's not possible, though.

"We're better than good," replies Mom. "We're great." She heads for the door and pauses. "Your father and I will work the store this morning." On reflex, Mom looks to the carpet. Which makes sense, considering how our family store is located on the building's first floor, right under this office. "Give us a yell if you need anything."

"I will."

Long after Mom's left, I still watch the closed door. With every passing second, a weight of worry settles more deeply into my soul.

All members of the Magicorum get pulled into a fairy tale life template. Mine's Cinderella. So I can't help but notice some facts.

Fact one. Marchesa has two nasty daughters who are my age.

Fact two. Marchesa also stares at Dad with googly eyes that make me want to puke.

Fact three. Mom has been sick for a really long time.

I've seen the Disney movie here. In short order, I'm heading into the *not too pleasant phase* of the Cinderella tale. This is the part where my parents are gone and I'm stuck with a frenemy stepmother who names her kid Agatha. Other Cinderellas may sing at their window and hope for the best.

Me? I've got a plan.

Which leads to the best part of my day: the jewel heist.

2. CHAPTER TWO

ELLE

*R*efocusing on my computer, I fire up Magiweb, which is the secret internet for our kind. Scanning through message boards, I look for lost valuables. My goal? Find stolen jewels that I can return for a reward. I've been saving up for the *evil step-mother-n-sisters* stage of my life. Becoming a servant in my own house? Not an option.

I flip through the best boards for lost jewels.

JewelFinders.magic
WheresMyStuff.fae
VampLost.shadowcoe

Each site is the same—there are no new listings. So I check some web chats. A particular conversation catches my eye.

GemBabe1000 - Any new bounty jewels out there?
HuntAndFound - Nothing. Only Q of H crown in TP-CP

In regular speak, *TP-CP* means the Turtle Pond in Central Park. And the *Q of H* stuff? That's the Queen of Hearts. She's part fae. Part Vampire. All badass.

Here's the deal. The Queen of Hearts is so powerful, people are always asking for her help. The good news is that the queen can do almost anything. The bad news is that she may develop an unhealthy interest in your love life along the way. I'd never ask her for help. But reaping a reward? Count me in.

> *GemBabe1000 - How long has that crown been sunk*
> *HuntAndFound - 100s of yrs*
> *GemBabe1000 - No one will ever go after that thing*

I rub my palms together. *Ha! I am SO going after that crown.*

After shutting off my computer, I head downstairs. Once there, I speed through the warehouse part of the first floor. It's a maze of metal shelves crammed with boxes of stuff. Soon I reach the building's front ... and a wooden door with a small window.

The entrance to Cynder Mercantile.

I enter the room. Sure enough, my parents stand inside. The shop itself is a small wooden space lined with fancy shelves, all of them overflowing with hand-made stuff, like blown glass bowls, lace doilies, or carved statuettes. The artists who make these pieces live on the upper levels of our building.

The radio plays a song, *Do You Believe In Magic?* It's an ancient and corny tune, but my parents sway in sync as they stock the shelves. So sweet.

An itchy feeling crawls up my neck. *Someone's watching us.* I look backward and sure enough, Marchesa stares at Dad through the little window in the warehouse door. Marchesa's a tall lady with loops of brown hair that are piled high atop her head. In my opinion, she always looks like someone just offered her a small turd to eat. Right now, that regular poop-look combines with a longing stare in Dad's direction.

Ick, ick, ick.

I take care to step into her line of sight, blocking any view of Dad. *Take that, creepster.*

"Hey," I call. "You guys need any help?"

Dad spins around and grins. "Hey, yourself." My father is handsome in an earthy way with his brown hair, strong build and easy smile. I can almost picture Marchesa craning her neck for a better view.

"How's my Ellie Belly?" Dad asks.

I mock-gasp. "You did *not* say that."

"You were such a chubby baby, what else could I call you?"

I roll my eyes. "Elle?"

"Come here and give your old man a hug."

So I do. Dad gives the best hugs; they're always full of love and warmth. That's just how Declan Cynder is in general. My father's a giving type of person. In fact, Dad founded Cynder Mercantile to help desperate artists from the magical world. Meanwhile, the rest of his life centers on me and Mom. It's a pretty awesome set-up.

Mom stares pointedly at my purse. "Where are you off to?"

"A walk in central park." I'm wearing jeans, Doc Martens, and a Disney Princesses T-shirt. Therefore, my *morning stroll* story is totally believable, if I do say so myself.

Dad frowns. "Are you sure it's safe to go alone?"

"I'm a careful girl," I reply. "I just want some air." *And a crown.*

My parents share a long stare before Mom focuses on me again. "It's fine. Bring your phone and be back by lunch."

"You got it. Thanks!"

And with that, I'm off to find the Queen of Hearts' crown. Afterward, there will be a major reward in store for me. And goodness knows, I need it.

This is one Cinderella life template who's kicking butt and taking charge.

3. CHAPTER THREE

ALEC - AGE FIFTEEN

J loiter before a construction site on Manhattan's Upper West Side. A sign on the chain-link fence reads, *Coming Soon: the L Center.*

Reporter Rosa Langstrom stands beside the wooden placard. She smacks her lips and smoothes her short black hair. "Ready to shoot?" she asks her cameraman.

"One sec," says the guy.

I'd keep walking, but the L Center stands for the Le Charme Center and I'm none other than Alec Le Charme. Color me curious.

"Ready," says the guy.

Rosa grins for the camera. "For seven years now, New Yorkers have seen this sign." She gestures toward the placard behind her. "The L Center is notorious for constantly being under construction. In fact, there have been no less than four complete rebuilds of this place. It's a strange legacy for what's arguably the most famous jewelry company in the world, Le Charme. But here at the Magicorum News Network, we've uncovered inside information that this eternal construction site may actually be finished soon. Why? There's one simple reason. Alec Le Charme."

Called it.

Is it strange that I'm standing on the sidewalk while a reporter does a story on me? Not too odd. Plus, I'm a pro at hiding in plain sight. I wear a baseball cap, sunglasses, and jeans. More importantly, I slump while keeping a blank face. It's a skill.

Rosa goes on. "Le Charme Jewelers was founded in 1643 by the famous gem caster, Charles Le Charme. For any of you living under a rock, casters—meaning witches and wizards—are part of the Magicorum. As a gem caster, Charles was the perfect man to start a jewelry company. All the Le Charmes follow a Cinderella life template. The first-born son always has a Glass Slipper Ball during his eighteenth year. It's when he chooses his wife."

I fight the urge to roll my eyes. For centuries, the oldest sons in my family have been marrying someone they meet at their Glass Slipper Ball. That behavior ends with me.

Rosa continues. "As everyone knows, Diamond and Legend Le Charme have one child, their fifteen-year-old son, Alec. His eighteenth birthday ball will be here before we know it. And that's a big reason to finish this construction. You heard it first here, folks. Now in other Magicorum news… a new season of Real Warlocks of Manhattan has just been given the green light…"

While the reporter keeps talking, I join the pace of foot traffic on the sidewalk. Soon, I approach the back gate to the construction site itself. There I find a familiar mini house that holds Gerry, our wrinkly guard. Like always, Gerry watches a small black and white television.

I pause before the window. "Hello."

Gerry smacks his lips. Without making eye contact, he points toward the small tray under the Plexiglas window. "Identification." I slide my company key card over. Gerry picks up the card and chuckles. "You sneak up on me every time."

"It's my superpower." Gerry slides my ID back; I scoop it from the tray. "Is Legend here yet?" Some parents are called Mom and Dad. Mine are always Diamond and Legend.

"Arrived a few minutes ago," answers Gerry. He bats at a little bobblehead Yankees figure on his tabletop. As behavior goes, it's a little weird, but that's Gerry.

I scan the deserted construction site. "Any word on the crew coming back?"

"Not that I've seen."

"Right."

I set my hands into the pockets of my baseball-style jacket, march onto the backlot, and wonder. Could that newscaster be right? Is construction starting up again? If so, it wouldn't the first time the L Center was reimagined. Legend regularly drags me here to share his latest schemes. All of which leads to one question.

What's Legend up to this time?

4 . CHAPTER FOUR

ALEC

$\mathcal{M}$inutes later, I step through a long and rectangular space that's made from concrete. My father waits in the center of the chamber. Like always, Legend is all blond hair, blue eyes, and irresistible charm that's wrapped in an Armani suit. I'm a younger version of Legend, only in jeans. If I think about it too much, that fact is more than a little creepy.

Legend throws his arms open wide. "Alec!"

"Hey, Legend."

"Can you see it? This place will soon become the main studio for the Le Charme Lady Extravaganza!"

I knew the L Center would have a hotel, restaurants, and shops. That's it, though.

"Did you just say studio?" I ask.

"It's my new plan. Obviously, you'll have your Glass Slipper Ball here when you're eighteen." Legend shoots me a sly grin. "Which is when you'll find a bride."

"Maybe." We have this discussion regularly. Legend and I have agreed to disagree.

"Until then, we'll hold an annual event right in this studio. Each year, we'll award some young woman the title of Le Charme Lady."

I frown. "We do that already. I'd hardly call it an event, though. It's more of a dinner."

"But that's what's changing. We'll transform that dinner into a massive extravaganza. And it will be held right here, along with a big audience and cameras. So I'll ask you again. Can you see it?"

I step around in a slow circle. There's a lot of concrete, open steel beams, and piles of lumber. Previous plans had this space being built out into a series of bowling alleys. I kick a nail across the floor. "Not really."

"Bah! The new Le Charme Lady Extravaganza will become the greatest event ever. The Oscars? Emmies? They'll be seen as nothing compared to the Le Charme Lady Extravaganza."

Tilting my head, I contemplate the new idea. "And this helps us sell jewelry ... how?"

"Branding, my son. Branding."

"Sure." I try moving the conversation onto more solid ground. "Did you see the pics I sent? Tiffany's has a new line of silver necklaces. Maybe we should put some money into designing stuff like that. I mean, the Le Charme catalog still includes crowns. We're in desperate need of some updates."

"You're so literal, Alec. Try to see the big picture." Legend snaps his fingers. "I've got it." He rushes over to a nearby wall. There, my father pulls paper off a tall object. Turns out, it's a mirror. "I'll let none other than Charles Le Charme explain things to you directly."

My eyes widen. Charles Le Charme is my forebear and the original founder of Le Charme Jewelers. Somehow, Charles wrangled himself a home in the Faerie Lands. Essentially, it makes him immortal. "How did Charles get his own magic mirror?"

"It's not a mirror," corrects Legend. "This is a portal from the human world directly into Charles' home in the Faerie Lands. He's agreed to visit Earth once a year for the Le Charme Lady Extravaganza. The press will go insane!"

A figure appears in the mirror. It's a man with a high wig and long blue coat. He looks like he could have stepped out of the Versailles court of Louis the Sun King, mostly because he actually did. No doubt about it. This is Charles Le Charme.

Charles steps through the mirror. One second, he's an image. The next, he's a living guy. He rounds on my father and beams. "Legend!"

"Charles!" They share a long and inexplicable laugh. Legend gestures in my direction. "Explain to my son about our plans."

"Surely." Charles points to a short wall of the long and rectangular space. "We'll build a great stage over there. Imagine a winding staircase that loops down from the rafters. That's where the contestants will walk down."

I tilt my head. "So they're contestants now."

"Of course!" Charles continues. "On stage left, we'll have the Queen of Hearts. There will be an empty spotlight on the right—that will be for you. And in the center will stand the Master of Ceremonies. Me."

Legend nods toward a stretch of the floor just before the imaginary stage. "Your mother and I will be on a judges panel. Our table will be down here. We'll ask questions of each contestant."

"Are you with me?" asks Charles. "Got the layout?"

"Basically." What I'm having trouble with is how Charles talks like he's younger than I am. But that's living the Faerie Lands for you. It messes with your brain.

"Here's how the event will actually work," says Charles. "The contestants will step down the staircase. Behind them, a video will play of their lives. Once the lady in question reaches the main stage, I'll say something charming." He pauses, waiting for a comment.

"Wow," I say.

"It will be stunning!" cries Legend.

"Once I'm done, your family will ask some questions. That will go on until we've met all the contestants. Then, in the end, the ladies will return for one final moment. You."

"Me." *I hate this idea.*

"You!" yells Legend. I've never seen my father this worked up.

Charles continues. "Yes, you step on stage and … drumroll! Who will Alec Le Charme ask to be the next Le Charme Lady?"

A foul taste fills my mouth. "I hate this idea. I'm no reward."

"You're simply giving out the title," says Legend. "We have sponsorships lined up for these ladies. I'm talking clothing, toys, energy drinks, you name it. The Le Charme Lady will become a wealthy woman."

I've heard my father's plans before. Legend builds up new ideas—

along with parts of the L Center—and then tears them all down again. But this is the first time Legend has gotten our founder out of retirement. I tap my chin and think things through. There's one big question here.

"Has the Queen of Hearts agreed?" I ask.

Charles bobs his bows. "I can handle her. We made a bet years ago. I'm winning. That means I get what I want out of her." Charles turns to Legend. "Which reminds me. What are we doing for Alec's Glass Slipper Ball?"

I fold my arms over my chest. "I'm not having one."

Charles pales. "What?"

"That's what the boy *believes*," explains Legend. "We've agreed to disagree for now. And years remain before he's eighteen."

Charles lowers his voice to a whisper. It's an odd choice, considering how I'm standing right here and can catch every word. "You've got some strength in terms of *mind vise* spells. Just make it happen."

Legend stiffens. "This is my son."

I appreciate my father's statement, by the way. Gem casters develop specialties. Legend knows how to control other people's minds. It's not a pleasant process, either. All the more reason why I'm ticked off that Charles even raises the possibility.

I focus on Charles. "Do you know who I am?"

"A spoiled child?" asks Charles.

"I'm the warden of all caster magic. I develop my own gems and spells. That means I'm no one you can bully."

Charles fluffs his already-puffy collar. "Whatever you say. Just be ready when we hold the first Le Charme Lady Extravaganza in six weeks."

Calculations spin through my mind. "That will mean tons of overtime work for construction. Can we really afford it?"

"Just use magic," says Charles.

I shoot Charles a warning look. "You haven't been on Earth in a while. The MITRE agency tracks the use of magic in human affairs. We can get in big trouble if we do this with spells. Humans expect fair competition. We pay workers in cash, not cheat with magic. It's why humans see us as celebrities *and not threats*. We need to keep it that way."

"Don't worry about MITRE," says Charles. "If you do as Legend and I dictate, then we *may* give you the option *not* to marry at your Glass Slipper Ball."

"That's not your option to give."

Legend gasps. "Alec!"

Charles frowns. "I disagree, mon petit chou."

Sadly enough, Charles may be right. I can't ignore the fact that no fewer than twelve Le Charme sons have gotten married at their Glass Slipper Balls, including my father.

All of which is why I spend my spare time developing fresh gems and spells. I refuse to be forced into anything. When I marry, it will be because I love someone with all my heart, end of story.

5. CHAPTER FIVE

ELLE

*L*eaving Cynder Mercantile behind, I high tail it to Central Park. Soon I reach the Turtle Pond. It's still pretty early, so no one's here yet. This is what's so cool about Central Park, by the way. It's actually a lot of little parks. Places like this pond feel all cozy and deserted.

Or in my case, safe to cast a spell.

Closing my eyes, I pull on the fae power within me. Mom and I are *swarm fae*. It means we can make creatures group up and do stuff. For instance, I could inspire a bunch of mice to clean the floors. Don't get too excited, though. Mice suck at housework.

Which brings me back to the present moment. What I need now is some turtle-shaped assistance.

A haze of silver light materializes over my right palm. *Yes!* The spell is starting. I command the magic into the water while I think through my desire.

Come to me. Aid me.

Tiny glistening particles of fairy dust tumble off my hand and onto the still pond. Moments pass. The nearby trees rustle in the morning breeze. The low murmur of far-off voices and car horns seems to turn deafeningly loud.

At last, a dozen turtles pop their heads above the water. The largest speaks in a rumbly voice. "I am Ironshell."

I grin. I can't really practice my fae magic—that could blow my cover—so I wasn't sure this spell would work. And when I do cast swarm spells, it's either on mice or pigeons. Turtles are a new one for me.

"Nice to meet you." I wave. "I'm Elle."

"You require our help?"

"Yes, there's a crown at the bottom of the pond. I'd like you to bring it to me, if you don't mind." Fact is, my magic could just force the turtles to help out. But I like to be polite. Also, you never know who's actually an evil wizard enchanted to be a tortoise or something.

"What?" Ironshell gives me one of those shocked turtle faces where he gulps for air. "You mean the Queen of Hearts' crown?"

"That's the one."

"Are you certain? There are many kinds of fae in the Faerie Lands, such as pixies, sprites, fairies, and elves."

"Don't forget the shadowcoe," adds another turtle.

"That's right," confirms Ironshell. "Trolls, vampires, and dwarves are all natives of the Faerie Lands as well. Yet none of them is more dangerous than the Queen of Hearts."

"And no reward will be better, am I right?"

"Possibly."

"Definitely. I'm not leaving here without the crown." I could try to enchant the thing out of the pool, but that would involve using my father's magic. Which I've never so much as touched. "I really need your help here."

"As you command." Ironshell pops under the water; his other buddies follow. A long minute ticks by. The surface of the pond churns as the turtles do their thing.

Splash!

A blob of brown goop breaks through the water's surface to land beside my feet with a plop. Within all the slime, I make out the gleam of rubies.

So far, so good.

Kneeling down, I pull on my fae magic once more. This time, the silver dust cascades from my hand to cover the blob of goo. Wherever the magic touches, the scummy bits melt away. Seconds later, there's only a tall crown that's covered in rubies. A giant heart-shaped gem marks the front.

"You better run on now," says Ironshell. "It is not safe to carry such jewels."

I chuckle. It's far less safe for a fairy warden to openly use her magic, but there's no way I'm volunteering that fact out loud. I slip the crown into my purse. It's a tight fit, but it works.

"Thank you, Ironshell."

"Be safe, Elle." With that, my new buddy vanishes under the water once more. I check my watch. That only took twenty minutes. This morning's so-called *walk in the park* is going great.

From here, it's a short hike to Central Park's Belvedere Castle. It's a small structure made of gray stone that sits atop a low hill.

And it's where the Queen of Hearts keeps court.

6. CHAPTER SIX

ELLE

*a*s I close in on Belvedere Castle, I pull on my powers of fae sight. For me, this is much less dangerous than casting an actual spell. Even the least powerful fairy can see the truth of the world around them. And what do we view?

A Faerie Land reality that overlaps with the human one.

Scanning the world around me, I call to its parallel fae nature. Flecks of silver light gleam in my eyes. My powers come to life.

Everything changes.

The thin walkway beneath my feet overlaps with another image: a grand street made of white stone. The woods of Central Park flicker between their regular brown trunks and green branches … into tall white trees with red, heart-shaped leaves. The small structure of Belvedere Castle slowly morphs into a massive palace. Warriors in red armor flank either side of the entrance. These are the queen's infamous Vampire Guard.

As I close in on the palace gate, more of the human world fades away. By the time I'm facing an actual guard, I'm completely inside the Faerie Lands.

"State your name," orders the guard.

"Elle Cynder," I reply.

The guard now does something I didn't expect. He steps backward. "Go on inside. She's expecting you."

My first reaction is shock, but I quickly hide that under a mask of casual confidence. When facing a vampire fairy queen, it's important not to cower.

"Excellent," I state.

The heavy wooden gate swings open, revealing the palace's interior ... as well as a cat.

And this is not just any feline. It's the Cheshire Cat of *Alice in Wonderland* fame. The creature tilts its head. "Hello, Elle."

Turns out, the Cheshire Cat has a deep and rumbly voice. Not what I expected, but on this feline? It totally works.

"Hi, uh..."

"Call me Chesh. It's what everyone does." The cat spins about and saunters into the palace proper. I follow behind and for the first time, I wonder if this is the best idea.

The interior of the palace is all white stone inlaid with red, heart-shaped tiles. Chesh and I enter the receiving room, which holds a vaulted ceiling and tons of courtiers. Everyone dresses in medieval style, like they stepped off a deck of cards.

In the center of the chamber, the Queen of Hearts sits on a red throne that rests atop a raised platform. She's tall and curvy with cocoa skin and long red hair. The folds of her crimson gown roll down the steps leading to her throne. Her red wings flutter as I enter. Everyone quiets.

Uh oh.

I give my best courtesy. "Greetings, your Majesty. My name is Elle and I've brought your—"

"I know why you're here," interrupts the queen. She raises her arm; the crown flies out of my purse to land directly onto her outstretched hand. The queen scans the item as if it were no more than a trinket she found on the street. "Why did you uncover this?"

I shrug. "There's a reward."

"And why would you want that?" The queen grins, and there's no missing the fangs that mark her as a vampire.

"I'm a Cinderella life template. Rewards will come in handy."

"So you're preparing for the worst." The queen narrows her eyes. "You could use magic."

"I'm a fairy without wings. I don't have that much magic. No one does these days."

"I do, but you're right about the rest of the world." The queen scans me slowly from head to toe. "You're curious. Far more than any Alice life templates I've met in ages."

My heart swells with pride. Turns out, it's nice to get complements from a queen. "Thank you."

"Who are your parents?"

"Rae and Declan Cynder."

The queen stands. "Did you say Rae and Declan Cynder?"

I feel like there's a trap in this question, but I can't imagine what it could be. "Yes."

"Oh, this is good. Too, too good. I'll provide your reward, and it's a prophecy."

That trap-feeling grows larger. The queen didn't even cast a spell or anything. "How do you know this prophecy off the top of your head?"

"Believe me, I do. So, do you accept that as your reward?"

Fae are tricky, but something about the gleam in the queen's eyes reminds me of someone. Oh, right. That would be me. The queen is crafty but not evil. At least, not at this very moment. Plus, I've already risked a ton to come over here. What's one more thing?

"Yes, I'd like to hear the prophecy."

"Perfect." The queen slowly retakes her throne. "My vision for you is this. You'll lose your parents and the Lady Marchesa will become your stepmother. Do you disagree?"

"I'm a Cinderella life template. It's not like the thought never crossed my mind." *And Marchesa also has two daughters, let's not forget that part. Totally template-ready.*

"Here's what you do *not* know," adds the queen. "Your stepmother will form an alliance with none other than Legend Le Charme in order to keep you from your true love."

"*The* Legend Le Charme?" I ask. "Of the Le Charme Jewelry fortune? As in the husband of Diamond Le Charme?" I don't know these two personally, obviously. But their faces get plastered on the tabloids at least once a week.

"That's what I said," repeats the queen. "Marchesa and Legend Le Charme."

"So those two will team up and separate me from my true love. And then what?"

The queen sighs. "Then nothing. That's it."

Frustration corkscrews up my back. It may be reckless of me to get angry, but that's a pretty crappy reward. After all, her crown sat at the bottom of a pond for centuries. "You don't have anything else for me?"

Chesh sidles to the top step of the queen's dais. "Curiouser and curiouser," he says.

The queen runs her fingertips down Chesh's back. The cat does that move where he arches his spine and pokes his tail in the air. The queen leans in closer to Chesh. "Elle doesn't know the whole story, does she?"

I raise my hand. "I'm standing right here. Would love the whole story."

Chesh slowly licks his forepaws. "Think of it this way, Elle. The Queen of Hearts fixes problems. Anything. She could clear the way for you and your true love."

The queen grins. "I may even have reasons to want to help you."

"But not for free," adds Chesh.

"Never for free," agrees the queen. "I have a reputation to think of."

"Elle must find something else of value for your Majesty," says Chesh. "It's the only way to secure your aid." Chesh then smiles in a way that makes my stomach sink to my toes. In that moment, one thing becomes absolutely clear.

It's time to leave.

I make my goodbyes and run-walk out of the chamber. And for whatever reason, the Queen of Hearts allows me to go without saying another word.

That might be the most troubling part of all.

7. CHAPTER SEVEN

ALEC - DAYS LATER

I lounge on the couch in my family's penthouse. This is my favorite spot since it sports a fireplace and awesome view of Manhattan. And let's not forget the kick-ass gaming station that's set into one wall.

My buddy Knox is camped out on the same couch, too. We're playing a new game called Magicorum Killers. Humans can pretend they're a shifter, witch, or fairy and then go fight evildoers. It's hilarious, considering how I'm a wizard and Knox is a shifter. We're also wardens of magic, which makes us tops in power for our Magicorum type.

Long story short, there definitely are times when Knox and I must kick some troll butt or whatever. It's just bizarre to see it on screen. And did I mention that I'm seriously losing this game? My skills are way off this afternoon. Not that I'll admit such a thing to Knox.

I shoot my buddy a snide grin. "My controller's broken."

"Is not. I just kicked your ass, fair and square." Knox is tall and ripped, same as me. Early growth spurts go with the whole warden situation. Unlike me, Knox has black hair, heavy brows, and a super-short temper. I'm more of the blond-haired, blue-eyed, and charming type.

"Best out of nine," I counter.

Knox shrugs. "Whatever you say."

Once we restart, I keep screwing up all the electronic spells. It's like my fingers won't move fast enough or something. On-screen, a pack of vampires corners me in short order.

A note on vamps. It's funny how humans know all about the Magicorum, but they're oblivious to trolls, vampires, and the like. Sure, humans sense the danger when a vamp or whatever is near, but that's it. The reason? Those supernatural folks—what we call the shadowcoe—are experts at staying hidden. Good for them.

In the game, I'm finally able to take down the vamps. Still, something feels off. On reflex, I pause everything and look to Knox. A question falls from my mouth. "Do you ever think about our fairy tale life templates?"

One great thing about Knox: when he isn't enraged, my bud is super calm. At this point, anyone else would complain that I stopped the game. Knox stays totally chill.

"Nah," Knox replies. "I think about how to kick Jules' ass, only worse than I'm kicking yours." Jules is the leader of a group of zombie-mummies who murdered Knox's parents.

"Makes sense. Normally, I'm right with you. Unless my parents are going on about my Glass Slipper Ball, I don't think about my life template at all."

Knox tilts his head. The movement reminds me of the massive black wolf he carries inside him. "What's up?"

I debate about lying or restarting the game. Once again, those are my plans. But different words tumble from my mouth, all on their own. "I had this crazy dream last night."

"Was it a dream … or a magical message?"

"Hard to tell. I saw the Queen of Hearts."

Knox's upper lip curls with a look I like to call his *protective growl.* "She's dangerous."

"The queen told me that Legend would one day form an evil alliance to keep me from my true love."

"Huh." Knox purses his lips. "Not a surprise that the Queen of Hearts would get interested in a warden's love life. But Legend forming an evil alliance against *you*?" Knox gives me a look that says, *we both know who he really wants to hurt.*

As if on cue, my father saunters into the room. Legend is all blonde hair, blue eyes, and magnetic charm. Tonight Dad looks like an older surfer in a three-piece suit.

Beside Legend stands my mother, Diamond. She moves with a ballet dancer's grace, mostly because she used to be one. Her long brown hair falls in waves down her back. My mother looks runway-ready, even if she's wearing a sweatsuit, which is what she sports today.

Speaking of Diamond, she rounds on me. "Tell your father that he needs to attend the Le Charme grand opening in New Jersey."

Legend lifts his chin. "Tell your mother that I'll attend when the opening is actually scheduled."

Welcome to the ongoing battle over Le Charme Jewelers that is my parents' existence. Once in a while, I get in the middle of their marital war. Whenever I'm dragged into such a fight, I find it's easiest to put on my mental armor and battle fast.

I look to my mother. "Diamond, he'll go to the opening." Next, I focus on my father. "Legend, she knows you hate Jersey, so don't try to weasel out at the last minute." My gaze flicks between them. "Are we done here?"

Without another word, my parents march off to their separate rooms, slamming doors behind them as they go. Normally, this scene would prompt me to want to punch someone. For some reason, their actions today only remind me of the Queen of Hearts.

I return my focus to Knox. "About that dream."

"What about it?"

"It makes me wonder. My parents both have life templates for the Cinderella story."

"Yeah."

"The queen talked about my true love. That's Cinderella template stuff. But with my parents?" I hitch my thumb in the direction where they marched off. "I don't think they're each other's true loves."

"I get that." Knox itches his neck. It's a move that means he's thinking something through. "Unless you say their one true love isn't a person. It could be Le Charme Jewelers."

Those words are totally foreign and familiar, all at once. "What makes you say that?"

"Because I've known you forever? It's the only thing your parents really care about ... outside of you. I mean, stop me if I'm wrong. I'm just your friendly neighborhood werewolf."

"No, you're not wrong."

"And?" prompts Knox.

I lean back into the couch and admit the awful truth. "I don't want to turn out like them."

"I get that, too."

All of a sudden, it feels like the walls of this spacious penthouse press in around me. "Do you think we're locked into our fairy tale life template?"

Knox bares his teeth. It's the face he makes when disgusted. "Fate ... Fairy tale life templates ... Those are things adults talk about because they screwed up their own lives and want an excuse." Knox fixes me with his most serious stare. "You get what I mean, yeah?"

Nodding, I try to process all this. Are fairy tale templates real? And do my parents truly love Le Charme Jewelers most of all? Good questions. Yet whatever the answer, I meant what I said to Knox.

I do not want to end up like them.

"So." I raise my not-so-broken controller. "Are we playing best of nine or what?"

Knox chuckles. "Prepare to get your ass kicked."

"Maybe." And somehow, it feels like that statement is about far more than this game.

8. CHAPTER EIGHT

ELLE

For a week after my Queen of Hearts adventure, I feel super groggy. Turns out, facing vampire queens is a real energy drain.

Lesson learned.

This morning marks day three of my sleep deprivation fest. I drag my bum out of bed and into the kitchen. It's a neat space with lots of white tile and mint-colored appliances. On the counter, I find an empty coffee cup and bagel crumbs, but no sign of Dad.

Odd. I check the clock.

9:06 AM

Dad's normally cleaned up his dishes and stuff by now. *Huh.* Thuds sound from below. That's where the store is located. Dad must be there. But why?

The truth hits me. Agatha and Ivy were supposed to work the shop this morning. Marchesa thought it would be good for them to have a summer job. Of course, the sisters rarely show up. Dad's probably hustling to cover for them. Customers expect the doors to open at 9 AM.

Time to step in.

After marching downstairs, I make my way through the first-floor warehouse. Sure enough, I find Dad in the store and fiddling with the register. His hair sticks up at odd angles; his T-shirt's on inside-out; and his eyes are totally bloodshot. Long story short, my father's the very definition of the word *frazzled*.

"What's the access code for this thing again?" Dad pounds random numbers onto the register's keyboard.

"Hey there," I say gently. "What's up?"

Dad braces his arms on the countertop. "Your mother had a rough night. I need to open the store."

Part of me wants to ask what he means by saying *rough night*. But Dad needs sleep far more than *question and answer* time.

I step up to the register. "I'll get it."

"You sure?"

"Absolutely."

"Thanks, Ellie Belly." Dad takes off at double speed.

The front door swings open, sending a wave of summer heat into the small space. A woman enters. Everything about this human screams New York, from her fashion model strut to her grey suit, matching heels, and long black hair. An access badge dangles from her pocket that reads, *Ms. Coco Tao, MingMart Inc.* My brows lift. MingMart is *the* new hot retailer in the city.

"Is this Cynder Mercantile?" asks Coco. Living in New York, you get a feel for accents. Hers carries a touch of Mandarin.

"Yes, it is."

By the way, the store's full name is *Cynder Mercantile of Manhattan's Second Avenue.* Not catchy, but my folks are experts in magic, not wordplay.

Coco slowly scans the room. I picture things from her eyes. It's a small wooden space packed with hand-made stuff. Then there's me, a fifteen-year-old whose blonde hair is tied off into pigtails. I stand behind a tall wooden counter wearing pajama bottoms and a hoodie.

Not my best day, fashion-wise.

"Aren't you rather young to be running a store?" asks Coco. "I saw adults in here the other day."

"Those were my parents. And I'm fifteen. That's a legal age to work in New York."

"Ah." She eyes my fuzzy bunny slippers and ... *yeah, I get it.* No matter what the age, I'm not your typical salesgirl.

"Look, it's my parents' place and our regular help is late, so here I am." I'd explain how we live upstairs, but *meh.* This is New York. We don't over-share.

"*Chirp, chirp.*"

My eyes widen. *That can't be ...*

"*Chirp, chirp.*"

It is.

The top two floors of our building are studio spaces. The artists up there make stuff; then we sell it down here. Although *artist* really isn't the right word for them. They're more enchanted objects; we call them animates. And that chirp comes from none other than Ooks, our enchanted statue of a baby phoenix. Clearly, Ooks has broken loose again.

Where can that little phoenix be hiding? I scan the nearby shelves. The store isn't that big. A small statue can't hide forever.

"*Chirp, chirp.*"

Yipes. That's Ooks again.

Coco taps her chin. "Interesting."

"*CHIRP, CHIRP, CHIRP!*"

Wow, Ooks is on a tear this morning.

I plaster on an innocent stare. Did Coco hear anything? When it comes to magic, most humans notice zero. At least, not right away. Eventually, humans do sense that something is off, however. And that's when animates like Ooks end up in the trash. It's also why Cynder Mercantile was formed. Dad wants to give animates a future outside of a dumpster.

"Your parents should write a book." Coco holds up an imaginary novel. "The title could be, *Inspiring Children.* My son won't finish his homework, let alone run a store. Mark my words. That would be a best seller."

"Um, okay." I exhale. *Coco didn't notice Ooks. Good.*

Speaking of the baby phoenix, the four-inch-tall porcelain statue hops onto the countertop. Ooks is all red feathers with a long tail that curls under her in a graceful arc. Her head looks more like a dove than a hawk; that's how you know she's a baby.

Coco steps closer. "That's a unique piece. Is it ... moving?"

Sure enough, Ooks jumps up and down on the counter. That's

how it looks to me, anyway. Coco just sees a small sculpture that twitches in a non-existent breeze.

"How could it move?" I throw up my hands. "That makes no sense."

This is a classic way to derail humans, by the way. They want everything to be logical. Magic isn't.

I point to a random wall. "Besides, there's much cooler stuff over there."

Coco turns to look, which is great. Sadly, Ooks takes the opportunity to leap atop Coco's head. Wincing, I wonder if Coco will notice. She doesn't. Animates can be very sneaky that way.

"Oh, those are gorgeous." Coco heads over to a shelf stocked with hand-blown glass statues. "I'd love to meet your supplier for this. We need new goods for MingMart's private customers."

This triggers my standard speech for just such an occasion. "Everything here is made by New York artists who only work with Cynder. Sorry."

"Can we work through Cynder on volume discounts? I have an event coming up where these would be perfect." She lowers her voice. "It's for the Le Charme family."

"Sure, you can ask my parents." I scoop up a business card from the counter and hand it over.

"Thank you. I'll be in touch." Coco steps toward the exit. While Coco's back is turned, I take the opportunity to jump up and scoop Ooks down. Thankfully, Coco still notices zero. Just to be safe, I watch until the door fully swings shut and Coco is gone.

Whew.

A voice sounds behind me, making me almost jump out of my skin. "Good morning, Elle."

Spinning around, I find Jacoby. He's a dark elf who works with Doc Eight, one of the Cynder animates. Jacoby looks about my age, but you never really know with elves. His hair is short, dark, and tousled. It's a look that offsets the strong bone structure of his pale face. Per usual, Jacoby wears jeans and a T-shirt. To humans, Jacoby seems like one of them. Only folks like me notice his pointed ears and silver irises.

"I've told you a hundred times," I groan. "Don't materialize behind me like that."

A sneaky smile curls his mouth. "I can't help it. I'm a *classic*."

When it comes to fairy tale life templates, most fae live by *the classic* pattern, which means a life of mischief. Jacoby steps a little closer. "What's your life template, Elle?"

Ooks hops off my hand to skitter behind the carved pumpkin display. I don't blame the phoenix for avoiding a dark fae. After all, these elves trick humans into stepping off cliffs *for fun*. That said, I've known Jacoby forever. He's harmless.

"I'm a Cinderella template. You know that."

"Sometimes, I wonder." Jacoby sets a strand of hair behind my ear. "I wish you'd confide in me." His silver eyes get all dreamy and sweet. You can't knock elves for looks.

Even so, I'm not telling him a thing. I'm the warden of all fae magic. And with any luck, no one will discover that fact. Especially Jacoby. I take a half step backward.

"You're such a drama elf. I'm boring old Elle, nothing else."

"You're fae."

"Barely. I don't even have wings. No one's interested in a fairy who can't fly."

Technically, my parents had my wings removed when I was a baby. Brilliant move, by the way. Most fae wardens don't live past age ten. I'm some kind of record.

"I grew up in the Faerie Lands," says Jacoby. "They might get interested in you. Best to be prepared. I could help you, if you let me."

I consider how to tell him *no* for the hundredth time when the door opens once more. At last, Ivy and Agatha walk inside. I go to grab Jacoby's hand—those sisters are much less nasty with him around—but the dark elf has already vanished.

Thanks for nothing, Jacoby.

"Hello, Ellie Belly." That's Ivy, by the way. She stands tall, bright-eyed, and blonde with the same pinched features and perma-scowl as her mother, Marchesa. Like always, Ivy wears a bright plaid dress.

"Hel—"

"Quiet, Agatha."

"Lo," finishes Agatha. Like always, Marchesa's youngest daughter dresses like she's in a witness protection program. Today that means a boxy dress, floppy hat, and big sunglasses. All black. I'm pretty sure she's pale with long brown hair under everything, but you never know.

Ivy slowly scans me from head to toe. "You look rather sloppy today, even for you."

I shouldn't let Ivy get to me, and I don't. *Mostly.*

"Guess what?" asks Ivy. She communicates a lot in questions, by the way. It's as annoying as it seems. "We didn't plan on working this morning."

"Well, you were both on the list," I state.

Ivy sighs. "I can't believe the schedule was so unclear."

"Ask your mother," I counter. "She made it."

Which is true. Marchesa is supposed to help run Cynder Mercantile, but nothing she touches ever seems to go right. Even so, my parents won't fire her.

Ivy checks her watch. "The party starts now, right?"

I shake my head. The animates are throwing my parents some kind of celebration today. Leave it to Ivy and Agatha to try and show up right before things start.

"Nope," I reply. "It starts at noon."

"Oh, noon?" asks Ivy.

I force a grin. "That's what the slobby girl said."

Ivy twiddles her fingers at me. "Since you've got things covered, Agatha and I will hit the warehouse until noon. Ta!"

Fact: I happen to know that to Ivy and Agatha, the definition of *warehouse hitting* means hiding behind the wall of wooden pumpkins while playing Bubble Breaker on their phones. Now, it's true that I could force those two to stay and work with me in the store, but that's more hassle than it's worth. So I simply watch as the sisters step out the back door. *Buh-bye.*

I've got time to kill before noon, so I hang by the register. After a few minutes, Ooks comes back out of hiding to chirp and dance across the counter. There's nothing cuter than a baby phoenix doing the cha cha. Sunbeams shift across the store. The gentle music of car horns and voices echoes in from the street. With every passing second, more warmth and happiness seeps across my chest.

Cynder Mercantile is my little *cocoon of perfect*. Living upstairs with my parents… keeping my warden identity secret … taking online lessons … And helping the animates. It's a pretty awesome life, even if I do have to deal with Marchesa and her spawn.

At that thought, a ball of worry settles into my stomach. I'm a Cinderella. A perfect life isn't exactly in the cards for our kind. Still, I've got backup plans. I can handle whatever happens.

At least, I hope I can.

9. CHAPTER NINE

ELLE

$\mathcal{R}$ ight at noon, Mom opens the back door. "Ready, Elle?" She wears another sundress. Sadly, this one seems to hang even more loosely on her frame. My throat tightens. How much longer does she have?

"Almost," I reply. "Just need to lock up." I reach the front door and navigate our collection of bolt locks and key codes. "What's the plan for today?"

"We visit the fourth floor for a party of some kind. That's all I know. The animates are organizing everything."

"Whatever it is, I'm sure it will be nice." The animates adore my parents.

Once I'm done with the locks, I flip the sign to read *closed*. After that, I follow Mom through the back exit and into the warehouse itself.

"Did I tell you about our latest artist?" asks Mom.

"No." This isn't a surprise, though. Somehow, new animates always find their way to my parents.

"It's an enchanted violin. She's a Stradivarius."

I let out a low whistle. "She must have had a ton of emotion around her."

Here's the deal. When a human pours feelings into an object, part of their soul becomes attached to the item. Later, when an enchanter casts a spell on that same object, those traces of soul can get activated as well. If there's enough emotion, then the object comes alive. Permanently. We call those animates. They appear like objects to humans, but those with magic can see their true nature.

"Has she chosen a name yet?" I ask.

"Varrie," answers Mom.

"Oh, pretty."

While we chat, Mom and I pass through the maze of inventory shelves and then march up the back staircase. On the third floor, there's Harvest's studio. She's an enchanted scarecrow who carves things with a farm theme. This level also has animates who paint, sculpt, and do old-fashioned photography. As we climb up more steps, my pulse speeds.

I love the fourth floor. That's where the phoenixes work. I also love the story about our phoenix population. It goes like this.

Once upon a time, there was a human artist, Zander White, who lived in New Mexico and carved marble phoenixes. Zander put so much feeling into his creations, we now have a whole flock of his work living on our fourth floor. They're majestic creatures: eight feet tall with flowing red feathers and a long tail. Our phoenixes are also experts in glassblowing, which goes with the whole *rising up from fire* thing. Their leader is an alpha named Kokkivo.

The fourth floor is a wide space that's filled with a lot of tables—the phoenixes use them to cool new creations. Their enchanted furnace sits against the far wall. It's a dark mound with a circular, fiery mouth. I scan the scene. The only folks here are Kokkivo and Dad, who both stand by the furnace.

"Where's Blackaverre?" I ask.

Blackaverre is Mom's fairy godmother. Mine too, I suppose.

"Not sure," says Mom.

Some Cinderella trivia: ever wonder why the fairy godmother doesn't show up until the end of the story? It's because fairy godmothers follow the *classic* fairy life template. Which means they are supremely unreliable and prone to deceit.

Speaking of fairy godmothers, Blackaverre appears before us. She's a small blue creature with pink wings and pointed teeth. While hovering before Mom, Blackaverre bows wildly.

My mother beams. "You're so sweet."

Sweet isn't the word I'd use. Blackaverre likes to turn our cream cheese moldy for fun. Plus, she only speaks in broad hand gestures. It's like having a permanent mime on site.

Mom turns to me. "Don't you think Blackaverre is the best?"

Actually, I think my mother is the best. Mom stubbornly refuses to see anything but good in everyone she meets.

"Something like that," I say.

Blackaverre sticks out her tongue at me. I return the gesture. Mom laughs. "You two! Always playing about. I love it!"

See what I mean? It's literally impossible for my mother to be nasty. Or to see evil in others, for that matter. She's like a fairy miracle.

Kokkivo moves closer while fluttering his great wings. It's how Phoenixes say hello. It's also a welcome break from interacting with Blackaverre.

"Greetings, Elle and Rae." It's amazing how Kokkivo can talk with his long beak mouth, but he manages it perfectly.

"It's good to see you," says Mom.

"Greetings, Kokkivo." I wave. "Hey, Dad."

My father winks at me before focusing on Mom. "My Rae of sunshine." Dad positively beams as Mom approaches. He's had a chance to nap, shower, and change clothes. It's a much better look on him.

Mom leans against his shoulder. "My Declan." She turns to Kokkivo. "So what's all this about?"

"I need everyone present first." Kokkivo whistles.

Animates march onto our floor from every corner of the building. There's Harvest and her scarecrow crew. Jacoby materializes with Doc Eight, who's an enchanted set of medieval armor. There are also enspelled Greek statues (the guys all wear togas), life-sized paintings (you have to look at them straight on or you'll miss them), and even our new Stradivarius. Best of all, there are dozens of phoenixes.

Dad waves me closer. I stand beside him and Mom.

Marchesa and her daughters step out from the stairwell and rush over.

"Rae, you look gorgeous." That's Marchesa.

"Mr. and Mrs. Cynder, how can we thank you enough for including us?" asks Ivy.

This goes on for two full minutes. Kokkivo and I share a dry look. Technically, this is the animates' party. Marchesa is a powerful potion master, the same as her deceased husband. She doesn't see animates as legitimate life forms. It's rude.

"We're ready to begin," announces Kokkivo at length. "I've been elected spokesman for the Cynder animates."

By now, the floor is filled with about a hundred animates of all shapes and sizes. They let out a hearty cheer. I angle my body so I don't have to look at Marchesa, Ivy, and Agatha. No reason to let them ruin my day.

Kokkivo flaps his wings again, which makes the audience fall silent. "If it hadn't been for Declan and Rae Cynder, all of us animates would have been ruined. Am I right?"

More cheering follows.

Kokkivo continues. "We wanted to give something back to show our appreciation."

Dad shakes his head. "Rae and I don't want anything."

"Ah," counters Kokkivo. "But this gift isn't for you. It's to support Cynder Mercantile."

"What do you mean?" asks Mom.

"I've been working on a special glass treasure chest," explains Kokkivo. "It's tiny in size, but massive in power. All of us animates contributed a little of our life force into it. Once a day, the owner may open it and the box will provide whatever the store most needs. I call it *the Coffer of Wonders*."

Mom pops her hands over her mouth. "Oh, my. That's lovely."

I get a little misty, too. The animates know that things are turning dicey with Mom's illness. They're trying to keep the store going.

Kokkivo leans back his head and caws. All the other phoenixes do the same. At that call, a magical red mist surrounds Mom's hands. One moment, there's nothing in her palms. The next second, Mom holds a small box made of red glass.

"Go on," urges Kokkivo. "Use it."

Mom pulls off the box's lid. Dad then asks, "What do we need most for today?"

More red mist flows out of the Coffer of Wonders to fill the room. When the haze vanishes, the tables are all covered with cakes and punch.

Mom grins. "Oh, I love it!"

While we all dive into the food, Marchesa lurks in the shadows. I'd worry about it, but my parents are happy and enjoying their lovely gift from the animates. My little *cocoon of happy* surrounds me once more, and I'm going to enjoy it.

10. CHAPTER TEN

ELLE - MONTHS LATER

*D*elivery duty is the worst.

I march down Second Avenue while dragging a little red wagon behind me. Two large boxes lay stacked on the cart. And inside those containers? A thousand little glass slippers and tiny carved pumpkins. Today, it's my job to deliver them to the L Center.

The good news is that the center isn't far from Cynder Mercantile.

The bad news is that one of the wheels on my wagon snapped about a half-block ago. It's tempting to use magic, but this is precisely the kind of situation where I can't. Dozens of people fill the nearby stretch of sidewalk, and I'm not even counting those who can watch from buildings. The chances that someone would notice my spell are just too high.

As a result, my march to the L Center takes on a certain rhythm.

Drag.

Drag.

Drag.

Whump.

Drag.

Drag.

Drag.

Whump.

Then there's the jingle of glass. Wincing, I give the boxes a gentle shake. Did anything break? No.

Back to it, then.

Drag.

Drag.

Drag.

Whump.

It's not that hot outside—and I'm wearing shorts and a T-shirt—but even so, I sweat up a storm.

At last, I'm in the final stretch for the L Center's loading dock. I turn off the main sidewalk, navigate through a skinny alley, and then approach a small yard. The loading dock takes up one wall of this tiny space. As I haul my wagon along, I come to a major realization.

For a new place, the L Center has nothing but broken concrete back here. It's way bumpier than the regular sidewalk. Hasn't anyone delivered glass to this place before?

As I haul the wagon onto the edges of the yard, Jacoby materializes before me. He looks very non-sweaty and annoying.

"Hello, Elle. Fine day, isn't it?"

"Are you following me?"

"Never. I have..." He taps his cheek dramatically. "Yes, I'm following you. Things are awfully boring in Doc Eight's shop." He glances behind me. "Why are you using a broken wagon?"

"It wasn't broken when I left Cynder."

"Would you like some help?" asks Jacoby.

"I know what you think of as *help*, and the answer is *no*."

Six teenagers march into the yard. They're all wearing fancy gowns and have VIP passes hanging around their necks. Moving in unison, they turn to stare at me. All their irises flare with silver light.

"How may we serve you?" they ask in unison.

I round on Jacoby. "Who are these girls and why did you enchant them?"

Jacoby rolls his eyes. "I knew you wouldn't allow me to help directly, so I brought in some outside aid."

"They're all wearing ball gowns and high heels. They should not be schlepping boxes around."

"Um, they're human." Jacoby rolls his eyes again.

That's dark fae for you. And Jacoby's one of the nice ones.

"You're terrible," I counter.

"No, I'm interesting. And completely devoted to you, don't forget that part."

"Where did you find these girls anyway?" I lean in a little closer. "I don't think any of them are blinking. That can't be healthy."

"They're here for the Le Charme Extravaganza," says Jacoby.

I tilt my head. "And that's tonight?"

"Obviously. Didn't you notice everyone lined up in front of the L Center?"

"Not really. I was more focused on not breaking glass slippers." My eyes widen. "This isn't a Glass Slipper Ball, is it?"

"No, it's one of those where they award a new Le Charme Lady." He bobs his brows. "Why? Do you have your eye on Alec Le Charme?"

"That's a big *no*." Mostly because I've been breaking into his office to un-steal jewels. I read online that you should never date people you work with. In my opinion, Alec counts in that category.

I quickly scan the yard. There doesn't seem to be anyone around. (In my opinion, Jacoby and some enspelled humans don't count.) So I pull on a little of my fae magic and send it toward the girls. A tiny cloud of silver faerie dust flies off my fingertips and surrounds the teenagers. In my mind, I issue a command.

Move.

They start cooing.

"Oh crap," I groan.

Jacoby grins. "Did you enchant just them to act like pigeons?"

"I asked them to move. I really only know how to enspell two kinds of animals."

"Let me guess. One of those is pigeons."

I stick my tongue out at him. "Shut up."

Jacoby scans each girl in turn. They've started scratching at the concrete with their feet. "You know," says Jacoby. "I like them better this way."

That prickly feeling on my neck again.

Someone's watching us.

Turning, I see the outline of a guy standing in the back shadows of the loading dock. He's totally staring at this situation.

Oh, no.

This man must work here. I've been through the drill before. I'm supposed to just unload stuff, not stand around with six girls cooing like pigeons and an evil fae.

Things have gotten complicated.

11. CHAPTER ELEVEN

ALEC

For the last two hours, I've been meandering around the L Center. Why? We're holding the Le Charme Extravaganza tonight and my new best friend, Clarissa, is a Production Assistant trying to guide me to the dry run.

It hasn't been going well.

All the dry runs have been in the hotel complex, which is admittedly huge. Sadly, Clarissa gets lost easily. Eventually, Clarissa led me to the L's loading dock. Once here, she asked me to wait (again) while she tried to find someone to answer a few questions (again-again.) So I've been hanging by the back wall while staring out across a small and empty lot. In New York, this has been counting as a *Zen moment*.

A girl stepped out onto the concrete and my world turned upside down.

Which brings us to the present moment. I can't stop staring at this girl. She's singular in how she combines so much in a single glance: fierce and sweet, gentle and rough, lovely and strong. Beside her, a few boxes sit on a broken wagon. A bunch of human girls stand close by, along with an elf.

My pulse speeds. Every corner of my soul becomes awash with one thought. *How can I approach this girl?* The humans all wear passes for tonight's Le Charme Extravaganza. Clearly, I can't step out as Alec Le Charme.

A plan forms.

I scan the dock. Sure enough, a worker's jacket hangs on a nearby wall hook. True fact: it's amazing what you can get away with when you wear a uniform. I slip on the jacket and march out to meet the girl.

"Hello." I wave in her direction.

"Hey, I need to drop these off and..." She looks around. "Everyone's gone."

That's right. There was an elf and some humans here before. Lucky for me, they've all taken off.

I gesture toward the boxes. "May I assist?"

"That would be great." Her face brightens with a dazzling smile. Inside my soul, emotions shift. Desires align. Excitement rises.

This girl.

I hoist up one box on my shoulder. The other container goes under my arm. I could use magic, but these aren't too heavy. Soon I'm setting both boxes onto the edge of the loading dock.

The girl takes out a little scrap of paper. "Um, can you..."

"Sure, I'll sign for them." I scratch out my signature. For once, I'm glad my writing is an unreadable mess. I'm not ready to reveal who I really am. *Yet.*

"Thanks." She takes in a shaky breath. "I'm Elle."

I grin. "Elle."

She gestures to my jacket. "And you're Fred."

"I am?" I look down at the jacket. Sure enough, the name Fred is written on my chest. "I mean, I am."

Elle blushes. "Thanks for helping me with the boxes."

"Any time."

"I should probably get going." Elle takes a step backward, but the pavement here is really uneven. She missteps and starts to topple. On reflex, I move forward and catch her.

A second later, I've got Elle in my arms.

An electric charge pulses through me. Threads of connection wind between us. Is this magic? Do I really care?

The moment stretches on. I should really let Elle go. Yet I don't. It's not like I want to kiss her. I mean, I do want a kiss, but it's more than that. It's like we're meant to fit together. Letting go would be some kind of crime.

I shake my head. I'm only fifteen and Elle looks about the same age. That's too early to get feelings for someone, isn't it?

It takes an effort, but I release her. "You almost took a tumble there."

"Yes, thanks for your help. Again."

Think, think, think. There must be some way to keep her here.

I step closer again. "Are you hitting the Le Charme Extravaganza tonight?"

"No. I'm not much for cameras and crowds."

"Right. So what do you like?"

"RPG."

Role-Playing Games. This girl really is perfect.

I lean back on my heels. "Let me guess. Your fave these days is..." I tap my chin as if I need to think about this one. "Magicorum Killers."

"Oh yes!" Elle bobs a little on the balls of her feet. It's always amazing to meet someone who likes the same games. "I love the evil pixie option."

"I'm working it as a wizard. The spells trip up my fingers, though."

"It's not you. They're working on an upgrade for that. You want my opinion?"

"Absolutely."

"Shut off that wizard mode. Play the game as an evil pixie. You will kick everyone's ass." A mischievous gleams lights up her eyes when she says *kick everyone's ass.*

"And is ass kicking the point of playing?"

She laughs. "There's another?"

"Not in Magicorum Killers, that's for sure."

"You look so familiar, Fred." She frowns. "Have I seen you somewhere before?"

My arms are itching to reach out for her again. Maybe now is the moment to reveal who I really am. Something tells me Elle won't care either way.

A new voice interrupts us. "What's going on here?" The speaker lurks in the shadows of the loading docks, just as I did a few minutes ago. Still, there's no question who's joined us.

Diamond.

I raise my pointer finger toward Elle. "One sec." Next I turn around and shoot Diamond a quick wave. "Be right over." When I look back, Elle is gone. Her wagon sits on the concrete, broken and alone. That fact makes me a lot sadder than it should.

As I approach Diamond, I check over my shoulder every few steps. Nope. Elle stays gone. By the time I near Diamond, there's no mistaking the look of absolute rage that tightens my mother's features.

"Why is that girl here?" she asks.

I hand over the signed receipt. "She had an order from Ming-Mart. You asked Coco to get you the hottest stuff in giveaways for the press, remember? Big opening for L Center and all that."

"MingMart." Diamond glares at the spot where Elle just stood.

"All the girl did was drop off some boxes and go."

"You were talking to her."

Now I could tell the truth, but something makes me feel protective of Elle. "I signed a receipt, Diamond. That's hardly a deep conversation."

"That girl?" She points to the spot where Elle stood. "She's not for you. Ever."

I straighten my back. "Why?"

"Because I *said so*. And never breathe a word about this to your father."

"Why would I tell Legend about some random delivery girl?"

Diamond throws up her hands. "You're acting all kinds of strangely today. Why were you out here in the first place?"

"There's a new Production Assistant. We got a little lost. She told me to wait here while she figures out where I should be for the run through."

Diamond huffs out a breath. "That's because the actual set is open today. We aren't rehearsing in the hotel anymore."

"Well, Clarissa got confused."

"Oh, that makes sense." Diamond rubs her temples with her

fingertips. "I'm just worried about the show tonight, that's all. Let's find this Clarissa. We're late for the dry run as it is."

"Sure."

I wasn't lying to Diamond before, by the way. I'd never tell Legend about meeting Elle. Mostly because I want to see Elle again. Clearly, asking permission won't get me that. Magic might.

Whatever it takes, I'll find her.

12. CHAPTER TWELVE

ELLE

J hustle my butt down Second Avenue. *Poor Fred.* That guy is in deep trouble. I couldn't see who was calling to him, but whoever it was? They were seriously ticked off.

And it's all my fault.

Ah, well. It's probably for the best. I was getting way too chatty with Fred anyway. Plus, the guy definitely gave off some kind of magical signature. In other words, Fred is not human. And me? I'm the fae warden. Getting to know people with magic can only end with me getting exposed.

As I step along, I keep glancing back toward the L Center. Maybe I'm hoping Fred will step out and follow me.

Okay, I'm totally hoping Fred will appear.

He doesn't, though. Which is probably for the best. Fred is a distraction. It's time to move on and forget all about him.

And I will.

Maybe.

13. CHAPTER THIRTEEN

ALEC - HOURS LATER

*H*ours later, I stand backstage at the L Center. Our first show is almost finished. It went exactly as Charles described all those weeks ago.

Contestants step down a winding staircase.

Charles introduces them.

My parents ask questions.

Wash. Rinse. Repeat.

After a few hours of this, I walked out and named our new Le Charme Lady.

Now, we're at the part of the show called the parade of sponsors. This is where different celebrities come out to explain to the newest Le Charme Lady what she'll be talking up for the next year because—surprise, surprise—those celebrities are contracted to the exact same companies. Funny how that stuff works out.

While all that fun goes down, I keep standing at stage right. From here, I can see the show proper, but no one can see me. Well, not unless you count Knox, who keeps glaring in my direction while pulling on the collar of his tux.

"I can't believe you got me into this monkey suit," he grumbles.

"Honestly, I'm shocked you showed up at all."

"I rally, you know that. We wardens stick together."

On stage, another celebrity sponsor marches up to our newest winner. Knox frowns. "Is that—"

"Hemorrhoid cream. Yes."

Stage right is divided into sections. Knox and I stand in the area closest to the front. Curtains line up behind us. A new set drapes down every few yards. Voices sound. Some folks are chattering on the other side of the fabric closest to me and Knox.

"I don't know how Legend does it," says one guy. I recognize the voice. He's Ekon Streng, a senior enchanter (which means he turns objects into living things).

"I'll tell you how," says a second man. "Legend's latest mistress is none other than Amoura. Did you see her in that new movie, *Lovesick*? They say she'll win an Oscar."

I know this guy, too. It's Kwon Bai. He's another kind of wizard called a potion master.

When you have my life, this kind of thing happens more often than you'd think. It's true that my father isn't faithful. I hate it, but there's not much I can do. Even so, I don't want to stand around and listen to other people gossip about the situation. I'm about to cough and make my presence known.

That's when Kwon says something that makes my hair stand on end.

"Don't be too hard on Legend. It's that Le Charme curse, you know."

My gaze turns to Knox. My shifter buddy rolls his eyes and whispers one word. "Warden?"

No question what Knox means. As wardens, we're under a supernatural curse. We're supposed to find something called the Fountain of Magic. If we don't find it—and then we get married anyway—our spouse will sicken and die. It isn't something that I think about much. After all, I'm not a shifter. If Knox finds his life mate, then he's sunk. His wolf won't be happy until they have the equivalent of a shifter wedding. But me? I can stay a bachelor forever, no matter what my parents say about my Glass Slipper Ball.

Knox repeats the word. "Warden?"

"Probably," I whisper.

Inside, I'm not so sure. The thing is, the warden curse isn't specific to Le Charme. I'm a gemstone mage, so my tuxedo jacket is packed with hidden pockets and stones. Right now, all those gems feel extra heavy, like they'll tear through my coat and plunk onto the floor. It's my magic's way of telling me that something is wrong here.

Inside my pocket, I grip an emerald in my fist. This variety can have divining powers. In my mind, I ask a question.

What's wrong?

As a gem wizard, I do more than pull power from stones. We interact. In this case, the emerald replies in a warbling voice.

Danger, danger, danger.

I'm so focused on the message from my stone, I don't even notice when the show ends. At some point, my parents stand before me. I drop the stone and focus on my mother.

"What's this about a Le Charme curse?" I ask.

Diamond's nostrils flare. "Who told you that?"

"Kwon and Ekon were talking about it. I overheard."

"I'll have a chat with them." Diamond rounds on Legend. "This is *your* family's problem. I suggest you take Alec somewhere quiet to discuss."

Translation? *My mother wants no part of this.*

Which means it's bad.

Legend reaches into the pocket of his tuxedo coat and pulls out a handful of red gems. The stones glow in his hand. Tendrils of crimson mist swirl up around us.

My brows lift. "When Diamond said to discuss, I didn't think it meant this minute."

"It does."

The mist surrounds us and we're gone.

A moment later, we're back in my family's penthouse overlooking Manhattan. Legend dropped us off by the living room window. I type out a quick text to Knox.

MagicMan: Got called away. You can take off your straightjacket now.
FortMe: Thanks. Coming over to game.
MagicMan: Sounds like a plan.

I reset my cell into my jacket pocket and watch Legend pace around the living room floor.

"Want a drink?" asks my father. "I have soda and such."

"No, thanks."

Legend goes over to pour himself something alcoholic. After downing the shot, he refills his glass and heads over to the leather couch. "You'll want to sit down for this."

I cross the room while loosening my bow tie. All this while, my thoughts about a curse have led to one worry.

Shadowcoe.

These are dwarves, trolls, vampires and other beings that go bump in the night. Some have been helping out Le Charme for centuries.

Are they at risk?

I take a seat across Legend. "Does this have to do with our shadowcoe?"

"No." Legend downs a healthy gulp of his drink. "I'm sorry, son. You need to know our family secret. You see, there's a curse to being a Le Charme. All this wealth. Privilege. Attending West Lake Prep high school. But there's a dark side to the Cinderella myth for us. Know how long Le Charme has been around?"

"More than a three centuries, both here and in Europe."

"Quite right. In all that time, a son of Le Charme has always led this company. Each one has had a Glass Slipper Ball during his eighteenth year."

"Sure. I know that."

"Here's what you're unaware of. Each son of Le Charme walks into their glass slipper ball with one vow: never find his bride. Myself included. And each one walks out engaged, the deal sealed by the Queen of Hearts. It's what happens to us."

I scan my father's face. There's the camera-ready Legend, a guy who's all charm and glamour. This is a different man altogether. Whatever my father is saying, he believes it.

"So what happens?" I ask.

"We all start off trying to make things work, but they never do. Within a few weeks—*a month at most*—it's all over. Cinderella and her prince loathe each other."

I can't believe this. "You hate Diamond."

Legend sighs. "How can you truly love with someone that you met for two minutes? For some it's possible, but not the Le Charme boys."

I turn this news over in my mind. Some parts simply don't make sense. "I'm also the warden of all casters. I can't get married anyway."

"We'll see about that. The Le Charme name can not die out. As long as we solve this warden problem by the time of your eighteenth year, it's fine."

"And if we don't?" The thought hangs out there. *My bride will die.* I don't even get into the part where I don't want to get married at eighteen. The *death situation* should be enough to end this idea.

"I said we'd figure it out. And after we do, I've some ideas for you. Better a loveless marriage than one filled with hate, right?"

"Not sure what you mean." If there's one thing I've learned in life, it's this: never agree with Legend on something if you don't know all the particulars.

"Diamond and I believe that Le Charme jewelers must stay in business. We're working an option. Some folks in midtown have a magical item that might help us." He takes another gulp from his glass. "In any case, we'll find you a bride who's useful to Le Charme."

The word *useful* sticks in my brain. The stones in my pockets feel weighty once more. "Why would I need a bride to be *useful*? What aren't you telling me?"

"The company isn't going bankrupt, if that's what you mean."

"I didn't say it was."

Which makes the fact that Legend even brought up bankruptcy all the more sketchy.

"Son, I understand that the idea of a wife can be overwhelming at your age, but once you're eighteen…"

"I won't marry at eighteen."

Legend chuckles, but there's no humor in it. "We all say that. It's the nature of the curse."

As I watch Legend down the rest of his drink, I come to a big decision.

I don't believe in curses. I'll find a way out.

14. CHAPTER FOURTEEN

ELLE - TWO WEEKS LATER

*N*ew text flashes on my computer screen.

Congratulations, Elle Cynder! You have completed 52% of your freshman year of high school.

I'm about to close out the program when another message pops up.

As a Magicorum, you are required to check in with your local Denarii League.

The text goes on to explain how magic is fading from the world and Magicorum like me must be protected even if I'm challenged.

Challenged.

That's their way of saying I'm a fairy without wings. *Whatever.* The notice goes on to say that the Denarii league can help me, *blah blah blah*. There's even an address where I can stop by and meet my group facilitator.

Wow. That's so *not happening.*

I scan the fine print. To get out of these group sessions, my parents need to send proof that I'm living by a proper fairy tale life template. No a problem. I'll send Mom and Dad a link to the paper-work for this stuff; it'll be fine.

With my school work over, it's time for some fun. Gaming is tempting, but I still need money for what I call my *Cinderella's In Trouble Fund*. So I open a browser for Magiweb. Within seconds, I'm scanning through postings on a message board for lost valuables. One catches my eye.

Vampire coven seeks lost pendant. Reward $200.

Now in New York, $200 will cover lunch and a taxi ride to New Jersey. Still it's interesting. In my mind, lost jewels are like a puzzle. Who took the gems? Where might someone find them? And what if that someone was me? I keep on reading.

Jewel last seen in Manhattan. It's three perfect emeralds set into gold disc. Reverse side contains runes of protection. Family heirloom. See image below.

Magical runes? That means most stores wouldn't try to sell it. Not a lot of places would. The MITRE agency would be on your back in a hot minute. Only one human I know would carry this kind of item. *Dirty Leon*. If it's dangerous and magical, it often ends up in Dirty Leon's pawn shop.

I tap my chin and wonder. Dirty Leon's store is just up the street. What would happen if I stopped by? Would I find the pendant?

I might find trouble, but it's been a boring week.

Closing my eyes, I summon in my fae power and call out to my mousey friends.

Anyone nearby? Need some help here.

A minute later, one of my favorite animal buddies skitters across my desk. It's Gustav the mouse. He's a little grey guy with big eyes like black marbles. He sits back on his haunches.

"Do I look fat to you?" asks Gustav.

I shake my head. "I am not having this conversation with you again."

"So I'm fat."

"You are a sleek and gorgeous marsupial." Gustav needs fresh compliments. I have to look up new words online in my spare time.

Gustav runs his little hands over his pointed nose. "Thank you."

I tap the computer screen. "You see this pendant? I think it may be at Dirty Leon's. Can you go check out?"

Gustav sighs. "I'm not sure."

"I'll get you some Cheerios."

"And a candy bar?"

Now he's just getting greedy.

"How about we work out another outfit for Halloween?" I made Gustav wear a tiny shirt four years ago. He still lives in terror of it, considering that be believed it showed off his so-called *love handles*.

"I'll go! I'll go!" Gustav skitters off toward the window.

Once Gustav is gone, the door behind me swings open. The scent of rose-hips and rotting leaves wafts into the room. Only one person carries that particular stench. Marchesa. I quickly click back from the Magiweb to my online classes. The less Marchesa knows about my actual interests, the better.

"Don't mind me," she says. Like always, she wears a fitted black dress. "I'm just dusting." Marchesa then raises her dust cloth as evidence.

Totally believable. In another universe.

After that, Marchesa does zero in the way of actually removing anything that looks like dust from anywhere in my parent's office. Instead she checks behind chairs, scans inside filing cabinets, and generally snoops around.

No question what she's looking for.

"It's not here," I say.

"Whatever do you mean?"

"The Coffer of Wonders. My parents hid it."

"How clever of them. Do you know where it is? As the Office Manager, I should be aware."

"Well, as the teenage daughter, it's not on my *need to know* list. Can't help you."

Turning away, I pretend to be super busy with the computer. In reality, I keep reading the same line onscreen, over and over. Is

Marchesa trying to steal the Coffer of Wonders? I wouldn't put it past her.

"About the coffer," I begin.

"What?"

"It's bonded to the store, not my parents. It won't help a person. Just in case you're wondering."

Marchesa narrows her eyes. "Are you certain?"

"The animates want to keep Cynder going. It's my parents legacy. Helping a person ends when they die. Cynder can go on forever. That's why the coffer is aligned to the store." I keep scrolling the screen up and down like I'm actually reading stuff instead of fuming about what Marchesa might *really* be up to. "Kokkivo told me all about it."

Marchesa pauses. For a moment, I think she might leave. No such luck. Marchesa drags a rolling chair to my side.

Uh oh. This is going to be one of her *talks.*

Sure enough, Marchesa leans into my personal space. "Since we're alone, I'd like to have some girl time."

"Sorry." I put on my *disappointed face.* "No can do. I have really important school stuff I'm working on."

"Like what?"

"Tests. Reading. You know. School."

Marchesa keeps going like I didn't say a thing about having actual school work. "Look, I know it can't be easy for you. Your father is more a *prince of a man* than an actual prince." Marchesa gets this dreamy look in her eyes as she says that *prince of a ma*n part. *Eew.*

"Meaning Dad isn't rich. Got it."

"Your mother could have been the Cinderella of her own life story. Instead, she married your father and became the mother to *another* Cinderella. You know what that means." She sniffles. "I want to help."

"Good point. I have an idea there, as a matter of fact. You can stop saying things that upset Mom."

"Me?"

"You're always chatting about how Ivy and Agatha have all this stuff I don't. It makes Mom feel bad. So, you know, stop."

A look of rage flashes through Marchesa's eyes, but it's gone as quickly as it appeared. Still, I totally saw it.

Hate you right back.

Marchesa pats my shoulder. "If you need to talk, I'm here." At last, she leaves.

Thankfully.

Once Marchesa is gone, I plan out six different speeches where I verbally shred the *Frenemy Queen* into little bits of bitchy. At some point, I notice Gustav tapping my hand. I look down.

"Hey, Gustav."

"I have good news for you. I saw the pendant. It's at Dirty Leon's."

After that ugly encounter with Marchesa, I'm all jacked up on adrenaline. I need a mini adventure. After a little prep work, I'm ready to hit Dirty Leon's. To be specific, I pull out picture of Legend Le Charme that was cut from Midtown Magazine. It's something my father was experimenting on. To be specific, Dad was testing out a new enchanter spell. He wasn't totally happy with the results, so Dad chucked it into the trash.

Whereupon I rescued the pic.

And now? I have the perfect opportunity to use it.

15. CHAPTER FIFTEEN

ELLE

*M*inutes later, I stand before a tall brick building. The sign reads, *East Side Jewelers and Pawn Brokers*.

I push open the door. "Leon!"

The place is little more than a tiny room with a grungy counter set into the wall. Dirty Leon stands behind a Plexiglass window. He's got greasy dark hair and what looks like mustard caked onto his scraggy chin. The entire store smells like rotten dumpster.

"No way, Elle. No, no, no, no, no."

"What?"

"Not selling you anything," declares Leon.

"Why not?"

"I don't do business with kids."

In other words, Dirty Leon doesn't like me. Mostly because he's pretty sure I scam him on a regular basis. And in truth? I totally scam him on a regular basis. Hey, if he'd split reward money with me, I wouldn't have to con him.

I puff out my lower lip. "But I have lots of money, Leon."

"What do you want?"

"Got any green necklaces?"

"Yeah, I do." Leon pulls out a pendant from a shelf behind him. "Like this?"

That's it all right.

"Perfect," I state. "How much?"

"Four thousand."

"That's way too high, especially since the real thing cost zero."

"Zero?"

"It was stolen, Leon."

"So call the cops. I'm not a church here. People try to sell stuff, I help them."

"If you give it to me, then I'll return it to the owner and we can spit the reward. You know I'll keep my word."

Leon folds his arms over his chest. "Nope."

"Fine. I'll pay four thousand."

"Price just went up to eight thousand."

"Ha! I knew it." I point at his nose. "You just won't sell to me."

"Clever thing. I don't sell to any kids. You're all hustlers." Leon turns around and resets the pendant into a nearby box.

Fine.

Reaching behind me, I pull out the magazine picture from my back pocket. I can't wield enchanter energy, but my father sure can. Once I flatten out the image, my father's spell kicks into action. The pic twists in the air before speeding across the floor. With a whip-fast movement, the sheet slides under the door and out onto the sidewalk beyond.

Could there be easier ways for me to lift that pendant? Sure.

Are there ways which are more fun? Not that I can think of, and I focus on this stuff a lot.

The door slams open.

I gasp. "Oh, no! It's Legend Le Charme!"

Leon pales. "*The* Legend Le Charme?"

Sure enough, it sure looks like Legend Le Charme. Dad used magic to blow up the picture from the magazine and make it come alive. It's even visible to Leon, who has zero in the way of magic himself. So long as you look at Legend straight on, he looks like the real thing.

In other words, my daddy's a badass enchanter.

"Yes, it is I, Legend Le Charme, owner of Le Charme Jewelers."

Leon tilts his head. "People pose as Le Charme. Is this some kind of hustle?"

"Moi? Un Poseur?" Fake Legend reaches into pocket. "Check out these gemstones. I have miles of them back at my amazing palace."

"Palace?" Leon scoffs. "Don't you live in a hi-rise? There was a dinner party there last week."

Uh oh. Who would have thought Leon was a fan?

"Of course," says Fake Legend. "We just call it the palace because it's so palatial inside."

I nod. That's a pretty good comeback. More points for Dad.

I slap on my most innocent face. "Why are you here, guy who is obviously Legend Le Charme?"

"I wish to buy this particular pendant," says Fake Legend.

"Oh, no! I came here to buy it." I sniffle. "You can't take it away!"

Leon narrows his eyes. "How much are you willing to pay?"

"Let me see the pendant, kind sir," says Fake Legend.

Leon pulls out the item from its nearby box. The pendant dangles from his hand. "What do you think?"

Fake Legend sighs. "That's clearly rather low quality. I know these things. But, I'll give you four—"

I cough.

"Thir—"

Cough cough.

"Twe—"

COUGH.

"Ten. Ten dollars."

I fan myself with my hands. "Hoo, I think I had a fur ball there. All better now, though." I slam down a twenty. "No! I can't let this rich creep take away what is certain to be my favorite necklace. I'll pay twenty."

Leon gestures toward Fake Legend. "This is a good customer. A fair customer. Sold for ten dollars."

Fake Legend holds out his hand. Leon grabs my twenty and sets the pendant onto the animate's palm. After that, Leon turns to me and grins.

Eew. Looks like Leon had parsley with lunch.

"Take that," declares Leon.

I ball my hands into fists. "Leon, you thief!"

Fake Legend now walks backward-style out of the store. It's an odd way to move, but it's not like turning around is an option. I help to cover up the move by continuing to glare hot death at Leon.

Once Fake Legend is outside, I stomp out of the store in a huff.

"Got you that time, Elle!" calls Leon.

Sure you did.

Once outside, I find Fake Legend is, once again, a small and crumpled-up piece of paper. I scoop up the wad and peep inside. There's the pendant, just like I'd hoped.

Yes!

Pulling out my cell, I text to the number from the online ad. And yes, I have an alias for just such occasions.

> *BountyHunterBabe: I have the pendant.*
> *VampTheVamp: Excellent.*

I read the name over and over. That alias is familiar.

> *BountyHunterBabe: Vlad, is that you? It's Elle.*
> *VampTheVamp: It IS me! Should've known you'd deliver*
> *BountyHunterBabe: Hey, I'm awesome*
> *VampTheVamp: Where do you want to meet*

Which raises a good question. I can't meet Vlad in my home neighborhood—there are simply too many chances to get discovered. An address pops into my head; it's the one from the Denarii League. So I type it in before texting my parents that I'll be home in an hour. Vlad agrees.

Time to meet my vampire buddy.

16. CHAPTER SIXTEEN

ELLE

*a*n hour later, I hang in an alley of Midtown Manhattan. A flash rain just ended, so it's one of those summer afternoons where sunshine turns the sidewalk all steamy. New York is the best.

Any minute now, it will be time to hand over my un-stolen necklace to Vlad. The worst part about vamps? The drama. Vlad is especially bad in this department. Don't get me wrong. Vlad's also one of my best customers. He just needs to leave the cape at home.

Sure enough, Vlad stalks down the sidewalk. He looks like something from a black and white movie, what with his slicked-back hair, super-pale skin, and shiny cape wrapped across his arm-slash-face. Normally, anyone with a smidgeon of magic attracts tourists like shmears to a bagel. But Vlad is so *over the top* that he looks more like a human groupie than a real vamp. It's a common problem. There are very few old, nasty and subtle vampires left.

Vlad stalks into the alley. "Mmm cmm ummm whmm fmmm tmm?"

"I can't understand you with that cape over your mouth."

"Oh." Vlad lowers his arm. "Do you know if the weather is fine today?"

I roll my eyes. "It's me, Vlad."

"Elle, we're supposed to use the pass phrases. This is a secret mission for us Magicorum."

Vlad looks so miserable that I can't help but play along. "What's the weather today? All sunshine, all the time."

Vlad makes an 'o' face, which is meant to look like he's exhaling with relief. He doesn't need to breathe anymore, but I do appreciate the attempt to look alive.

"Do you have the pendant?" he asks.

I open my purse. "It's in here."

Vlad reaches for the tiny velvet bag. "Thanks."

I close my Gucci. "Payment?"

Vlad reaches into his cape and pulls out a hefty envelope. I scoop it from his hands and scan the contents. Two hundred.

"All right, you're good to go." I hand over the item in question.

"Great. My coven will be thrilled to have this back, you know. It's an heirloom."

"Pleasure to do business with you."

Vlad takes off; I jam the envelope into my purse. That's when Jacoby materializes at the alley's exit. His face is angry and thunder.

"Hi Jacoby." I step toward the sidewalk. Jacoby doesn't move. "You need to let me pass."

"No." In the dim alley, Jacoby's eyes flare with silver light. He's really ticked.

"What's the problem?"

"Did you visit the Queen of Hearts?"

I set my fist on my hip. "So what if I did?"

He steps closer. "You should have asked me for company. Protection."

"I can handle myself."

Jacoby does that predator move where he backs me up against a wall. He frames his hands on either side of my head. "Allow me to accompany you home."

A fluttery feeling spreads throughout my stomach. Not that I'll let Jacoby know he's getting to me, though.

"Look," I declare. "This stalking stuff is a little weird. Okay, a lot weird."

"Not where I come from. It's the not-killing-you part that's strange." He leans in, stopping when his mouth is inches from mine. Is this about to be my first kiss? I could do worse than Jacoby.

Nah. It's the principle of the thing. Stalker behavior should not get rewarded.

"Mom says I should never have become friends with you. She told me having a dark elf as a buddy is like taking on a life-sized barnacle. There's no scraping you off."

"And yet, you went ahead and befriended me anyway. I keep an eye on you for one reason, Elle. Not every Cinderella meets her prince, you know. Some fall for very charming elves."

All of a sudden, it's very hard to pull in a breath. "Do they?"

"If you gave me a chance, you might find I'm the love of your life."

Words from the Queen of Hearts through my head. Marchesa and Legend Le Charme will try to stop me from being with my true love. Is that Jacoby?

A small smile rounds Jacoby's mouth. Does he guess what I'm thinking? Probably. Dark elves have all sorts of odd powers.

Jacoby pushes away from the wall. "We can talk about it another time. I'm patient. Not to mention how we both have many long years ahead of us."

Not for the first time, I find Jacoby to be a living riddle.

And like Mom says, a life-sized barnacle.

17. CHAPTER SEVENTEEN

ALEC

For days, my chat with Legend after the Le Charme Extravaganza rattles around my brain.

Is Le Charme Jewelers going bankrupt?

If that's true, it could mean trouble for our dwarves. They've mined our jewels for centuries. And considering where they work, it's not like I can text to see if they're all right. And if my parents know I'm visiting them, then Legend and Diamond will definitely want to come along. I can't let that happen.

Well, not if I want the honest truth.

As a result, checking on the dwarves becomes a matter of waiting until the penthouse is empty so I can use our enchanted portal and visit them solo.

Not as easy at it sounds.

If Diamond is out of the penthouse, then Legend is here. And vice versa. Long story short, it's taken a few weeks, but at last, the penthouse is empty.

And I'm off to visit the dwarves. Finally.

I step into the library. It's a two-story tall room lined with shelves of leather-bound books. The place is also packed with leather couches, candelabras, and Persian rugs. A large chair sits in one corner. It's a simple thing, almost laughable in this ornate room.

It's by far the most powerful object in our entire penthouse.

After sitting on that chair, I pull out a small red gem from my pocket. Gripping the stone in my hand, I reach out to the gem with my mind.

Ready?

The stone replies in a sultry female voice that only I can hear.

Always. What do you want?

Take me to the dwarves.

Anything for you.

The stone glows red in my fist. Crimson mist appears on the floor surrounding the chair. An electric charge of power fills the air.

The chair transforms.

A series of red circlets surround the chair. The round shapes spin faster and faster, creating a sphere of power around the chair itself.

Both chair and orb hurtle through the earth.

It takes a few minutes, but the chair eventually stops. Instead of hanging out in the ornate library, I now stand in a low cavern lined with torches. A line of fifty dwarves hack away at the walls with picks. Once I rise, they all pause from their work, turn around, and fall to their knees before me.

"Our prince," the murmur.

"Please stand," I state. Kneeling is part of their traditional greeting, but it's still awkward.

Their leader, Wilhelm, is the first to rise. The rest follow. Wilhelm is a stout dude who stands about four feet tall. He wears a brown tunic to match his long beard. "It's the little prince! You've gotten so big. How old are you now, forty?"

"Fifteen," I say. "But that's like forty in dwarf years, am I right?"

"Sure enough." Wilhelm steps closer.

"You look leaner." I scan the other dwarves. "You all do. What are they feeding you?"

"Not as much as before." Wilhelm sets his thumbs into his leather belt. "We understand; funds are tight."

I frown. "That wasn't always true."

"No. Time was, Le Charme was swimming in gold. We ate off silver plates the day you were born." He pats my shoulder. "Come, let me show you our latest stones."

With that, I go through the requisite tour of their latest rocks. To dwarves, each tiny gem is like one of their children. Wilhelm explains in detail which stones are for what settings. A pile of over-sized gems catches my eye.

"What are those?" I ask.

"Discarded stones. Those don't perfectly fit Le Charme designs. We set them aside for later."

I'd ask him what he means by *perfectly fit*, but that would start an hour-long lecture on stone quality and settings. All of which is inter-esting, but I can't hang out here for long. My parents are due back any minute.

"So you've been setting aside these stones for how long?" I ask.

"Only a thousand years or so."

My brows lift. "One thousand years?"

"We're dwarves. We don't toss good stone."

I'd never heard that before; I set the thought aside for later. "Thanks for the tour. I'll look into the food situation for you."

Wilhelm's face reddens. "Don't do anything! We don't wish to worry Legend and Diamond. We're doing our part, that's all."

You can bet I won't worry Legend and Diamond. Something is going on with Le Charme, and if I press too much, I'll get more happy talk.

When it comes to the dwarves, I'll take care of this myself.

◆

18. CHAPTER EIGHTEEN

ALEC

a few minutes later, I'm back in the penthouse library. My heart sinks when I see how the room has changed.

Now Legend and Diamond are here. They do not look happy.

"What did the dwarves tell you?" asks Diamond.

"Nothing." I rise from the chair and dust off my pants. "They just showed me the latest stones they're digging up, that's all."

"Did they say we're bankrupt?" asks Legend. "We aren't."

"My family just secured a new line of credit," adds Diamond.

I set my hand on a nearby shelf and go into what I consider a causal pose. "They showed me some new stones. That's it."

My parents share a long look. *Not good.*

Legend is the first to speak. "If you wish to help the dwarves, then you must adjust to the idea of the Le Charme curse."

"You're getting married at eighteen," adds Diamond.

This conversation is getting ugly, fast. I will not stand around fighting about whether I'll marry at eighteen. Yes, I could use magic to distract things, but my parents would see that coming a mile away.

So I use technology instead. What my parents don't know about cell phones is a lot.

I glance down at my phone. "Knox is on his way. He plans to let himself into the penthouse to play video games. I better go." My parents won't keep me here if Knox is around. He has werewolf hearing.

"Here's the thing," says Diamond. "We don't have funds to lavish extras on the dwarves. They aren't entirely necessary. It's not like we're selling out of jewels."

"Of course, our current inventory is still incredibly popular," adds Legend.

"Yes, and we're doing very well," states Diamond. "As a company."

Surprise prickles across my skin. These are my parents, taking in tandem and riffing off each other's sentences. It's a little upsetting.

A lot upsetting, actually. Mostly because I know what's coming next.

Legend grins. "All that we're saying is this: keep an open mind about the curse."

And that would be what I was expecting.

19 . CHAPTER NINETEEN

ELLE - DAYS LATER

I wake up to the sound of Second Avenue traffic. *Ah, sweet music.* Yawning, I slog myself to the kitchen. There's no sign of Dad. *Huh.* Normally, he's up by now. I walk around our apartment. No sign of anyone.

I'm about to knock on my parent's door when Dad steps out of their bedroom. His eyes are rimmed with tears.

"How is she?" I ask.

"Let's talk in the kitchen."

The world takes on a dream-like gleam. I sleepwalk into the kitchen. Once we're there, Dad leans against the counter. He grips the countertop like it's the only thing keeping him upright.

"Your mother is getting worse. I have to make plans." He sighs. "And you don't like Marchesa and her daughters."

A chill crawls up my neck. This is it. The moment I've dreaded. It's really here.

I swallow past the lump of sorrow that just lodged in my throat. "We aren't best friends or anything, no."

"The girls are young for their age." Dad stares at the floor. "I know you have differences. But I'm asking you to look past all that." His shoulders shake with a held-in sob. "Things are really hard now."

I step closer. When I next speak, I take care to keep my voice in a soothing tone. "There are other things we can do."

"I know what you think. This is the fairy tale life template at work. You're a Cinderella. I'm your my father. The template says that I'll end up with Marchesa." His chin wobbles. "I don't know what will happen, Ellie Belly. All I know is that right now, Marchesa and her daughters are running Cynder. I need them."

I've never seen my father more miserable. At this point, I can't deny him anything. "Sure, Dad. I'll try harder."

"And Ellie? Some things are just destined. Fighting them is useless."

I hug my elbows. "I don't agree."

All the sorrow in the world shines out in his face as he speaks two final words. "You will."

20. CHAPTER TWENTY

ELLE - SIX MONTHS LATER

I'm wearing black.

Again.

Which makes sense. Again. After all, today marks my second funeral in six months.

I grip a little card with my father's picture on it. Looking down, I stare at the words along the top.

In loving memory of Declan Cynder.

I've another card just like this one back on my dresser. Only that version reads Raelyn Cynder and is dated three months ago. My dresser also holds a wedding invitation (of sorts). It's a hand-written Post-It that Dad left on my computer. On it, my father wrote the date we'd all meet at the court house for his second marriage. Marchesa and Declan tied the knot one month after Mom died.

And now, two months after that second wedding, my father is dead. The coroner said Dad's heart just gave out.

That sounds about right.

I meander about my family's apartment. With every step, my body feels more numb. Voices echo around me. A few phrases seep into my mind.

Where would you like the flowers, Lady Cynder?
Sign here, Ivy.
It was a beautiful ceremony, Agatha.

I stand in a corner of my own living room. No one speaks to me. That's fine. I don't want to talk anyway. I simply stare at the little card and try not to weep.

At some point, the visitors take off. Marchesa asks me to help her move some boxes around in the basement. It's not a place I visit much, but fine. I gave my word to Dad.

I'll try.

Marchesa and I step down into a concrete room. There are no boxes here—only a bare mattress in the corner. My breath catches. Marchesa closes the door behind her.

She isn't.

She wouldn't.

There's the click of a lock turning.

She just did.

Marchesa glares at me. Hatred blazes in her brown eyes. "My best friend Rae is gone. Declan married me and then died of a broken heart. This marks my second time as a widow. It makes me miserable."

"This hasn't been a picnic for me, either."

"I'd disagree. Life has been rather easy for you, Elle Cynder. But now? It's time to balance the scales. You'll learn what it's like to suffer."

I blink hard, trying to process what I'm hearing. Sure, you can suspect that someone loathes you. But then there's having that someone lock you in a basement and talk about making you suffer.

"My family tried to help you. Doesn't that mean anything?"

"*Help me?*" Marchesa's voice takes on a hysterical edge. "You know nothing. Declan was my only true love. Rae stole him away. That ruined my life."

That's a shocker. "I know you three hung out when you were young... but Mom stealing Dad away? Why would she do that?"

"Because she could. Everyone adored Rae. So your mother did

what all spoiled women do … she took what she wanted and left others to pay the price."

"Price." Like *suffer*, it's all I can do to keep repeating things here.

"My first husband was horrible, and that's all on Rae. She had other choices than Declan. Scads of men worshipped Raelyn Livie. Yet me? I only had one chance. Declan. And Rae took him. I should have lived *her* life. My daughters should have been *you!*"

Memories flicker through my mind. Mom and Dad always gave Marchesa and her daughters a free pass. Now it all makes sense.

"My parents bought into your personal pity party. If my Dad loved you, he would have chosen you, end of story. He didn't."

"Declan truly loved me! Rae just dazzled him."

Rage overtakes my mind. "Dad only felt sorry for you and we both know it. I can't believe you manipulated my parents all these years, using your *fake crush* on my father to leech off their kindness."

Okay, that was really harsh, but it's also totally true.

Marchesa's eyes flare with rage once more. After that, she turns strangely calm. "I am done with your attitude," she declares. "Let's discuss your false identity as Abigail Smythe."

Now I have multiple false identities. It goes with the whole *jewel bounty hunter* thing. I checked the Abigail Smythe accounts this morning. They were emptied but the funds moved to another account. I didn't remember doing it, but I balance a lot of numbers.

"What about Abigail Smythe?" I ask.

"I've discovered your sad attempt to save money. All your bank accounts have been drained."

It's on the tip of my tongue to say draining money isn't too scary, but there's no need to point that out. Clearly, Marchesa's unaware that her plan failed.

"Welcome to your new home." Turning, Marchesa leaves the basement. The door lock clicks behind her.

I pull my cell from my pocket. Dead. Well, Marchesa gets points for actually doing that part right. Still, she thinks she's locked me up with no way to call for help.

She's wrong.

My parents always said to hide my true powers. Right now, that advice will save my life. If Marchesa knew what I could really do, I'd be dead already.

Closing my eyes, I summon my fae powers. In my mind, I send a message to Gustav.

Need some help, bud.

An hour passes before I hear the familiar scritch-scratch of mousey feet on the basement floor. By this point, I've taken to sitting on my mattress with my back resting against the wall. Gustav hops up onto my knee.

"So sorry I'm late." When Gustav speaks, his voice is even higher than usual. The little guy is pretty upset.

"Not to worry. I knew you'd get here eventually."

"You shouldn't have waited. Marchesa could have done *who knows what* to you. Why not use fairy dust to open the door?"

"I know how to reach out to you and some pigeons down the block. That's it."

"Why not enchant the door to open?"

"I'm not sure I even have any enchanter powers."

Gustav grips his tail tightly. "When I think about what could have happened—"

"But it didn't," I state. "How about getting me the key to that door?"

"Of course." Gustav runs off. A few minutes later, he returns while dragging along a key with his tail.

"Thanks." I take the key in my hand. "Can you tell me when the coast is clear?"

"Absolutely." One thing about mice, they can flatten themselves like pancakes and it doesn't even hurt. Gustav slips under the door. This time, only a few minutes pass before he returns.

"How's it looking?" I whisper.

"You can go if you leave right now. Just stick to the far-left warehouse wall. It's dark there. And that will lead you to the back door."

"Thanks again, Gustav." Holding the key tightly in my grip, I step up to the door. Sure enough, the door opens with the quietest of clicks.

With that done, I march off into the shadows and my future.

PRESENT DAY

1. CHAPTER ONE

ELLE - AGE EIGHTEEN

*M*y alarm blares. Rolling over, I grab my cell and turn off the noise. Blinking, I scan the time.

7AM

What a strange dream. I was back with the Queen of Hearts. She told me how Marchesa and Legend Le Charme would block me from my true love.

I remember that prophecy. Meeting the Queen of Hearts isn't something you forget. The prophecy is seared in my memory, too.

I'll be blocked from my true love.

What a load of crap that turned out to be. My days are split between online classes and jewel un-thievery. There's no true love in sight. Yes, Jacoby's still around, but if I were in love with him I'd know it.

At least, I think I would.

Propping a pillow under my head, I look out across my apartment in Greenwich Village. It's a single room with a high ceiling, big window, and loft up top (that's where I'm cuddled up now).

Yawning, I slide out of bed and climb down the loft ladder. After hitting the bathroom and pouring myself a bowl of cereal, I head over to the couch, open my laptop, and launch my online classes. Text flashes across the screen.

Congratulations! You've finished junior year of high school.

My brows lift. All my final essays and exams were due last week. It wasn't clear how long it would take to grade everything, but looks like that's done now.

It's official. I'm now a high school senior. Not bad for someone who's eighteen and has never set foot inside a typical school.

I grab my cell and type out a quick message to my best friend, Bry.

OnlyCallMeElle: Graduated today. You?

By the way, Bry is short for Bryar Rose. She's pretty awesome.

Here's how I met the best girl in New York. After my parents died, there was no one to verify my fairy tale life template anymore. I had to start attending Denarii League meetings. That's where I met Bry. She's a Sleeping Beauty life template and a super cool girl. Sadly, I can't tell her the truth about my being a warden. Or about a lot, really. But she's the best friend I've ever had and I love her to pieces.

Bry's also taking the same online classes that I am. She might have graduated as well.

MyOwnBry: oh, lemme check

Minutes pass before my cell phone gets the *dot-animation* thing. Bry is typing back.

MyOwnBry: Me 2!!!

Grinning, I send her some pics of supermodels saying, *you're fabulous.* Bry is the fashion type. She texts me back with some little animated ninjas because I'm so stealthy.

Did I mention Bry is the best? She is.

OnlyCallMeElle: What r u doing today
MyOwnBry: auntie lockdown :(

Technically, Bry is *always* on auntie lockdown. Those ladies barely let her leave their penthouse. I swear, if the Denarii League weren't such pests about their support groups, I don't think Bry would ever leave her room.

That said, I can work some of my fairy charm and get the aunties to set Bry loose. Yet I have to be careful about that stuff. If I use too much magic around the infamous aunties, they might figure out I'm a warden. Plus they could also realize they're being manipulated and shut me down. If that happened, I'm not sure Bry would ever see daylight again.

Back to the *auntie lockdown* thing. It's also part of the code between me and Bry. It means that her aunties are in an especially bad mood. So bad in fact, that even I couldn't charm Bry outside. On days like these, Bry likes to hang in her room, eat ice cream, and surf the web. I respect that.

> *OnlyCallMeElle: text me if u need help*
> *MyOwnBry: will do*

It's a bummer that Bry can't get out today, but my schedule will move forward.

Time to un-steal jewelry.

Puling up my laptop, I check the Magiweb once more. *Nothing new. Boo.*

That said, there is one wedding ring listing that I've been tracking. The ad is still live, which means it hasn't been found yet. And the bounty is a sweet two grand. Only trouble is, I'm not sure where the stolen item could be.

I know who can check, though. Mice may suck at housework, but they totally rock at surveillance. I close my eyes and pull on my inner magic.

> *Gustav? Are you around?*

In reply, there's the unmistakable sound of tiny claws on my velvet couch. Gustav crawls up onto my knee. His marble-black eyes blink up at me.

"I found it," he says in his squeaky mouse voice.

No question what *it* is in the scenario. *The wedding ring.*

"Where?"

"It's in Alec Le Charme's office." He flicks his little hands over his face. "Again."

"Huh. Let me check his schedule." By that I mean, surf the web. The paparazzi keep tabs on where the so-called Le Charme prince can be sighted. In fact, the Magicorum News Network has a special section called, *Where in the world is Alec Le Charme?* I hit that site first, but there isn't anything specific.

Next up: surfing general celebrity sites. Which, since the internet is a time suck, leads to my checking out tons of pictures of Mister Fancy Pants himself. I swear, the guy must sleep in formalwear. There's Alec in a tuxedo at a charity auction. Alec in a suit jacket during a store opening. And Alec in a ... baseball cap?

I freeze. Inspect the picture four times. Blink a lot. Then I read the caption aloud. "In a rare shot, we catch Alec Le Charme hiding from the cameras on Fifth Avenue. Who knew he even owned jeans, let alone a Yankees cap? Nice try at hiding, but we see you, Alec!"

A jolt of realization moves through me.

I can't believe I never realized this before.

That's him.

Fred from the L Center.

Fred, the guy I daydream about to this day. *Mister Cutie McGamester.* Honestly, I don't fire up Magicorum Killers without imagining Fred beside me, trying to kick my ass at level twenty-eight. In my fantasy, Fred never wins, by the way. But it would be great to have someone try. And now there's no avoiding the truth.

Fred is Alec Le Charme.

This is a problem.

As in, I can't keep stealing stuff from him. It's asking for trouble. Bry is Magicorum, but she's a pretty low profile girl. But Alec is super famous and a gem caster to boot. Those guys are the top of the wizard food chain. They can do pretty much every potion master or enchanter spell ... plus a lot more.

Long story short, there is no way I can go anywhere near Alec Le

Charme ever again. Sure, I've just been un-stealing stuff from his office and leaving piles of ash on the desk, but that is now off limits.

Forbidden.

Taboo.

Done.

And I keep that vow for all of two minutes before coming to a another, far more momentous decision: I'm still a girl with bills to pay. And I'm stealthy chick, too. Just look at all my ninja animations from Bry.

What's the problem? I can totally sneak into Alec Le Charme's office again. My bank account will thank me.

And that's it. The only reason I'm going near Alec Le Charme is cold hard cash.

If I keep thinking that enough, I might even start to believe it.

2. CHAPTER TWO

ELLE

*N*ow that I've decided to un-steal that wedding ring, it's time to check some things. Namely, gear.

Next stop: *my super secret thievery supply area.*

Basically, that's a fancy name for a lock-box I keep under the sink. I open the thing and unfortunately, I am all out of key cards and other goodies. That means I must visit my Doc Eight. And as a side consequence, I'll see Doc's assistant, Jacoby.

Mysterious fact: ever since I learned that Fred is actually Alec, my stomach has been doing flip flops. Yet visiting Doc Eight means seeing Jacoby. Somehow, that reality doesn't make my stomach flip, let alone flop. It could mean something.

But I decide it means nothing.

With that important revelation behind me, I take off for Doc Eight's place. Soon, I stand before a super-skinny storefront in the Village. Basically, it's nothing but a small building squashed between two tall apartment complexes. The place has a red door with the words *Henry's Emporium* written above in loopy script. I pull on the handle and step inside.

As I march across the threshold, I'm surrounded by red mist. My ears pop from the change in air pressure as magic transports me to somewhere that is most definitely not a closet-shaped space in the Village.

A second later, I stand inside a large chamber made of charcoal-colored stone. Large wooden chests line the floor. A variety of medieval-style weapons hang on the walls. The scent of cut grass hangs in the air. I'm pretty sure this is somewhere upstate, but Doc is always cagey about his actual location.

Speaking of Doc, an enchanted suit of armor stomps toward me. As always, the helm is drawn down. "Elle!"

I wave. "Hey, Doc!"

A pouf of air rolls across the room. That's all the warning I get before Jacoby materializes beside me. He's all silver eyes and sneaky intent. Over the years, he's certainly built out into a grown guy. Most elves are more willowy. Jacoby's relatively ripped.

"Good morning, Elle." Jacoby winks. "What can I do for you?"

At this moment, I realize something important. Jacoby may not inspire my stomach to flip-flop. But he does generate zings of attraction. Dude is dangerous.

I turn to Doc. "I need supplies for a new gig."

"As you wish, Milady." Like always, Doc's voice sounds like he's talking inside a massive tin can. Which—let's face it—he totally is. Doc stomps over to one of the wooden chests and rummages around inside. "The usual supplies?"

"Yes, please." That means enchanted key cards, lock picks and the like.

Jacoby folds his arms over his chest. He wears a black-T-shirt and jeans today. Why can't he dress like Legolas? It's really hard to ignore him this way.

"You're purposely not looking at me," says Jacoby.

"No, I'm just very interested in what Doc is doing."

"He's bending over a wooden chest. That's interesting to you?"

I set my fist on my hip. "Infinitely."

Jacoby moves so quickly, he's a blur. One second, the dark elf is beside me. The next moment, we're nose to nose.

"Infinitely," repeats Jacoby. His voice is low and growly. That zing of attraction moves through me again.

This is all very confusing.

Taking a pointed step away from Jacoby, I focus on Doc instead. "Doc, I've started going to these Denarii league meetings and made a friend. I'm worried about her. Her eighteenth birthday is coming up and you know what that means."

Doc nods. "If anything goes wrong on a fairy tale life template, it takes place at eighteen."

"So, do you have any new weapons? You know, just in case?"

"Do I ever!"

Jacoby gives me a sideways look. "I know what you're trying to do," he whispers.

Good one of us does.

Doc goes through a bunch of the new weapons on the walls. There's an enchanted gun that's particularly cool. Eventually, we stop talking about the Doc's new stuff and get back to my key cards and stuff. In short order, my purse is crammed with fresh supplies for tonight's visit to Alec Le Charme's office.

"How much do I owe you?" I ask.

"Nothing."

"You can't mean that."

"I was rusting in a basement, left to rot. Your parents found me, cleaned me up, and gave me a purpose." Behind Doc Eight, Jacoby mouths the words to this speech in tandem because Doc says this all the time.

And yes, it's a little funny to see Jacoby pantomime it.

"But you need to let me pay you," I counter.

"No." And this time, the word has an extra-long and metallic echo to it.

"What about the other animates? Maybe I can pay them instead." I haven't kept in touch with them because Marchesa and her spawn still live in the Cynder building. But I could find a way to get them some gold if they needed it.

Clang!

Doc slams his fist onto his open palm. "I won't have this conversation any longer. All the other Cynder animates are fine."

Jacoby steps into my line of vision again. "Fascinating as this conversation is, you two have it every time. Perhaps a change of subject is in order?" He taps his chin. "Hmm." His eyes widen. "I have it. You mentioned a group before?"

"The Denarii league."

"Perhaps I could join you at these meetings. I may be able to help protect your friend."

I consider that offer for a hot second, then dismiss it. "Look, you're way too much of a prankster."

"You really think I'd try to cause mischief if some battle were at hand?" asks Jacoby.

"No, You'd totally fight."

"Exactly."

"It's just *all the rest of the time* that you'd be a pain. I've finally made a friend and you are NOT screwing it up."

"Then where are you attending school?"

"Why do you ask?"

Jacoby shrugs. "No reason."

"You're not trailing me to school. I still take classes online."

"Then I'll protect you at home."

I roll my eyes. "Jacoby."

He gives me one of his dazzling and elfy grins. "Can't blame me for trying."

"Goodbye, Jacoby." I turn to Doc. "Thank you, kind Doctor."

With that, I high tail it out the door and back to my heist. Mostly because Jacoby's many offers of protection were starting to become tempting.

And that's trouble.

3. CHAPTER THREE

ALEC - AGE EIGHTEEN

Mmm-psh ... Mmm-psh ... Mmm-psh!

The beat of this techno music is so loud, I can hardly hear myself think.

I'd turn it down, but this is my party.

And to be honest? Most days, I'd rather not think anyway.

I saunter about Knox's apartment and work the room. There are kids here from West Lake Prep, which is my Magicorum high school. Some up-and-coming stars and starlets hang by the back wall. And a new heavy metal band from Korea has camped out by the front door. All of them seem at home in what amounts to a concrete room with a great view of Manhattan.

From the corner of my eye, I catch a flash of blonde hair. A band of excitement tightens about my chest.

Is that Elle?

I make my way over to the girl in question. Her back is facing me, but I'm able to slip through the crowd so I can get a good look at her face. My heart sinks.

Not Elle.

Knox stalks up to my side. "Looking for someone?" he asks.

Werewolves and their damned sense of smell. With one whiff, Knox can tell what I'm thinking. "Always."

"You've got half of Manhattan in your apartment," says Knox.

"It's *your* apartment," I correct.

"Legend and Diamond pay the bills and ignore the parties, so let's call it a draw."

"They have their reasons." Mostly, my parents are still pushing for the whole Le Charme curse situation. They believe that giving me nice cars and a free apartment will smooth over my eventual disappointment when I get engaged. They're wrong, of course. The warden curse is still out there, so there are no plans to set up my Glass Slipper Ball. And I like it that way, thank you very much.

A stocky figure catches my eye. "Is that?"

"Yeah," says Knox. "It's Wilhelm."

The rest of the crowd doesn't notice the dwarf, but that's because shadowcoe carry extreme magic for just such purposes. You won't see Wilhelm unless he wants you to.

Speaking of Wilhelm, the lead dwarf winks at Knox.

"Back at you," says Knox. My best friend shoots Wilhelm a thumbs-up.

Here's what that's all about. Knox and his werewolves have been supplying the dwarves with fresh meat for years. My parents can't complain since it's a gift from a warden. The whole thing is one of my better ideas, if I do say so myself. I'm still tracking down why Le Charme can't afford to feed its own people, but that's turning out to be tricky. Let's just say that my parents are very good at hiding things.

All that aside, it's super unusual for Wilhelm to visit the Earth's surface. I look to Knox. "I'll talk to Wilhelm in the library."

"Sure thing," says Knox.

I take off through the crowd. The library has been magically soundproofed and warded about a dozen times over, so it's a good spot to chat. Within a few minutes, I stand in a snug room that sports lots of exposed wood, leather chairs and books. This is officially Knox's place but I do keep my own bedroom and library. After all, I need a place to crash. Plus, no self-respecting wizard sleeps too far away from his spell book collection.

Wilhelm slips into the room and closes the door. He looks as dwarfy as ever with his leather cap and long tunic. I can't imagine what would be important enough to lure him away from his dig.

"What's up?" I ask.

Wilhelm raises his arm. On his outstretched palm, there sits a thumb drive. I do a double take.

Wait, a thumb drive?

"Is that..." I gesture toward Wilhelm's hand.

"It is."

"I thought you were, you know..." I don't even know where to begin.

"Only interested in jewels?" asks Wilhelm.

"That."

"We hit an internet backbone years ago. If it's underground, it's dwarf business."

I slowly nod. "Okay, that makes sense."

"So we tapped into the web and, eventually, the Le Charme network. Turns out, data is interesting to dig through too." He wiggles his hand in a way that says, *take it.*

I scoop the drive from Wilhelm. "What's on this?"

"Video from the Le Charme security cameras. Diamond has been deleting it."

Interesting. If Diamond has been deleting footage, there's one likely reason why. Legend brings some of his lady friends to the building. Maybe there are some things Diamond wants to keep private. I shake my head. "I don't need to see footage of Legend *getting it on* in his office."

"It's not that," says Wilhelm. "Do you have a laptop in here?"

Now, I thought the fact that Wilhelm brought me a thumb drive was a shocker. Now hearing him use the word *laptop* in a sentence? For some reason, that stuns me even more. I think of Wilhelm holding a pickaxe and talking up the finer points of gemstone quality.

"This is all very strange."

"There's a reason we're called shadowcoe," says Wilhelm. "We hide things you simply can't imagine."

All of which brings this to an even greater level of odd. Shadowcoe conceal things from humans, but they're hiding stuff from Magicorum as well? My head gets a little woozy at the thought.

Focus, Alec. Thumb drive first.

I scan the room. My laptop sits in its regular spot on a nearby shelf. After firing up the machine, I look through the files on the drive. As Wilhelm said, they're all videos.

I click on the first one. My world turns upside down. It's Elle. My Elle. And she's in my office at Le Charme. I magnify the image just to be sure.

Yes, it's Elle all right.

"This girl." Wilhelm taps the screen. "She's been breaking in to take jewels from your office."

"I'm never there," I explain. "The office is more to keep up appearances than anything else."

"Appearances of what?"

"Interest in Le Charme, mostly. I'm never there, so folks toss boxes in there all the time. My place is warded and locked, so it's a good spot to stash stuff. I don't care."

"We looked into the items she's been taking. Most recently, it was a lost wedding ring."

I loop up from the laptop. "Lost?"

"Meaning stolen. Does that happen often?"

I bob my head and think this through. "We have a desk of heirloom jewelry in the store. It's supposed to be old pieces that are bought at auction or whatever. Sometimes stolen stuff gets in there, but we're supposed to call the authorities."

"Looks like this girl might be taking matters into her own hands."

My gaze locks on the laptop screen. This time, the video shows Elle and a friend breaking into my office. *And are they...*

I lean in for a closer look, just to be sure what I'm seeing.

Yup. I'm not hallucinating. Elle and her buddy are definitely jumping on my couch. I can't help but grin.

Elle. It's really Elle.

Wilhelm folds his arms over his chest. "Any idea why Diamond would want to hide this?"

"What does your *data dig* tell you?"

"Nothing." Wilhelm's gaze turns intense. "It's like this. My people are loyal, but when it comes to stealing jewels? That's something we can't abide."

"You want to go after this girl?"

"No, she's not a thief. She's clearly taking already stolen jewels. We figure she's after the reward." Wilhelm steps closer. "What we're worried about is Diamond."

My eyes widen. Suddenly, Wilhelm's visit makes a ton of sense. Dwarves value jewels above all else. It would never occur to them that Diamond wouldn't be involved in stealing something so precious.

"You don't have to worry," I explain. "Diamond isn't involved in stealing jewels. It's this girl." I tap the screen. "Diamond doesn't want me to have anything to do with her."

Wilhelm's brows pull together. "But the girl rescues stolen stones."

"Diamond doesn't see it that way. I don't know why she hates Elle. She just does."

Wilhelm makes a harrumphing noise. It's a single sound, there's a ton of meaning inside it. Essentially, Wilhelm thinks I'm being super naive. "If there's nothing else," says Wilhelm. "I'll be off."

"Thanks, Wilhelm."

"Keep a *weather eye* out on those stones."

"I promise."

With that, Wilhelm vanishes. One second, he's there. The next? No sign.

With Wilhelm gone, I bring back the image of Elle on screen. Reaching into the pocket of my sports jacket, I pull out a handful of gems. While focusing on the picture of Elle, I pull on the power inside the stones and ask a question in my mind.

When will she return?

These jewels speak to me in a low rumble. Their voices are so deep, my ribs seem to vibrate from the tone.

Your office. Two weeks from today.

Jolts of happy zing through my heart. I reset the stones in my pocket and head out to find Knox. My best friend hangs in the kitchen. I find him leaning against a wall, his arms crossed over his chest. Knox stares out at the crowd with a predatory glare. Every so often, a partygoer steps by him, careful to keep a safe distance.

I walk up and grin. "Making new friends?"

"I'd rather be out hunting Jules and you know it." He inhales. "You're happy. What's up?"

Now, I could confess here. For instance, I might admit how I cast dozens of spells to find Elle over the years. None of them worked. Or I could share how every girl I meet gets judged against Elle's memory. Which is true. I might state how even at this moment, invisible bonds pull me back to her. And all about girl I met for two minutes three years ago.

It's like this. There are some things that belong in my heart. Elle's one of them. Even Knox doesn't know the full extent of my feelings. Call it intuition, but something tells me she needs protecting ... even from me.

On second thought, especially from me. What if the media got word I'd been obsessing about someone? Elle's life would be turned upside down. I won't let that happen.

Knox clears his throat. I realize I've been staring out into the partygoers for a beat too long. Grinning, I refocus on my friend. "Something interesting will happen at my office in two weeks. Care to join me?"

"No."

"Too bad. You're hanging with me anyway."

Knox takes in another deep breath. "Don't look now. Your latest flames are here."

"How many?"

"Four."

"You keep better track than I do."

"Not by choice. You attract ladies who love strong perfume." He says the words *strong perfume* the way someone else might say *electric chair.*

Confession time. Turns out, my parents do know me quite well. Getting this apartment for Knox has been a rather nice distraction for me. There have been lots of parties. And a lot of trying to find Elle and, failing that, discover a way to forget her.

Let's just say I've enjoyed turning eighteen.

Speaking of which, one of the ladies in question steps up. She's cute and blonde with freckles. What's her name again? *Cici, that's it.*

Cici strolls up and gives me a quick peck on the lips. "Hey, Alec."

Knox waves. "Bye, Alec." He moves with wolf speed into the crowd.

"I've missed you," says Cici. "When will we get together again?"

"About that. I'm taken now. Sorry."

Cici's mouth falls open. "You're dating someone?"

"I am."

"Who?"

"You'll know when she does," I say with a wink. As answers go, it's cryptic and accurate, all at one.

Next I announce the party's closing down early. After all, I've got two weeks before I see Elle again. I need to make sure I have my rest and all that.

Plus—if I'm being honest—the real reason for the party has ended. I suppose some small corner of me always hoped that Elle would walk through my door one night. Now that I know where she'll be in two weeks? That door is closed until further notice.

4. CHAPTER FOUR

ALEC - TWO WEEKS LATER

*T*wo weeks pass. I've never been great at waiting. And when I'm anxious, I find there's nothing more irritating than paparazzi in my face. Sure, they've been following me around my whole life. But since I turned eighteen? Locusts are more subtle. And it's always the same questions.

Excited for your Glass Slipper Ball?
Chosen your bride yet?
Give us a name, Alec!

A few times, I came close to casting a silencer spell. But MITRE has already been snooping around our offices. There's no need to make headlines about what the agency calls *aggressive magic*.

At last, the big night arrives. Knox and I lounge on the couch in my office. I even dragged the thing further into the shadows so no one would notice us. The only source of light is a single lamp over my desk.

We haven't been hanging out for long when voices sound in the outer hallway. It's Legend and a woman. Whoever it is, the lady's not my mother.

"Oh, Legend!" The woman speaks with a southern twang. That's new.

"Should I... keep my hands away?" he asks.

Some dots connect in my mind. *Keep Your Hands to Yourself* is a new hit single from the singer Cassidy Audacity. She's in town for her tour.

"*Unless I ask you to play*," she sings in reply.

Oh, that's Cassidy Audacity all right. I stifle the urge to groan.

"Allow me to show you to my private elevator," says Legend. Footsteps sound, followed by the ding of an elevator closing.

They're gone.

A long moment passes before Knox speaks. "Want to talk about it?"

"Nah." I sigh. "Thanks for asking, though."

"I'm here. You know that." Knox leans back into the couch. "I'm bored as hell, but I'm here."

"Cassidy Audacity isn't shocking?"

Knox chuckles. "I've known Legend for years, remember?"

"True. The only time you got interested was when Legend dated the actress who plays Mighty Woman."

"Best Saturday morning TV show ever," says Knox. "Legend ruined it for me, but I've forgiven him."

"You're a class act, Knox."

The ding of the elevator sounds again. Knox and I fall silent. My buddy tilts his head. I've seen that move before. Knox is leaning into his shifter hearing.

If I thought it was hard to wait two weeks, these next few seconds are close to impossible. Is Elle coming at last? I strain to hear the sound of footsteps. Nothing. Then again, I'm no shifter.

Knox looks to me and gives the barest of nods. It takes everything in me not to cheer.

Elle is on her way!

Knox kicks back onto the couch. "Who is she?" he whispers.

"She?" I ask innocently.

"That footstep is too light to be a guy."

I place my pointer finger across my lips in the universal movement for *shh*.

Knox rolls his eyes. "Next time, pick up girls on your own. You're more than capable."

And Knox has a point. I dragged him here as my wingman without being honest about it. I vow to make it up to the guy. Later. Right now, it's time to see Elle again.

A figure slips into the office. She's curvy and young with brown hair. Not Elle. I reach into my pocket, ready to cast a spell and figure out what went wrong.

That's when I notice it. Knox is sitting up. He's also doing that werewolf-sniffing thing again. For the record, I've never seen Knox act this way around a girl before.

The mystery girl digs around in a box on my desk. *Interesting.* Knox and I have been trying to solve the problem of my first curse, which is the one where wardens can't marry without killing their spouses. And the particular containers that our visitor is opening?

It holds papyri from Ancient Egypt.

As a matter of fact, I have a sideline acquiring papyri. With any luck, I might uncover information about the so-called Fountain of Magic (and how to break my warden curse.) So far, I haven't had too much luck though. The stuff uses its own language of hieroglyphs. I can barely manage English, let alone some new text from ancient Egypt.

And, if I'm being honest, I'm pretty happy with the warden's curse. It stops me from worrying about my Le Charme version. But tinkering with papyri keeps my parents happy. And who knows? Maybe some day I will want to marry. It's possible.

The girl opens the box, pulls out papyri, and takes digital photos. Then she reseals the container with ease. Impressive, but not as entertaining as watching Knox lose his mind beside me. The guy's almost hyperventilating.

All of which adds up to one thing. Elle isn't here, but I've seen this girl before. She's definitely Elle's buddy. So I simply must chat her up. And if that means Mister Smooth Shifter loses his mind a little? That's just an extra bonus.

The girl finishes resealing the box and freezes. No question about it. She's sensed that we're here. I rise and get ready for the fireworks.

Little by little, the girl turns to face me. "Hey."

"Hello. I'm Alec." And I smile.

"I came here to take pictures of your papyri. I'll just leave now."

"I was waiting for the jewel thief," I explain. "Normally, she comes here with you."

The girl lifts her chin. "I don't know what you're talking about."

I hold his hands up, palms forward. "Your friend isn't in any trouble. I've started running checks on the pieces she takes." *Or rather, my dwarves have.* "They're all stolen jewels with a bounty on them. Le Charme would have returned them if the company were aware."

The girl sets her fist on her hip. "Your parents totally knew."

"You're right. My parents knew." *After all, Diamond took the time to have the footage destroyed.* "But I didn't."

"And?"

"I'm ready to work with her."

"And why would you want to do that?"

"Every time she steals something, she leaves a little pile of cinders on my desk. The cleaning staff have been complaining."

The girl steps toward the door. "This is me leaving."

I move to block her path. A shiver visibly rolls up the girl's back. She glances over in the general direction of where Knox hides in the shadows.

"Back off," she declares. "I said I was going."

I haven't spent years talking down jittery fans not to know how to deal with this situation. It's important to continue the conversation.

"How come you want to steal my papyri anyway?" I ask.

"I make digital photos of them. There's a difference."

"Why not ask my office for access?"

"I did. Many times."

"Let me guess. Your requests got routed through my parents."

"That they did."

"Well, ask me this time. You'll get a different answer."

"No one else should look at those papyri. They're ours." That would be Knox, snarling from the shadows. Over the years, I've learned the nature of his different growls. This particular variety says he's fighting with himself.

Knox is interested in the girl. Oh, this is too good.

"If we're having a group discussion, why don't you come out of the shadows?" I ask.

Setting my hand back into my pocket, I toy with some gems there. It's something I do when thinking things through. And in this case? There's one conclusion to be made.

"Oh, I like her," I state. "We should work with her directly."

"No," grumps Knox.

The girl glares in Knox's direction again. "Quiet, you. I'm talking here."

I can't help but chuckle. "Oh, we're definitely working together."

"Working with you on what?" she asks.

"The papyri, of course," I reply. "There's a code in them. We're trying to break it."

"A code?" At this point, the girl's phone rings. She raises her pointer finger. "One sec. I have to get this."

"You're taking a call?" asks Alec. "Right now?"

"You always this fast?" The girl says it with a smile and a wink, though.

It's a quiet room and a loud phone. Long story short, I can hear the voice through the earpiece. "Hey, Bry."

Every nerve in my body goes on alert. It's been three years since I heard that particular tone, but I'll never forget it. Elle. And her friend is named Bry. Good to know.

"Hey," says Bry.

"Your aunties are on hold right now. I told them you're in the shower at my place. Normally, that would make them hang up, but they wanted to stay on the line until you got out. I said I'd take them off hold once you were done. You ready?"

"Sure. Patch them through."

Now, I understand having intrusive guardians. In this case, it seems Bry's aunties are pains in the neck. I wasn't kidding before. I do like this Bry. This makes me even more intrigued.

"You got it," says Elle. "Oh, how's it going with the heist?"

"It's going."

"That good, eh?"

Bry glances my way. "I'll explain later. Patch them through now, or they may actually be tempted to use magic."

"You got it," says Elle.

At this point, there's a lot of high-pitched chatter on the other end of the call. I don't catch all of it, but I do make out the words *homework* and *episode*, as well as Bry's claim that Miss Chang is not teaching her martial arts.

I know a lie when I hear one. Bry is totally learning martial arts. That makes her even more interesting.

Bry paces the floor. With each step, she gets closer to Knox. At this point, I wish I had popcorn and a soda. A rather enjoyable show will begin any second now.

Sure enough, Bry gets too close. Knox growls.

"What's that noise?" asks the voice on the phone.

"Oh that? We're watching Animal Planet."

"It was terrifying." The voice has a warble to it. Must be Bry's auntie.

That exchange is followed by even more yammering from the auntie in question. Bry gives her a minute before cutting the call short.

"Love you all," says Bry. "Buh-bye." She ends the call and turns to me once more. "Sorry about that."

"Can't they trace you?" I ask.

"Duh. This is a burner. My friend has the real phone."

"Your friend named Elle."

How much do I love saying the name Elle out loud? Very much, indeed.

"Like you didn't know." Bry slips her hand into her purse and pulls out a can of mace. "I'm going to leave now. This is the last time I'll say it."

"Please." This time, I give her my very best smile. "I waited patiently while you rifled through my things. I didn't even call security. The least you can do is answer a few questions before you mace my face off."

"Fine. Ask your questions."

"How old are you?"

Here's what that question is all about. If Knox is interested in Bry, then the girl must be part of the Magicorum. And for those of us who are shifters, casters, or fae? Turning eighteen is a major birthday. As I've learned too well, turning eighteen means marriage. Sure, I'm fighting this but I'm an exception. By asking Bry her age, I'm just providing Knox with important information.

And yes, I'm being a bit of a busybody matchmaker. What re friends for?

"That's rather personal," says Bry. "How old are you?"

"Eighteen. And you are?"

Bry shrugs. "I'm eighteen."

"You're eighteen?"

"That's what I said."

"Right now?" Knox asks this one from the shadows. Classy.

"My birthday is in three days."

Bingo. In other words, if Knox wants this girl, he better get moving. Am I a great matchmaker or what?

And move Knox does. My friend hauls his butt off the couch and steps into the light. There's no mistaking the energy and interest that sparks between him and Bry. I should know. I experienced the same thing with Elle three years ago.

"What... What's your name?" Bry asks.

"Knox."

"Knox. Like the gelatin?"

"Like the fort."

"Oh."

I roll my eyes. *Master of charm, that's my Knox.*

"What's *your* name?" Knox asks.

I'm tempted to shoot the guy a thumbs up. Asking for names is a very normal way to get to know another person. Much better than growling. I consider this progress.

"Bryar Rose."

"You're not safe here, Bryar Rose."

At this point, Knox actually snarls. I roll my eyes once more. Was I really about to congratulate my friend on his social skills? Forget it. That growl is the equivalent of interpersonal dynamite. I've seen this move before, and most folks run for the exits. After all, Knox is a warden and badass. In this case, he's also being a douchebag. I wince, waiting for Bry to hightail it out of my office.

That isn't what happens.

Bry steps closer to Knox. "I can handle myself."

"No, you need to leave." Knox points to door. "Don't ever come back. You got me?"

Bry turns to me. "You wanted to talk?"

I blink hard, not believing what I'm seeing. Bry still isn't running. *How wonderful.* "Yes, I did."

"Well, I'm listening."

"When you were on the phone just now, you said something about tutors. Are you one of the Magicorum that can't go to a regular school?"

"Why do you ask?"

"I attend a school called West Lake Prep. Heard of it?"

"Maybe."

You don't grow up in retail and not know when someone's interested in a particular *whatever*. And the idea of West Lake Prep definitely appeals to Bry. I want to get closer to Elle, which means keeping Bry around. And if watching Knox actually fall for a girl happens along the way? That only adds to the fun.

"I'm a student there," I explain. "Going into my senior year, as a matter of fact."

"And?" Bry prompts.

"My parents are on the school's board. You want in? You're definitely accepted, so long as you join the summer internship program at Le Charme."

Knox rounds on me. "You don't have a summer internship program."

"Quiet, Knox. I just made it up." I refocus to Bry. "But I assure you, my parents will do this for me. They're dying for me to take an interest in the business. They'll be thrilled if I organize some interns."

And when I say *interns*, I mean both Elle and Bry, obviously. Of course, it may take some doing to hide Elle from Diamond. But the dwarves already think Elle is a heroine for returning stolen jewels. I'm sure they can work their magic on our video tracking systems.

"But what if someone says I'm not qualified for West Lake?" asks Bry.

"We have ways around that. We're a private institution and not subject to all the government rules and regulations. Plus, if you were awarded a scholarship..." I allow the logic to hang out there.

Knox's face darkens. "You don't have a scholarship program, either."

"I said, quiet." I stay focused on Bry. "So, what do you think?"

"If I take your internship, are there more papyri I can read?"

"Sure, I'll even give you everything we have on the code."

"How will you do that? You ship all the papyri away."

"They're shipped, but to another floor. All the original papyri are stored right here in this building."

Bry frowns. "I thought you sent them somewhere else."

"You thought wrong. In fact, I hereby declare that your internship job will be to research all the papyri in our archives and work on breaking the code."

"What's the code about?" asks Bry.

"That's a good question, isn't it? Once you break the code, you can tell us." It's a lie, but warden business is our own.

"What do I get in exchange for all this?" asks Bry.

"Le Charme will pay you a wildly inappropriate salary, whether or not you crack one word of the hidden code. We even have furnished apartments here in the building. You could work round the clock, if you wanted to. That's what interests you, doesn't it? The papyri in our collection and being independent?"

"Possibly."

Oh, she's interested all right. I flash yet another in my collection of compelling grins. "So, consider it."

Knox steps between me and Bry. He spies the edge of a brochure in Bry's bag. The title is something about Magicorum and the Denarii league. *Uh oh.* Knox's favorite past time is trying to kill Jules. Failing that, Knox takes down Jules' minions ... and many of those folks are in that league.

Knox plucks the brochure from Bry's bag. "You really think you're in the Magicorum, yeah?"

"I know that I am." Bry snatches the brochure back. "Don't touch my stuff."

Knox rubs his chin. This Denarii thing has him worried, clearly. No one gets more protective than a shifter. Even if Knox thinks he doesn't like Bry, he'll want her safe.

"If you're in the Magicorum, then what's your fairy tale template?"

I open my mouth, ready to point out that it's obvious how Bry is part of the Magciorum. Yet I can imagine where Knox is coming from here. No doubt, part of him hopes she's not Magicorum and this attraction is all some fluke.

Been there, tried to rationalize that.

"Not answering," says Bry.

Knox works his *I'm an alpha warden stare* on the girl. In my opinion, this tactic is far more effective than growling. Bry takes in a deep breath.

"My template is Sleeping Beauty."

"Then why are you after all these papyri?" asks Knox. "Shouldn't you be out in the woods looking for your prince?"

"I have other interests." Bry looks to me once more. "I'd like to find out more about your internship."

"No," says Knox. "She wouldn't."

"Yes." Bry counters. "She would. Don't order me around." As she says those last four words, Bry pokes Knox in the chest. My buddy's eyes widen. For shifters, touch is important. Pretty sure Knox is debating whether or not to kiss Bry at this point. With his alpha shifter power, most girls would just kiss him first.

Again, Bry surprises.

Bry steps away from Knox and looks to me. "Like I said, Alec. I'll be in touch."

How did she walk away? Shifter mojo is next to impossible to ignore. Hell, I have trouble with Knox sometimes. What's going on here?

My eyes widen. It could be a *life mate thing*. When shifters find their mate, it can break all the rules. Perhaps that's why Bry can walk away so easily. It's something to consider after. For now, I have an internship to finalize.

"Stop by my office anytime," I tell Bry. "Only it's preferable if you visit during working hours. I'm here every day during the summer." *Or I will be now that Elle may be stopping by.* "All they do is pay me to dress up and surf the web. I'd love some good company."

"Hey, I'm here with you," growls Knox.

I wink. "Like I said. I'd love some good company."

"I'll stop by." Bry shoots one last glare in Knox's direction before hustling herself out the door. Knox watches her leave, his body still as a statue.

He's got it bad, all right.

"An internship." I round on Knox. "Tell me that wasn't brilliant."

"You cannot hire her."

"Why not? I like her. And if she can get something new of out those papyri, we need to try."

"We'll figure it out on our own."

"If there's some secret in there, our people haven't found it in the last—what is it again?—oh yeah, that's right. Two thousand years. I don't see the harm in giving Bryar Rose a chance. Besides, she'll just keep trying to copy them illegally otherwise."

"No."

"No?"

"You heard me."

"We'll drop the subject… for now." Mostly because I have a spell to cast. Since Bry called Elle, the room still holds a bit of their mutual energy. It's not the kind of thing a junior wizard could use in a spell.

Then again, I'm not a junior wizard.

And I will find Elle.

5. CHAPTER FIVE

ELLE

I'm not freaking out.

   I'm not freaking out.

I'm not freaking out.

Okay, I'm freaking out.

It's the day after Bry got discovered breaking into Alec Le Charme's office. I'm now back in Alec's office or the first day of our internship.

Yipes.

Bry is off playing with her papyri. Alec has a pretty fancy lunch laid out… just for the two of us.

Trouble is, people keep walking by the glass door and staring. It's a little nerve wracking.

All right. It's a *lot* nerve wracking.

Alec sets his hands in his pockets. It's like he's posing for the cover of a magazine or something. He gestures across the low coffee table that sits across from his couch. The thing is covered in fancy plates with little silver domes on top. And does one of those have a Bunsen burner under it? It does.

"About lunch." Alec points across the food once more. "We have a choice of steak, chicken, salad and…" Alec peeps under one of the little domes. "Falafel. I wasn't sure if you were vegan."

"Oh." I try not to notice how the hallway outside Alec's office is getting more clogged with people. Total fail. "Are you not in here much or something?"

"In this office, you mean?"

"Yes."

"To do actual work?"

"Yes again."

"No. Never. I mean, sometimes I have to sit at the desk because there's a photo shoot or something, so I keep a pile of Sudoku in the top drawer. It looks like I'm signing contracts."

"Is that why everyone is staring at us?"

Alec turns. "Oh, I hadn't noticed that."

"I guess you wouldn't." I sidestep toward the wall and take care to keep my back toward the window. A flash of light comes from the hallway. "Did someone just take our picture?"

Alec frowns. "I'm afraid they did."

My self-preservation instinct kicks into high gear. "Look, this was a bad idea. You're Alec Le Charme and I'm not someone who should ever be in the spotlight. At all." I scoop up my purse from a nearby table. "I should probably go."

Alec shoots me a million watt smile. "Want to get something incognito?"

"You? Incognito?" But even as I ask the question, I remember how Alec popped on a baseball cap and became Fred.

This might work.

"What about the food?" I ask.

"Office buildings are essentially the same as vulture packs. The moment I leave the premises, they will pick over the leavings within minutes."

I tilt my head, unsure. "Really?"

"Oh yes. And to answer your other question, going incognito is one of my greatest skills." Alec bobs his brows. "Prepare to be dazzled." Spinning about, he marches up to the door and pulls it open. Reaching into his pocket, Alec pulls out a handful of gemstones and grips them in his fist. Closing his eyes, he focuses on his spell. A plume of red mist bursts out from his hand and fills the entire hallway. After that, the air clears. Alec turns to me. "Let's go."

I tilt my head. "What did you do?"

"Nothing too evil." He winks.

Now I have to see.

I step up to the door, glance out into the hallway and smile. Everyone is frozen in place. A light dusting of red covers them. "You cast a time stop."

"It will only last another minute." Alec steps into the hallway and gestures toward the back of the building. "I expect you know where the private family elevators are?"

"I do." Mostly because I break in here all the time.

We reach the elevators. Just as the silver doors close on us, everyone on the floor comes back to life. Leaning against the elevator wall, I try to jam my hands in my pockets. But this suit doesn't have any. So annoying.

"So what's next?" I ask.

"The dazzling will continue," says Alec.

We step out into the sub-basement. There Alec keeps a leather bomber jacket, baseball cap, and sunglasses. He swaps out his suit jacket for the casual ensemble and does another magazine style pose, this time where he leans against the wall with his right shoulder. "What do you think?"

"I'd never recognize you... Fred."

Alec whips off the sunglasses. "So you remember that?"

I shrug. "Of course."

"I never forgot it, either." Alec steps closer. My stomach decides to practice aerobics again. "And MingMart would not disclose their supplier. I even tried magic. Nothing."

A zing of happy moves through my soul. *He tried to find me.* "That was probably my parents. They cast lots of security spells over my identity."

"It was some good stuff. I'm a warden."

There's no hiding the mini gasp I let out. "You are? No one writes about that."

"I keep a low profile." Alec leans in even closer. "And you read about me?"

"You're hard to miss." I don't mean to say this, but my lips seem to move on their own. "I'm a warden, too."

"No way. You hide it really well."

"I'm sure you get why."

"Of course."

I want to face palm myself. Hanging around Alec is dangerous. Now I just told him I'm the warden of fae magic. How dumb is that? "It has to stay secret."

"I'd never risk you." Alec is usually such a player. Not in this moment, though. Nothing but sincerity shines in his blue eyes. "You need to know that."

The force of his emotion slams into me. I want to say a million things, like how I've never forgotten him ... how he awakens my heart ... And how happy I am in this moment. All those thoughts wrap into a single word. "Thanks."

A flash of red light floods the basement. The next thing I know, there's a dwarf standing between me and Alec. I step backward in shock. Words tumble from my mouth. "I've never met a dwarf before." And this is a real dwarfy-looking dwarf, if you know what I mean. Huge brown beard. Long tunic. Pointy-toed boots. The whole deal.

"I'm Wilhelm."

Alec sighs. "Why are you here?"

Wilhelm arrows his eyes at me. "I wish to discover your intentions toward our Prince."

Now I'm really lost. "Prince?"

"Wilhelm and his crew are pledged to serve the Le Charme family," Alec explains. "We're a Cinderella template, so that makes me their *you know what.*"

Wilhelm dramatically scans the empty basement, as if spies could be lurking in any random corner. "We serve Le Charme by digging up jewels... and information."

My eyes widen. "Were you the ones who cracked the internet backbone under the Russian Embassy?"

Wilhelm puffs out his chest. "Why, yes."

I nod, impressed. "I heard it was a dwarven job, but no one knew there was a senior crew operating in Manhattan."

"We've been here since the Le Charmes came over form Europe." Wilhelm clears his throat. "But enough about my crew." He wags a meaty finger in my direction. "Answer the question. What are your intentions?"

"Nothing but good stuff."

"And you'll respect his innate decency?" asks Wilhelm.

Alec groans, but there's no real anger in it. I focus on Wilhelm. "Absolutely," I reply. "His decency is safe with me."

"I suppose it's all right." Wilhelm pulls off his cute pointy hat and rubs his bald head. "Not sure why the Queen of Hearts is up in arms about you two."

All the blood in my body seems to sink to my toes. I'd forgotten about the Queen of Hearts. "What do you know about that?"

"Nothing you need be concerned about." Another flash of red light illuminates the basement. When the brightness is gone, so is Wilhelm.

Alec pretends to be very interested in wiping dust off his sunglasses. "Sorry about that."

"No, Wilhelm is sweet. It's clear he cares about you." And because I can't help myself, I add one more question. "Does he do that a lot?"

"That's the first time," says Alec.

"Oh," I say. And that's all I can get out at the moment.

"I should be honest here," says Alec. "Wilhelm knows I had a dream about the Queen of Hearts ages ago. She said that Legend would keep my from my true love."

"Oh," I say again.

And this would be the perfect place to add in how I actually met the Queen of Hearts. She told me the same thing, only the queen added that it would be none other than Marchesa and Legend who would try to spoil my love life.

But I can't get the words out.

Sadly, that confession feels sealed behind a heavy wall. A memory appears. I'm in the Cynder basement with Marchesa. She's tried to lock me in. Both my parents are gone. Sorrow weighs into my soul with such force, it's like I can't breathe.

So much pain. And I bricked it away years ago.

I haven't really gone past that wall ever since.

Yes, there's Bry. But having someone like Alec in my life? That's more than a new friend. It explodes my whole life. It could rip down that wall. All the hurt would escape and overwhelm. And if things with Alec didn't work out? I don't know that I'd have the strength to build myself up again.

"Elle? Can you hear me?" It's Alec.

I clear my throat. "Yes?"

"You seemed a little lost just then. I hope the stuff about the Queen of Hearts didn't upset you. If Wilhelm says not to worry, then we're safe. Really."

"No, it's fine." I force on a smile. "I just need some lunch."

"Sure," says Alec. But a question lingers in his eyes. "Why don't we head out the back alley exit? There's a hot dog cart not far from here. We could get something to eat and chat."

I take in a deep breath and clear my thoughts. "That sounds perfect."

As we step outside, my thoughts go back to Bry. All these feelings for Alec remind me how much I already care for my best friend. And her eighteenth birthday is coming up. Again, that's never a great date for anyone with a fairy tale life template. No matter what, I've got to keep my eye on her.

And protect my heart.

6. CHAPTER SIX

a shadow falls over Elle's face. I step closer. Every impulse in my being wants to enfold her in my arms. Still there's no missing the chill around her. It's not a physical sense of cold, mind you. It's more something inside.

"What's wrong?" I ask.

"It's nothing." She forces a smile. "Let's get some lunch."

I slip in my sunglasses. "Hot dogs, here we come!" I push out the back door.

Together, Elle and I step into the alley and merge with the foot traffic on the sidewalk. My disguise works and happily, there are no fans or paparazzi to bother us.

Now we can get down to business.

I've spent years wondering what happened to Elle. All we had was a small chat by a loading dock. At last, I can fill in the blanks.

"What's your favorite color?" I ask.

Elle's blue eyes dance with humor. "Color?" she echoes.

"Yes, I want to know all about you."

Her cheeks redden. "It might be the same for me. Curious, you know."

"Perfect." Seeing Elle blush brings out my mischievous side. "How about we play *Truth or Dare?*"

"What? You mean that we either answer a question honestly... or perform any dare the other person demands? Are you honestly suggesting we play a game popular with eight-year-olds everywhere?"

I make my best *poor you* face. "Scared, huh?"

"Bring it on."

"Huh." I tap my chin dramatically. "Why were you sad before?"

"Before?" Elle asks the question as if she's confused, but I think she knows exactly what I'm talking about. And I could back off. Yet I still want to know everything about this girl.

"In the basement," I explain. "You seemed a little blue."

Elle nods slowly. "Okay. The answer to your question is orange."

"What?" I shake my head. "You were unhappy about orange?"

"No. Your first question was my favorite color." Elle wags her finger at me. "You can't switch now."

"Fair enough." I chuckle. "Your turn."

"Truth or dare?"

No question. "Truth."

Elle eyes me for a long moment. "When is your Glass Slipper Ball?"

I set my hands over my heart and stagger. "Ouch."

"Not your favorite subject?"

"Let's say it's a tough topic with my parents." I sigh. "Right now, it's scheduled for Valentine's Day. That's right before my nineteenth birthday. It's traditional for Queen of Hearts to bind a couple at the ball."

Elle hugs her elbows. "Bind?"

"It's a magical marriage. Normally a real wedding follows a few weeks after the ball."

"I don't know a lot about the Queen of Hearts. Why would she bother with your family's marriage ceremonies?"

"It's unclear. And believe me, I've read everything I can find on the subject. The founder of Le Charme Jewelers, Charles, once said he won a bet with the queen. Other than that, I know nothing."

At this point, it's on the tip of my tongue to share about the family curse, but I hold back. I did promise my father to keep it secret. But also? I'm unsure how I really feel about the whole thing. Before, I hated the idea. Yet now that Elle is back in my life? Things might be changing.

We reach the hot dog cart. "Here we are! Your lunch, Milady."

Elle grins. "Can't wait."

We get our grub and hoof it over to Central Park. There's a spot along the sidewalk with a bench and overarching trees. We take our seats. For a time, we eat in friendly silence. Then I ask the question. "Truth or dare?"

At this point, Elle had the hotdog halfway to her mouth. She pauses. "Dare."

"I challenge you to a Magicorum Killer tournament."

Her eyes widen. "Right now?"

"Oh, darn. We'll have to do that later, won't we?" I wink. "My turn again."

"Truth or dare?" asks Elle.

My phone starts blaring with beeps and chimes. I pull it out and turn it off. "This is a very important game," I explain. "I can't be interrupted."

Elle takes out her cell and does the same. "Mine's off too." She resets her cell into her bag. "Enough stalling. Truth or dare?"

I lean in close enough that Elle's breath fans out over my mouth. "Dare."

"Go with me to Cynder Mercantile." She worries her lower lip with her teeth. "Okay, that was a little odd."

"Not at all. What's Cynder Mercantile?"

"It's my parent's old store. They're gone now." Elle's voice quakes as she says those last three words.

"I'm so sorry, Elle."

"Cynder was their business and I'd like to see how it's running. I haven't visited because of my stepmother and sisters." A shiver rolls across her shoulders. "They're everything you can imagine from the fairy tale life template. And I don't have enough magic to go alone and stay hidden. Fae warden and all that."

"Of course," I say. "That's a second dare we'll have to save for another time, though. I'll need to gather a special set of gems."

"Thanks." Elle sets down her hotdog. "I was worried about Bry before. I mean, back in the basement."

I shift my position so all my focus is on Elle. No question about it. It's a big deal for Elle to trust me with this. "What about Bry?"

"She's turning eighteen. It's a big day for anyone with a fairy tale life template. Her aunties want her to marry some douchebag named Philpott."

I wince. "Knox won't be happy about that."

"You think they'll get together?"

"I'll put it to you this way. Knox is very protective. End of story."

"That's…" Elle looks into the line of trees and gasps. "Jacoby."

"Who?"

A guy steps out from the park. He's a dark elf of the handsome variety. I'm talking silver irises, pointed ears and heavy frame. Not very elf-like as these types go. "I'm Jacoby," he says with a grin that's the definition of the word *smug.*

"I'm Alec."

"I knew that," says Jacoby. "Everyone knows that."

Elle rolls her eyes. "What are you doing here, Jacoby?"

The elf takes a seat on our bench, careful to position himself on the other side of Elle. He sets his arm across the back of the bench and across Elle's shoulders. It's a mark of possession.

Are these two together?

Elle scooches closer to me. It's a very clear move that says, *you don't own me.* I can't help but grin. And if my smile is as smug as Jacoby's, so be it.

Speaking of Jacoby, Elle shoots a frustrated look in his direction. "I know Jacoby from my parents' store."

"Consider me a concerned and very good friend," says Jacoby. "Which is why I'm here today. I've found out some information about your new buddy Bryar Rose."

"What about her?"

"Trouble coming for her eighteenth," says Jacoby. "I got word from an animate. Very reliable. It's a mannequin from a Wicca supply store in Salem, Mass. Now that she's enchanted and alive, she gets tons of visions of the future. It seems you and Bryar Rose will fight evildoers and the go on a great journey."

Elle gives Jacoby the side eye. "That's not very specific."

"I'm afraid that's what I have for you." Jacoby gives me a knowing glance as he speaks his next bit. "I'll return when I know more." Without saying another word, he vanishes.

Elle groans. "That's Jacoby. Always materializing and disappearing at odd times. I should have warned you before. My parents sold items made by artist animates. I've a rather odd collection of buddies from that era."

"I can't wait to meet them all," I say. And I mean it. "Now we need to have a Magicorum Killers competition *and* a visit to your parent's store."

"That we do," confirms Elle.

A warm sense of satisfaction spreads inside me. Two dates with Elle and a pleasant lunch. The odd visit from Jacoby aside, this marks my best workday ever as a fake Vice President of Le Charme jewelers.

7. CHAPTER SEVEN

ELLE

*A*lec and I walk back from lunch. My brain is all foggy, and not because of Jacoby's surprise visit.

I can't believe I did all that.

How could I risk my security and tell Alec I'm a warden, too? Even Bry doesn't know. But that's not even the worst thing I did today.

Why did I ask Alec to visit Cynder Mercantile?

It wasn't anything I planned to do. The question just fell out of my mouth. Sure, I think about the store all the time. I wonder about the animates as well. Jacoby says they're all fine, but he's not exactly Mister Honest. And I'd rather see things for myself.

If there's one consolation, it's how Bry turns eighteen soon. That should keep all of us busy for a while. Maybe Alec will forget I ever gave him that dare.

Somehow I doubt it, though.

8. CHAPTER EIGHT

ALEC - TWO MONTHS LATER

*K*nox and I are back at our favorite gaming couch in my parent's penthouse. We've almost finished level twenty on Magicorum Killers. I've been playing with Elle, too, only we've hit level thirty-seven.

Slam!

The main door whips open.

"Alec!" It's Diamond calling to me from the front foyer. Based on the note of anxiety in her voice, she is not happy.

Knox pauses the game. "Want me to stay?"

"ALEC!" This time, there's some serious hysteria going on.

"Nah, you better go. Tell Bry I say hi."

Between me, Knox, Elle, and Bry, we've had quite a few adventures over the last few months. Knox and Bry are now officially an item. Turns out, she's a werewolf just like Knox.

"I will." Knox strides from the room just as Diamond comes in. Knox does his *chin-nod thing* in my mother's direction. "Hey, Diamond."

She doesn't even acknowledge him. *Oh, this shall be ugly.*

Diamond stands before me, her face at least three shades of red. She wears a long trench coat and carries a large satchel. After opening the bag, she pulls out a photograph. "What's this?"

I reach out my hand; Diamond places the photo on my palm. It's a picture of me, Knox, Elle, and Bry. There are also a ton of dead zombie-mummies around us. Long story short, Knox finally got to watch his life-long nemesis, Jules, get totally destroyed.

Did I say we've had an exciting few months? It's true.

I hold out the picture and make a great show of examining it. "Do you have someone following me?"

"Both you and your father. Seems I can't trust either of you."

"That's exceedingly rude, Diamond." But I say that with a smile. You can get away with a lot when you smile.

"Stop avoiding the issue. What is this?"

"I fought some zombie-mummies. It's not like we don't have one locked up in the sub-basement." And we do. Another long story. "Knox has a new girlfriend. She got in some trouble. I helped."

"And this?" Diamond hands me another picture. This one shows the four of us in Egypt posing before the pyramids.

"I took a long weekend in Egypt." As I speak, I'm careful to keep my voice casual. "It's another *Knox thing*. His girlfriend is rather prone to trouble. But it's all good now." I reach for the gaming controller. "If you don't mind, I'm almost done with my level here."

Diamond moves to block my view of the screen. "I don't care about Knox's girlfriend." Diamond pulls out yet another pic. It shows Elle and Bry in West Lake Prep. We all started going there in the fall so we could spend our senior year together. I arranged it and thought I'd been pretty subtle about the whole thing. Guess not.

"So?" asks Diamond.

"We all go to the same school," I confirm. "It's not like there are a million versions of Magicorum high. Everyone ends up at West Lake Prep."

"That's not what I mean." Diamond taps the image. "What about *her?*"

Sure enough, Diamond points to Elle.

It's an effort to keep my features blank, but I manage it. I squint at the image as if noticing Elle for the first time. "She's buddies with Knox's girlfriend."

"This is the same girl you chatted up back at the L Center," explains Mom. "It was right before the first Le Charme Extravaganza. You were fifteen. Don't you remember?"

Of course, I remember. But I'm not admitting that to Diamond. All of a sudden, that dream warning from the Queen of Hearts appears in my mind's eye, written in red letters.

Legend will keep you apart fro your true love.

I set the dream aside. There's enough to deal with right now.

"That was years ago." I lean back on the couch and kick my legs out. "What's this all about?"

Diamond pulls another picture from her satchel and hands it over. It's a snapshot of Elle in a ball gown, only something about the image doesn't look quite right.

"What's this?" I ask.

"That's Raelyn Livie. She was your father's *first choice* for his Glass Slipper Ball."

I tilt my head. "His first choice? I'd no idea he'd made a choice for anyone at all. I thought he walked in, met you, and the rest just happened."

Sort of. I don't add in all the stuff about the Le Charme curse. Mom doesn't handle that topic well, to say the least.

"Yes, your father had a first choice." Diamond grips the photo with more force. "He proposed to Raelyn two hours before his Glass Slipper Ball."

The couch seems to turn liquid beneath me. "I must have heard you wrong. Did you say Legend proposed to someone else?"

"Yes, Raelyn turned him down and married Declan Cynder." Diamond then pulls out the image of the pyramids. "That's Raelyn's daughter, Elle."

I can't believe this. "Elle's mother was Legend's first love?"

"Yes, and you're traipsing around with her. That's completely unacceptable. Do we understand each other?"

"Knox is my best buddy. Bryar Rose is his mate. Elle is Bry's best friend. I can't avoid this girl."

"Listen to me, son. I don't care what you do or where you go. We got Knox an apartment so you can have parties and that's fine. But Elle Cynder?" Mom grabs all the photos and jams them back into her satchel. "She's off limits."

Diamond stomps out of the room. I slump back against the couch. So that's why Diamond lost it when she first saw Elle. My father proposed to Elle's mother.

Whoa.

I rub my neck and think things through. Cut Elle out of my life entirely? Never. Clearly, my father made his mistake and lost his love.

There's no way I'm losing mine.

9. CHAPTER NINE

ELLE

*T*he past few months have been a trip. I made it through fighting zombie mummies... jetting overseas for the first time... and acing an odd experience with the pyramids. Plus, I did it all with Alec, Bry, and Knox.

Which means I can do this.

I can walk back into high school again.

Nearby, happy students chatter away. Everyone looks like regular teenagers in school uniforms. They aren't. Sure, there's the occasional human in the mix. Still, most students are Magicorum. I spy weres, fairies, and magic users in the crowd. Alec waits across the walkway. As usual, he's swamped with his many admirers. Everyone knows his Glass Slipper Ball takes place on Valentine's Day. Right now, all the buzz is about the school's Autumn Masquerade. Word is, whoever Alec takes to that will certainly be his bride.

I try not to think about it too much.

Bry and Knox stand nearby. Her head leans on his shoulder as a parade of weres march by them both. Basically, Bry and Knox are the total power couple of the shifter community now. Their buds, Hollywood and Abe, keep bowing and calling them *your Majesties*. And considering how Knox is the known warden of magic, that makes sense. Bry is no slouch in the power department, either. Weres sense this stuff, and it makes them submit.

Sadly, it's not the same deal with the fae.

I've spent my whole life hiding the fact that I'm the warden of fae magic. As of today, only Alec, Bry, and Knox know the truth. And after our experience at the pyramids, I lost a lot of my power. So why am I purposely hanging out with fae by attending this school?

There's only one reason I'm here, and he's chatting up fans across the walkway.

I am so screwed.

A group of fae seniors walk by. Everyone calls them the Three Seasons, mostly because they're named Autumn, Winter, and Spring. There used to be the Four Seasons, but Summer graduated last year. There's no missing their whispers, mostly because they're not trying to keep their voices too low.

She doesn't even have wings.
How did she get into West Lake Prep anyway?
I heard it's because the shifters feel sorry for her.

On reflex, my hands ball into fists. I'm half fairy, so you'd think I like my kind. Yet outside of my mother, I haven't met anyone from the Faerie Lands who doesn't suck.

Bry steps to my side. "What's wrong?"

"What makes you ask that?"

This is one of my best tricks, by the way: answer a question with another question. It's a great way to avoid communicating anything that's a downer. And Bry is so smiley today, I hate to rain on her *happy shifter parade.*

When we first started school, Bry was relegated to studying in the basement. Long story. Now she's in regular shifter classes and the equivalent of a queen. No one deserves happiness more than Bry.

"Come on." Bry sighs. "I can scent your worry."

"You can? Weird."

"Don't avoid the question, Elle. I know most of your tricks. You taught them to me." When she next speaks, her voice is very low. "What are you anxious about? I have a few ideas."

"Anxious? Me? No way. I can handle the *no wing* comments."

Bry gasps. "The fairies are teasing you about not having wings?"

"All day long. You have shifter hearing. I figured you knew."

Knox steps up. Now *his nose* is telling him there's trouble. "What's wrong?"

"I'm fine. You guys get back to your scene."

Knox frowns. "You're worried that magic isn't returning to the world, yeah?"

This time I answer a question with another question, and it's not on purpose. "What?"

"We had all those adventures in Egypt," says Bry. "That should have boosted the number of Magicorum around."

"Or made the ones who are here more powerful," adds Knox. "That hasn't happened. I just guessed that's what was bugging you. Bry and I talk about it all the time."

The bell rings, signaling us to enter the school. We all wear enchanted bracelets that hide our true nature. On the exterior, West Lake Prep looks like a brownstone with a short flight of steps leading to a single wooden door. The students look like humans, too. Yet once you cross the threshold, the glamour vanishes. Everyone's outfit changes. The shifters wear leather. The magic users all sport robes. The fairies dress in neon outfits which contrast their wings.

As I step across the threshold, my own ensemble transforms as well. All of a sudden, I'm in jeans and a T-shirt. There's no need to dress like the rest of the fairies. If I'm not going to fit in, I might as well be comfortable.

Once again, I wonder why I'm here.

My gaze snaps to find Alec in the crowd. He's chatting up a group of no less than six girls. His eyes find mine. He gives me the barest of winks. I nod, blush, and hurry off to the fae section of the school.

My first class of the day is fae history. Turns out, everything I learned in my online classes was human stuff. Here at West Lake Prep, we learn about the Magicorum. Even so, most of this stuff I already knew from surfing Magiweb. When you retrieve magical jewels, learning comes along for the ride.

I enter the classroom. Like everywhere else in this section, it's painted in neon colors—green in this case. Loopy golden desk chairs line the floor. I slip into one in the back corner. There are about thirty other kids here, all of them in their seats. The trio of seniors from outside keep not-whispering about me. They really need a new hobby.

Our teacher for this class is Goldilocks, the principal of the fae school. She looks like a little cherub with blonde hair, but make no mistake. Goldilocks is evil. Our principal flits to the front of the class and slaps her enchanted lollipop against her palm. Everyone quiets.

"Good morning class."

"Good morning, Goldi," say the students.

"Every so often I introduce the new additions to our little community. There hasn't been anyone in ages, so I'm very excited for the news today." One of the Three Seasons raises her hand. Goldi gestures to her. "Yes, Autumn?"

"We've had a new girl for a while now." Autumn points to me. "It's Elle."

"You should introduce her," says Spring.

"Elle?" Goldi stares at me as if she's seeing me for the first time. "When did you get here?"

"A while ago."

"You don't have wings," says Goldi.

"I'm aware. It's my back."

Goldi's upper lip curls, as if she's being asked to scoop up sewage with her bare hands. "I suppose I should introduce you. Everyone, this is Elle. She doesn't have any wings and we don't know why she's here—"

"I heard it's a shifter thing," offers Winter. Every school has a group of popular kids who can interrupt anyone, including the Principal. At West Lake Prep, that's the Three Seasons.

"Huh." Goldi stares at me and shivers. "Moving on. What I really wanted to lead off with today is our newest student. Everyone please join me in welcoming Jacoby the dark elf!"

My stomach sinks. I quickly scan the windows and doors, trying to see if there's an easy escape route. No such luck.

I cross my fingers under my desk. Maybe this isn't *my* Jacoby. There are a ton of dark elves running around, right? It doesn't mean that the guy I've had confusing feelings about since forever is going to walk into my classroom at West Lake Prep.

Yet sure enough, it's my Jacoby who steps across the threshold.

Oh, crap.

Jacoby slides into the open seat next to mine. "Hello, Elle."

The principal starts going on and on about the various types of fae, including fairies, pixies and elves. She then talks about how elves are more important than everyone else. I pay scant attention at best. Why?

My day has just gotten worse.

It's not only that Jacoby is here. Blackaverre just appeared at the front of the classroom as well. I scan the other faces. Does anyone else see her? No. So that's good. It also means she's still my fairy godmother, but that's beside the point.

"What are you looking at?" asks Jacoby.

"Nothing," I counter. "And what are *you* doing here?"

"Learning. It's very important, don't you think?"

"I'm paying attention to class, thank you very much."

Winter starts whispering to Jacoby, which thankfully distracts the guy. Meanwhile, Blackaverre starts miming someone walking around super primly with her face scrunched up. Okay, so that's Marchesa. Then my fairy godmother starts making soundless *pow* noises while showing her hands blowing apart.

I mouth one name. *Marchesa?*

Blackaverre shakes her head. That's a *no*.

Another silent word follows. *Store?* I ask.

This time, Blackaverre nods. *Yes.*

In other words, there's trouble at Cynder Mercantile. Blackaverre is a *classic* fairy template, so it's possible she's lying. Even so, that's not a risk I can take. And in truth, I've been worried about Cynder for ages.

Time to face my past.

10. CHAPTER TEN

ALEC

$\mathcal{I}$ stand in the principals' office. The room supports all three of our mini-schools, but only the caster leader is here. Her name is Babs, and she's the only thing keeping me from what I want this morning.

And what I desire most is to check on Elle.

I shoot Babs my most winning smile. "I just need to deliver something to the school's fae wing." Although my family is pretty tight with the school, even I can't waltz into the fae area without a hall pass. Sure, I could cast a spell… but that's technically forbidden. All of which is why I save it for occasions when my natural charm can't get me what I want.

In other words, I don't cast spells at school very often.

Babs keeps scribbling away at the document before her. "Shouldn't you be in class?"

"I'm on study break. Just need to pop over for a moment." Mostly because Elle had little creases in her forehead this morning. That means she's really worried about something. I simply must make sure she's all right. Not that I'll announce this to Babs. There's enough of a spotlight on me already.

"And why should I let you go?"

"It's about the Autumn Masquerade. I have plans. Big plans."

Babs looks up from her writing. "You haven't invited anyone?"

Normally, a principal wouldn't care who I invite to the Autumn Masquerade, but I'm no typical student. I happen to know for a fact that the tabloids will pay four thousand human dollars for information on my Autumn Masquerade ball choice. Mostly because everyone thinks it will predict my lady for the Glass Slipper Ball.

"I've my eye on Winter. Don't tell anyone."

"Oh, I won't," says Babs. But the sneaky gleam in her eyes says she totally will. The principal picks up a hall pass from her desktop and hands it over. "Have fun."

I saunter out of the room with my hall pass in hand. It's a short walk over to my destination. Sure enough, I have to show my pass to the entrance guardians.

Not a problem.

Once inside, I slip on my sunglasses. I'm not being a douche, either. The walls here are so bright, you can damage your retinas. I quickly find the right classroom. I glance through the small window atop the neon door. From where I stand, I have an angled view to the students, while no one inside can see me.

The fae principal, Goldi, flits before the class. It's a group of students that include...

Hold on.

That Jacoby guy is here.

A memory appears. Jacoby is the dark fae who interrupted my lunch over the summer. After the excitement with zombie-mummies and Egypt, I'd forgotten all about him.

What's he doing sitting next to Elle?

The principal fawns all over Jacoby, too. Not a surprise. Elves are the top of the fae food chain. There are a few exceptions, like the Queen of Hearts. But in general, elves are a big deal. We only have four in the school.

Jacoby smiles at Elle; she blushes. An angry feeling winds through my soul, and it has an ugly name. Jealousy.

My phone buzzes. I check the screen.

CallMeElle: Remember our dare? Cynder Mercantile?

I exhale. Jacoby may be grinning at Elle, but she's thinking of me. Some of my jealousy unwinds. I type extra quickly.

MagicMan: absolutely
CallMeElle: can we go today

No question what my answer is here.

MagicMan: U got it

I force myself to exhale. Whoever this Jacoby guy is, Elle is taking *me* to see her parents' store, not him. That's got to stand for something.

Because with every passing day, I'm realizing one thing more and more. Elle is my everything.

11. CHAPTER ELEVEN

ELLE

*T*he rest of my school day, all the fae girls fawn over Jacoby. I get that he's an elf and everything, but sheesh. The Three Seasons encircle him the most, which is fine with me.

All in all, Jacoby is one too many things to focus on today. My real worry is Cynder Mercantile. That place is protected by the Cask of Wonders. Every day, Marchesa can open the magical container and get whatever the store needs. What could possibly have happened to cause trouble?

My last class of the day is fairy studies. Basically, it's yet another class about how everything in the Faerie Lands is ranked. Once again, I learn how elves are on the top of the social pyramid Jacoby gets asked to step to the front of the class and describe why he's so awesome.

It's about as fun as it sounds.

I'm thrilled when my phone vibrates again. Technically, handhelds aren't allowed in school. That said, the teachers don't really understand how they work, being that it's human tech and all. It took a while for me to figure out that everyone uses phones despite the ban. They're just super careful about it. Which is why I slip my cell onto my lap before checking the screen.

MagicMan: meet up at the front door?

CallMeElle: for what?
MagicMan: to walk over to your store

My eyes almost pop out of my head. Alec is a great guy, but if I meet up with him and then walk away from school together? I might as well sign off on any hope of privacy. My life would be picked apart by the tabloids for weeks. There's no way I'm explaining all that in a text, so I go for the easy way out.

CallMeElle: how about we meet at TP-CP? 3:30?
MagicMan: will do

The Turtle Pond is close to Cynder anyway, so that will work out well. I spend the rest of the school day thinking through what could be wrong. Perhaps someone cursed Cynder. My thoughts then turn to the animates. Harvest the scarecrow... Kokkivo and the phoenixes... and even Doc Eight... None of them would ever turn on the store, would they?

At last, the magical bells ring, signaling the end of class. I hightail it over to the central hall. Bry is already there with Knox and their pack. Their faces are all flushed.

"Hey, Bry!" I call. As I close in, I lower my voice. "What happened with you guys?"

"We had pack bonding this afternoon."

"Pack bonding?"

"The principal transported us to the Adirondacks and we all run around for a while." Bry fans herself with her hands. "I suppose we're still overheated."

"Sure, that makes sense."

Here's the thing. Bry could have died many times over during the past months. And I am so happy things worked out for her. But if I'm being honest with myself, it's also tough. I wish I had someone like Knox. Inside my soul, that old barrier looms ever larger. The hurt from my parents sits on one side, like a monster ready to pounce if I lower my defensive wall even an inch. Somewhere along the way, it even becomes more than a single barrier. There's now a fortress inside me. It's too big to tear down by this point. And ultimately? That's my choice.

When I next speak to Bry, it's as if I stand on one side of my castle wall, peering at her through a thin window. "I've got some running around to do after school. See you back at the apartment?" Bry and I now share a new place together.

Bry takes in a long breath. "Sure. Is everything okay?"

Not for the first time, I curse that crazy power of smell that werewolves have. "I'm fine. Honestly. See you by dinnertime."

Hollywood steps up. He's one of the more personable weres. "Did someone say dinner, your Majesty? Where are we all eating?"

With that question, both Knox and Bry are surrounded by excited shifters. Everyone wants to share a meal with the equivalent of their king and queen.

I sneak off for Central Park.

It's 3:30 PM on the nose when I approach the pond. Alec is already there and in his incognito mode. I wave as I approach.

"Hey!" I call.

Alec does that thing where his smile lights up his face. It really isn't fair, how handsome he is. My legs get a little wobbly beneath me. "Elle." There's a real sense of contentment as he speaks my name. I can't help but blush.

"My parents' store isn't far from here. Thanks again for doing this."

"Not a problem." He reaches into the pockets of his leather jacket and pulls out a handful of pink diamonds. "I got some special gems for the occasion. Found a new spell for us, too."

I kick at the ground. "You didn't have to do that."

"I'm a wizard. Any excuse to look through spell books is like caster Christmas." Every line of Alec's face softens with joy as he says the words *caster Christmas*.

"In any case," continues Alec, "the best spell for today may be an obfuscation enchantment."

I tilt my head. "What's that? A disguise?"

"Not exactly. I looked into spells that would change our appearance. But those are tricky. Some fairies are immune to disguises. And there are invisibility spells, but those have the same risks. Overall, those are low-level spells. Not too powerful. But obfuscation? That's high-level magic. It forces anyone to simply look away when we're near. We're not invisible so much as always avoided. Does that make sense?"

"Yes. I knew you'd figure out something great."

"For you?" Alec winks. "Anything."

And do I blush again when Alec says the word *anything*? You bet I do.

On reflex, I check around. There are some humans far away; they won't notice Alec's magic.

"Ready?" asks Alec.

"You know it."

Alec holds the stones in his hand. The pink diamonds emit tendrils of colored smoke from between his fingertips. The mist rolls out from his fist to cover both me and Alec.

A moment later, the two of us appear in black and white, like an old movie. It's way strange. And cool.

I hold up my arm. "This is amazing."

"Thank you." Alec offers me his arm. "Shall we?"

"Let's." I wrap my fingers around his forearm, and my hand sears with excitement where we touch. And this is just through his leather jacket. I can't imagine what it would be like to brush my fingertips across his bare skin.

At this point, I realize I've been rubbing Alec's forearm in a slow rhythm. It takes an effort, but I make myself stop. Forearm rubbing is not something friends do. And that's all Alec and I can ever be. Buddies.

It's easy to ignore the little voice inside me that wants something more. Like the rest of my heart, it's trapped inside that inner castle which holds all my pain.

And staying friends with Alec certainly won't bring the walls down.

At this point, I'm not sure anything will.

12. CHAPTER TWELVE

ELLE

*I*t's a short walk over to Cynder, but it's sure a wacky one.

Humans stride around us. Magicorum do too. Each time, folks simply sidestep me and Alec without so much as a glance in our direction. It's an intricate dance of magic. Combine that with how Alec and I are black and white while the world around us stays in color, and I almost forget the serious reason I'm meeting up with Alec today.

Almost.

Minutes later, Alec and I stand before Cynder Mercantile. The store's brick exterior is covered in graffiti. The door hangs cockeyed on its hinges. One solid push and you could get inside.

Who leaves opened doors in the city?

When I next speak, my voice comes out as a choked whisper. "This isn't how I left the place." Letting go of Alec's arm, I hug my elbows. "Can you cast a detection spell? There could be squatters in here... or worse."

"Absolutely." Alec reaches into his bomber jacket once more. This time, he pulls out a handful of rubies. The gems flare inside his palm. Red smoke surrounds his fist. The mist whips away from Alec to slide past the slightly opened door.

Alec closes his eyes. I've heard how gem casters do their magic. Alec is listening to the stones talk to him. After a few moments, he turns to me. "There are serious wards on this place. No humans are inside. I do detect one fairy, though."

"That's probably Blackaverre. She's my fairy godmother."

"You have a fairy godmother?"

"I didn't say she was a great one." I smile, but it's not one of the happy variety. "She's the one who warned me to come over today." I shake my head. "It's just… it looks like this place has been closed for a long time. Why would Blackaverre warn me now?"

Alec moves to stand before me. Normally, this guy is all glib charm. Now his face looks deadly serious. "We don't have to go inside if you don't want to."

"Thanks." I grip my elbows more tightly. "But I must check it out."

Alec's gaze turn even more intense, if that were possible. "I'll be right beside you."

It takes a force of will for me to turn and face the door once more. Raising my arm, I press my palm against the broken entrance. The wooden panel swings open with a long creak.

I step inside.

The store used to be all bright light and packed shelves. Now the windows are covered in graffiti. Shadows fill the room. The shelves are all empty and covered in dust. The check-out counter lopes to one side, like it will tumble over any second. Water has clearly been seeping onto the floor. The scent of mold is everywhere.

My head turns foggy with shock. "But Doc Eight told me things were fine."

Alec's hand glows red as he fires up another spell. "This place has been deserted for three years."

"That's when I ran away." My body turns numb as I step toward the back door. This is the entrance to the warehouse.

Once again, the panel swings open with the slightest touch. Inside, the place is just as empty as the store. One shelf holds a pair of glass slipper figurines and a single cracked wooden pumpkin. Those were some of the very items I delivered to the L Center all those years ago, on the day I met Alec. I scoop the items up and put them in my purse.

They're all I have left of Cynder.

Within my soul, the walls of my internal fortress thicken under this sight. How could anyone allow this to happen? Didn't the animates care? Wasn't the place safe?

I reach out and take Alec's hand. Some part of me is shocked he doesn't pull away. After all, that's what happened to my parents. They vanished. So did their legacy. But Alec stays beside me. His thumb moves over the back of my hand in slow and soothing arcs.

A knot of sorrow tightens in my throat. "My family lived upstairs," I say.

"Do you want to see it?" asks Alec.

"Yes."

"Then I'll be with you." He gives my hand a squeeze.

I keep moving forward, but it's as if I'm sleepwalking. The only thing tethering me to reality is the touch of Alec's skin. We make the long march up the stairs. I check the kitchen and bedrooms first. All stand stripped to the walls. The pictures, furniture, and memories—everything is gone.

"I'd like a moment alone, please."

"Sure," says Alec." I'll check out the office."

I step around the bedroom in slow circles, trying to force myself to remember what things looked like. So many memories are already fading. It's almost too much.

Don't dwell on it. Move on.

Straightening my shoulders, I leave my parents' bedroom and head over to their office. Alec already stands inside.

"How does it look?" I ask.

"Completely stripped."

I cross the threshold. "What about that safe?"

"Safe?" Alex turns around and stares at the new-looking safe in one corner. "That wasn't here when I entered before."

I step in for a closer look. "And there's no dust on it, either. Must be an enchantment." I frown. "But who would enchant a safe?"

"Whoever it is, they only wanted you to find it. I couldn't see the thing until you entered the room."

Memories appear. "On the day I left here, someone protected my money from my stepmother. I never found out who did it. And now, someone glamoured my parents' safe?"

"It must be the same person."

I nod. "But who?" I shake my head. "That's something to worry about later. I'd like to check out the safe now."

"Of course."

"Did your spell show it was boobytrapped or anything?"

"No, but you will need the combination."

"That's okay. I remember it."

Kneeling before the safe, I twist the spinlock and enter in the old combination from my parents. My hands tremble, so it takes me a few tries to get it right. Finally, there's the soft click of the lock releasing. I pull open the safe door. A pile of documents sits inside. I pull out the sheets, set them atop the safe, and scan the top one.

"What is it?" asks Alec.

"It's a record of the store's history. After I left, Marchesa sold off everything. She turned out all the animates, too."

"Maybe she needed the money."

"No, my parents had a gift called the Coffer of Wonders. It was created to protect this store. Once a day, the coffer could be opened. Then it would give whatever the store needed."

"Hmm." Alec rakes his hand through his hair. "Sounds like that coffer's like the most valuable thing in the store. Perhaps that's what your stepmother sold. It would get the most money."

My blood chills. It never occurred to me that someone would sell the Coffer of Wonders. It was a gift from the animates meant to keep my family's legacy alive.

Sadly, I can see Marchesa doing just that.

I flip through more pages. "Here's a contract," I state. "It's dated the same week Marchesa closed down the store." I scan further. "And you guessed right. It's all about selling the Coffer of Wonders." I turn the page. "They're putting it in magical escrow? I've never heard of that."

"We do that sometimes with very expensive jewels," explains Alec. "It protects the buyer and seller. The object goes to a third party until the deal closes. It should all be listed later in the document."

"Right." I read a little further. "Here it is. The Coffer of Wonders will be held by the Queen of Hearts until..." I pause, not believing what I'm seeing.

Alec steps to my side. "May I?"

"Sure."

Alec reads further. "It says the coffer will be released to the buyer on the day of my Glass Slipper Ball."

That chill in my veins turns downright arctic. "Your parents are buying the Coffer of Wonders? Why?"

Alec sighs. "Le Charme Jewelers hasn't been in good shape for years. Tons of money has been poured into the L Center, and that's not even the most pricey of my father's plans." He meets my gaze. "It would make sense that they'd want the Coffer of Wonders. The magic serves the business, yes?"

I nod. "It was made to keep Cynder Mercantile going."

"I'm so sorry."

I press my palms to my eyes and think. There's something I'm still missing here. The question hits me. "What does Marchesa get out of this?"

"My parents can't be paying her with human money," says Alec. "They don't have any."

I flip more pages and pause. It can't be true and yet it's written right there. "Your parents will receive the Coffer of Wonders for Le Charme Jewelers. In exchange, you'll be bonded to Ivy Cynder at your Glass Slipper Ball. The Queen of Hearts will make sure it all happens." I look to Alec. "Now it's my turn to be sorry."

Alec scoops up the documents. "This is unbelievable."

"Don't worry," I offer. "They can't make you do anything."

"The Queen of Hearts certainly can." Alec shakes his head. "That damned curse."

"You mean the one against wardens and marriage? That's over now. Our trip to Egypt fixed everything."

"Oh, I'm a lucky fellow," says Alec. "I have two curses in my life. The warden one is over, sure. But there's a second bit of evil. My father believes that there's another curse that's specific to the Le Charme family. It forces our men into loveless marriages. Looks like Legend is making sure it happens to me."

Looking up, I see a small birdlike figure that flits above the safe. "Blackaverre."

"Your fairy godmother is here?" asks Alec.

"Sadly." I glare in her direction. "She doesn't detect us, does she?"

"No, do you want her to?"

I nod.

Alec pulls out some more stones and casts a spell. Within seconds, he and I are visible once more.

In response, Blackaverre throws up her arms in a great show of spotting me for the first time.

"She doesn't talk?" asks Alec.

"Nope."

After that, Blackaverre zooms over and kisses the top of my head. She's making a big act of being happy to see me. I'm here, but I'm still not sure what Blackaverre is really up to.

I step away from the kiss fest on my hair. "There's no emergency. This place has been deserted for ages. Why am I really here?"

Blackaverre twiddles her fingers. A moment later, a small note-card appears on her palm. She hands the message to me and winks. After that, my so-called fairy godmother vanishes in a pouf of pink smoke.

"Typical," I grumble. I hold up the envelope. A name is written outside, Elle. I know that handwriting. "This is from Marchesa." I tear the message open and read the contents inside.

Elle, By now you've figured out that running away is pointless. I've known where you are for years, and I've been looking forward to this day. If you hadn't run across Alec on your own, I'd have made it happen, just so I can see the pain in your eyes when you lose him... just as I lost Declan. - Your dear stepmother

"What does it say?" asks Alec.

"My stepmother, Marchesa, has been planning this all along. Our meeting. You marrying Ivy. It's her revenge on me."

"Revenge. Why?"

"Marchesa wanted to my marry my father, Declan." I toss the note atop the safe. "She's always hated me. And now I understand why your parents need her Coffer of Wonders."

"There's more to it than that. My mother recently told me. She swore me to secrecy, but in light of this?" Alec gestures toward the pile of papers. "I'm not keeping secrets for her any longer." He turns to me once more. "My father wanted to marry your mother."

On reflex, my hand goes to my throat. "Legend proposed to Rae? *My* Rae? Are you sure?"

"Diamond showed me pictures."

"How long have you known?"

"About the proposal? Only a few days ago. But there were warning signs before. Diamond never liked it when I talked to you, even all those years ago at the L Center."

A memory appears. The woman's voice calling to the guy I thought was Fred. "I remember that. I thought you were in trouble from your boss at the loading dock."

"That was Diamond. My parents don't have a happy marriage. Diamond blames your mother. And as I said, the Le Charme company isn't in good shape, either. I'm sure Diamond jumped at the chance to hurt you and save Le Charme at the same time."

I stare at the pile of papers, my mind lost in thought. This is hopeless. Diamond and Legend Le Charme teaming up with Marchesa? My own fairy godmother helping her along? And there very well could be powerful magic driving this whole thing. Maybe Alec and I should accept all this and move on.

Then again, screw that idea.

My blood heats with a mixture of rage and determination. I turn to Alec. "You know what I think about all this?"

He tilts his head. "Tell me."

"That—" I point to the pile of papers "—is a pile of crap. No one pushes us around. And if my life gets ruined, I won't let it be Marchesa and her spawn who take me down. I'll make my own terrible mistakes, thank you very much."

A smile quirks Alec's mouth. "What are you thinking?"

"I met the Queen of Hearts years ago. You had a dream where she visited you. I think that old vampire-fairy doesn't like this whole *curse situation* for some reason." I toss the papers back inside the safe and slam the door. "Let's go see the Queen of Hearts. You're a warden. So am I. There must be something we can do to make her kill this curse. I, for one, will not stand around and just take this. What do you say?"

"I say *you're amazing, Elle Cynder.*" Alec reaches out and runs his finger along my jawline. "And I love this idea."

I open my mouth, ready to say, *I love you, Alec Le Charme.*

But thankfully, I'm able to close my yap before I do something that crazy. I've already lost so much, between my parents and now Cynder mercantile. Alec is a friend who holds my hand and tells me I'm amazing.

I simply won't risk losing Alec's friendship. But I will go with him to see the Queen of Hearts.

Alec closes his eyes. "It's my detection spell. The stones speak to me once more."

"What is it?" I ask.

"A troll has broken in through the back of the warehouse."

I stumble backward. Trolls are the assassins of the shadowcoe world.

And they don't hand out pretty deaths, either.

13. CHAPTER THIRTEEN

ELLE

*A*lec's words seem to float in a word bubble by his mouth, like he's a cartoon instead of a person.

A troll has broken in through the back of the warehouse.

Seeing cartoon bubble talk? That makes it official. I am beyond stressed-out today. Yet another telltale sign of my anxiety is how I still can't believe Alec's words, despite the fact that I still see them in a cartoon talk bubble.

"Trolls?" I ask. "How?"

"I noticed some vials in the kitchen. There's only one purpose for these particular containers. Your stepmother is a potion master, yes?"

"Sure."

"They're closely aligned with trolls. We better go."

Now, I know we should leave. Yet my feet feel rooted to the spot. Blackaverre betrayed me. She lured me here to let me know Marchesa's plan to ruin my life, followed up by a troll to actually do the ruining part. All of which adds up to one thing.

Blackaverre is in cahoots with Marchesa. Not that I'm surprised.

Okay, I'm a little surprised.

Blackaverre may hate me, but my mother is the equivalent of a fairy saint. Who helps someone that destroyed Mom's legacy? I understand having a *classic* fairy tale life template but sheesh.

I'm about to complain about Blackaverre when Alec steps into my line of vision and sets his hand over my mouth. No question what he means here. *Stay silent.*

I nod. *Got it.*

Alec glances toward the doorway. An electric sense of alarm rattles through my nervous system.

Little by little, I turn to face the doorway. A massive troll stands framed on the threshold.

Damn.

14. CHAPTER FOURTEEN

ALEC

The troll is a lanky fellow, with a hunched back and skin that's covered in green pustules. His wide face holds beady eyes. A small tuft of yellow hair juts from atop his head. Four small tusks stick out from his lower jaw, two on either side of his mouth. He holds a large club in his right hand.

"Kill Elle," grumbles the troll.

Reaching into my pocket, I pull out a fresh handful of rubies. "That won't happen."

A surge of power surrounds Elle. It's like the electric sense of lightning before a storm.

She's pulling in magic and a lot of it.

I set my hand on Elle's forearm. "Not safe," I whisper.

A thin cloud of fairy dust collects around Elle's hand. She stares at the enchanted mist that swirls around her fingers. "I can't just stand here."

"I won't let you expose yourself." I raise my hand. Rubies gleam inside my fist.

I mean it, too. Elle's the warden of fae magic. Shadowcoe are residents of the Faerie Lands. If Elle exposes her powers to even one troll, all of Faerie could know the truth about her and soon.

The stones glow more brightly. Crimson light shines through my closed fingers. "Do I have to get nasty here?"

Elle winks. "Tough guy."

"You know it."

The troll raises his club. "Kill Elle!" he cries.

Closing my eyes, I reach out to the stones in my fist.

Protect Elle.

A chorus of alto voices reply.

What shall we cast?

My thoughts instantly spin through all the possible spells I could cast in this moment. I do have a special black diamond that I'm creating. Although I haven't heard a voice back from that particular stone yet, I almost wish I were holding it in my fist right now. That could protect Elle like nothing else.

The name of the right spell appears. I focus on it in my mind's eye.

Night.

Wisps of red smoke spin out from my hand. For a moment, the tendrils whirl about my palm. A burst of white light fills the room.

Then my spell really kicks into action.

Cords of red mist whip out from my palm. Lines of crimson power whirl around the troll. The shadowcoe writhes under the mist, trying to wipe the spell off his skin.

Yet the red mist stays in place.

Next, the colored gaze soaks inside the troll. Another burst of light follows.

The spell ends.

The troll wobbles in place, then falls over and snores.

15. CHAPTER FIFTEEN

ALEC

*E*lle steps up to the sleeping troll. She kicks at it with her boot. "Cool," she breathes.

"You'll have to show me some of your fairy and enchanter magic one of these days."

"I can only do a few things with fairy dust," Elle knocks on the statue's arm. "And I don't think I have any enchanter magic."

"I disagree."

Elle spins about to face me. "What makes you say that?"

"We get along far too well." I grin. "And I'm a wizard."

Bzzzz... Bzzzz...

My phone goes nuts. I pull my cell from my pocket. Both Diamond and Legend are calling me. My parents dial from separate phones, but with the same purpose.

"Blackaverre," I state. "Do you think she's working with Marchesa?"

"Absolutely."

I turn my phone off. "And Marchesa is in league with my parents. Clearly, Diamond and Legend know something is going on. They're blowing up my phone."

"Should you see them?"

"No," I reply. "But if we'll visit to the queen, we better hurry. I have about an hour before my parents cast transport spells and show up in person." I point to the troll. "Plus this guy won't sleep for long. Trolls are very resistant to magic."

"Got it. Let's go." Elle scooches around the snoozing troll and heads for the stairs.

She's unstoppable.

And in some way I can't quite understand, she's also entirely mine.

ALEC

*E*lle and I step through Central Park. According to my spell books, folks like Elle can view the Faerie Lands without using a portal.

"What do you see here?" I ask.

Elle pauses. "You've never been to the Faerie Lands before?"

"No. You?"

"Once. It's not a place I want to visit."

I nod. Of course. She wouldn't wish to expose her warden nature. "So why go there at all?"

"Because someone from Faerie once listed a crown for bounty. The Queen of Hearts."

I can't believe what I'm hearing. "You un-stole something for the queen?"

Elle bobs her head from side to side—it means she's thinking things through before talking. "I'm not sure it was stolen, really, so much as planted in the human world. A test, if you like. The Queen of Hearts wanted to see if someone would find her crown and return it." She curtseys. "That would be me."

"Can you see her right now?"

Elle steps in a slow circle. "I see the world of faerie overlapping with this one." She gestures across a small patch of forest. "To me, those take up the same space as trees with white trunks and red leaves." She then points toward Belvedere Castle. "And there's a great white palace on top of that gray one."

To my eyes, Elle simply follows a footpath to Belvedere Castle. All of a sudden, an oval hole appears in the sky just above the trail. I've read about these, but never seen one.

A portal to the Faerie Lands.

I step around the connection to the human world and the Faerie Lands. If I stand right in front, there's a cut-out spot in the air which shows the reality Elle described. Through that portal—*that window*—there's a white forest of red-leafed trees. Beyond that, a low hill is topped by a majestic palace of white stone. Small red pennants flap from the peak of conical towers. yet unless I look at the portal straight-on, I can't see the vision at all.

Scanning Central Park, I find I can no longer see Elle. So I step through the portal. Once I'm on the other side, Elle appears again. This time, she waits on the wide path to the Queen of Hearts' palace.

"How was the trip?" asks Elle. "I've never taken anyone to the Faerie Lands before."

I grin. "Didn't even tickle."

Together, Elle and I march up to the white palace. I'd be nervous seeing the warriors outside. After all, everyone talks about the infamous Vampire Guard. Yet there's no battle. One guard casually comments that the queen is expecting us. That's it.

A pair of heavy wooden doors swing open. Elle doesn't seem surprised, so I figure this is standard stuff.

Once we move inside, a very fluffy Cheshire Cat awaits us in the main foyer. The place is all white marble with red hearts, so it's hard to miss a large cat.

"Hi, Chesh," says Elle.

"Greetings, Elle," says Chesh. The cat looks toward me. "Alec."

Now, it seemed a little odd that the queen knew we were coming, but I figured that had something to do with Elle being part-fairy. But having Chesh know my identity? I have to admit, that makes my skin crawl a little. What's the Queen of Hearts really up to here?

We follow Chesh into a formal reception hall. Courtiers stand around in their medieval best. A short flight of steps leads to a raised platform. And atop that small stage? There sits the Queen of Hearts on her red throne. She's beyond beautiful with her red hair, silver eyes, and ebony skin. Her crimson wings flicker behind her. In fact, the queen is so lovely, I almost don't notice her fangs.

Almost.

"Stop," says the queen.

Elle and I pause. This is the queen's court, after all. If she says halt, that's what you do.

The queen rises. "You may wonder why I have an interest in you both." She slowly steps down the stairs from her throne. Her long red gown trails behind her. "You'll gain no insights from me. Yet." She moves to stand before me. "Although, I suspect you might know a thing or two."

"I do, your Majesty."

"Tell me."

"Charles Le Charme—"

The queen bares her fangs and hisses.

"Not a fan of Charles," says Elle. "Got it."

"Charles said something to me once about winning a bargain."

"What did he say?"

"That the deal means you must attend our Le Charme Lady Extravaganza each year as well as enforce a bond at the Glass Slipper Ball."

The queen bares his fangs again. "Anything else?"

"No," I reply. "But I do suspect that whatever your deal is, it's the reason Charles now lives in the Faerie Lands."

"Good work," says the queen. "Most here lie to me. You haven't yet."

"No."

The queen steps before Elle. "And what do you know?"

"That I found your crown and you gave me a prophecy. That's it."

The queen retakes her throne. "You are right that I am on the losing side of a bargain with Charles. And I do so like to win." She straightens the folds of her gown. "So why are you here today?"

"You once said that Legend and Marchesa would, uh, cause me trouble one day. If that happened, you said you could help."

The queen looks to me. "Is that why you are here as well?"

"It is."

"Alec was honest with me. You—" the queen glares at Elle "—just made a lie of omission. I prophesied that Legend and Marchesa would try to keep you from your true love. I am the Queen of Hearts, not the patron of companies. Are you two here to save Cynder Mercantile and Le Charme Jewelers … or are you in pursuit of true love?"

Elle's eyes widen. "What difference does that make?"

"Don't be thick," corrects the queen. "My court, my rules. So which is it? Love or money?"

"Love." Elle and I reply in unison. My pulse speeds. We replied at once, and with the same answer. *Does Elle really feel the same way that I do?* I glance in her direction. Elle twists her fingers together at her waistline while staring pointedly at the floor. I haven't known Elle long, but that's a sure sign she's holding something back.

The queen smiles, a movement that shows off her fanged teeth. "I do not believe you. Convince me."

At last, Elle turns to me. Our gazes lock. There's no missing the look of raw longing in her eyes. My heart soars.

She cares.

The day we met, lines of connection wound between me and Elle. Now that unity of feeling grows stronger than ever. Elle looks away. I move to stand before her. Only inches separate us now. Setting my knuckle beneath her chin, I gently guide her gaze to meet mine.

Once again, sheer longing is written on every line of her being. Reaching forward, I cup her face in my hands.

"Yes?" I ask.

"Yes," she replies.

Leaning in, I gently press my lip against hers.

Then my world turns upside down.

17. CHAPTER SEVENTEEN

ELLE

*A*fter the queen asked for proof, I had the same thought Alec did. A kiss would do it. But I didn't have the nerve. Alec is my friend. He needs to stay that way. Then he stood before me with the sweetest look on his face and a one-word question. "Yes?"

There was only one answer. "Yes."

Now his mouth presses against mine and it's tearing my soul apart. Every cell in my body wants to deepen the kiss. On reflex, I reach up and grab Alec's wrists, holding him in place.

I never want it to end.

"That's enough," says the queen.

We break apart. The moment Alec's mouth is away from mine, I realize that was a colossal mistake. Alec is too important to risk our relationship over something as dumb as a kiss.

But then again, maybe it wasn't a real kiss.

Both of us want to save our companies, as the queen called it. We did what we had to do in order to make that happen. It doesn't mean anything more.

It never will.

ALEC

I've kissed my share of runway models, starlets, and lead singers. But nothing I've ever experienced compares with the act of simply pressing my mouth against Elle's. For a supreme moment, energy and emotion careened between us. You can't fake that. Elle cares for me. She just needs more time to become comfortable with the idea, that's all. And I understand why. She's lost so much. Opening up again must be terrifying.

The truth is clear. When it comes to Elle, waiting is worth it.

The Queen of Hearts drums her fingers on the armrest of her throne. "That kiss was a fine start, but how am I to truly test your resolve?" Her eyes widen in a pantomime of shock. "Oh, my. Chesh has gone missing."

The court echoes the queen's statement. There are many disinterested murmurs asking, *Where is Chesh?*

This is all some kind of false performance for them. What is the queen really playing at?

"Find Chesh," declares the queen. "If you do so, I'll consider fixing your problems." She waves her arm. "Now be gone!"

A flash of red light surrounds us. One moment, Elle and I stand in the queen's palace. The next, we wait outside Belvedere Castle in Central Park.

Elle rounds on me. "We need to find that cat."

"Agreed."

"I can use my swarm powers."

"I'll cast tracking spells."

A new voice sounds nearby. "You'll do nothing of the kind."

I fight the urge to groan. I know that tone anywhere. It's my father, Legend. Turning, I find him standing beside Diamond.

Damn. It's never good when these two team up.

Diamond glares at Elle. "Whatever Alec has told you, it won't happen," she declares.

I'm about to tell them both to back off when a cloud of red smoke surrounds me. It's a transport spell. My vision fades as does Central Park. The last thing I hear is Elle calling for me.

The sound simply breaks my heart.

*T*he transport spell yanks me away from Central Park. As the red haze fades, I find myself back at my parents' penthouse. Diamond and Legend stand nearby.

Legend flashes me a charismatic grin. "Why don't you have a seat?"

Diamond slides onto a leather chair across from my favorite gaming couch. "Trust us, you'll want to sit down."

I lean against the wall. *This is me, not sitting.* "I didn't get a chance to say goodbye to Elle."

Legend's smile doesn't falter. "We'll tell you the full truth now."

"Still not happy about being dragged away from Elle," I state. "Go on."

Legend slides down to sit on the armrest of Diamond's chair. It's strange to see my parents purposefully staying near each other. Yet another example of why this conversation will not be pleasant.

"We held off on sharing this before," begins Legend. "There was no deceit from Elle?"

My voice lowers. "Deceit from Elle? What do you mean?"

"We only want what's best for you," adds Diamond.

My pulse beats so hard, I can hear the whoosh of blood in my ears. "Disrespect Elle again, and I'll leave this room."

Legend holds up his hands, palms forward. It's the universal hand symbol for *calm down*. "Son, I know your mother told you about me and Raelyn."

The muscles in my throat tighten. "She did."

Legend sighs. "I've had years to think this over. There are two reasons why Raelyn refused my proposal."

As Legend says *refused my proposal*, Diamond visibly shudders. That cools my rage a little. Clearly, this isn't easy for my parents. They're both a little unhinged, but they do care about me.

"Raelyn turned me down because of the family curse," says Legend. "But there's more. Rae was a flighty girl. You know, the kind who gathered many admirers."

"Don't beat around the bush, Legend." Diamond looks toward me. "Rae lied and played with men's hearts."

"That is not Elle."

"Please," says Legend. "Haven't you seen her with other men?"

A memory appears. Jacoby. He showed up both at the park and at school.

"See?" asks Diamond. "He's not denying it. That means he knows it's true."

"I know nothing of the kind."

"Take a word of advice from someone who learned a lesson the hard way," says Legend. "You don't want this kind of pain. That's why your mother and I have been working so hard with Marchesa. We simply can't allow your life to be ruined like ours was."

"So what are you proposing?" *Because my parents wouldn't bring all this up unless they had a plan.*

"Your father and I discussed it," says Diamond. "We're willing to create a trust fund for Elle. Marchesa will assist. Elle will get Cynder Mercantile back. All her animates will be restored. Elle can even have her old fairy godmother in residence, if she likes. And Elle will always stay safe. No more troll attacks."

My brows lift. I haven't known Elle forever. Even so, I know she'd love this idea. "And what would you get in return?"

"Le Charme Jewelers will receive the Coffer of Wonders," declares Legend. "It will save our company."

"You want that, don't you?" asks Diamond. "It would keep Wilhelm and his crew safe."

I lace my fingers behind my neck and work this through. It's a lot of information for one chat. In the end, I decide to tell the truth. "I don't know what to say."

"Well." Diamond turns to Legend. "That's a start."

Legend stands. "All we want is for you to consider what we've said. In the meantime, you must stay away from Knox and Elle until your Glass Slipper Ball."

"And no casting spells or using human technology," says Diamond.

On reflex, I reach into my pockets. All my gemstones are gone. My cell is missing, too. Rage corkscrews up my spine. "You can't force me to stay away from anyone."

"We can't," says Legend. "Your magic is too powerful. But there are other ways to motivate you son. You are rather close to the dwarves."

I step forward, my throat tight with rage. "What did you do to them?"

"They're safe," says Diamond. "For now."

"We didn't want to do this," explains Legend. "It's the last resort."

I push off from the wall and stalk across the penthouse. Reaching the library, I sit in the transport chair. A fresh gemstone sits on the armrest. My fury burns brighter. Legend and Diamond left this stone for me.

They planned everything.

I set the stone into my fist. Soon overlapping rings of red power whip about the chair. One second, I'm in the library. The next, I'm underground.

I reach the dwarves' cave. The cavern lies empty, save for one figure who sits against the far wall. It's Wilhelm, and he's never looked sadder. I rush over to his side. "What's wrong? Where's your crew?"

"Your parents took them," says Wilhelm. He grabs my wrist. "Do whatever they say, Alec. I can't lose my brothers."

"Legend and Diamond wouldn't really hurt them." Yet even as I say the words, they come out as more of a question than a statement. With every passing moment, I'm realizing I don't really know my parents. It makes my love for Elle shine even more brightly.

Wilhelm's grip on my wrist tightens. "Promise me."

I meet his gaze straight-on. "I'll protect them with everything in me."

Wilhelm releases my hand. "Thank you."

All of a sudden, I feel like a sleepwalker. I stumble back to the chair and grip the stone once more. The transport spell kicks in. I return to the library. Both my parents are still there.

"So you've seen the truth," says Diamond.

When I speak, my voice drips with rage. "If anyone so much as scratches Wilhelm's crew—and that includes both of you—then I will make them pay. Do not forget I am the warden of all magic users. I can do things you can only guess at."

"We thought of that," says Legend. "Cast a single spell and they will hurt. Talk to Knox or Elle and the same will come to pass. Do you really want to risk that?"

"You know I don't."

Diamond lifts her chin. "This is about our very future, Alec. Le Charme is bigger than the three of us. It must be preserved, no matter what the cost."

I stagger backward. Once again, the truth stares me dead on through the eyes of my parents. They said it without any nuance. Le Charme is first. I'm not.

"Now," says Diamond. "Let's discuss what will happen at school."

"And at the Autumn Masquerade ball," adds Legend. "Let's not forget that."

My parents then list all the specifics of their plan. I can only half-process what they have to say. Obviously, they've been scheming about all this for some time. And with Elle's evil stepmother, no less. As they talk, I occasionally grunt a short phrase in reply.

Inside, I'm seething. I won't allow Wilhelm's crew to be hurt. And I won't be sacrificed to a loveless marriage... just another in a long line of Le Charme princes lost to hate.

Yet I don't know how to stop it. At all.

20. CHAPTER TWENTY

ELLE

*V*isiting the Queen of Hearts was a trip. But watching Diamond and Legend drag off Alec? That was a shocker. I pull out my phone and text Bry.

> CallMeElle: *You won't believe what just happened*
> MyOwnBry: *I was just about to text you the same thing*
> CallMeElle: *What's wrong? Are you and Knox okay?*
> MyOwnBry: *We are. Just need you here*
> CallMeElle: *Where r u*
> MyOwnBry: *Knox's place in Le Charme*

There's no question what *place* Bry is talking about—it's Knox's apartment in the Le Charme building. For a moment, I wish I knew the first thing about my enchanter powers. I could create a flying carpet or something to get me home quickly. Instead, I settle for running across the park.

By the time I reach the Le Charme building, I'm a sweaty mess. I hit the button for Knox's floor. The elevator seems to creep along slowly until we reach the right spot. The doors slowly open with a metallic hum. I jog to Knox's door and grip the handle. It's unlocked. My skin prickles over with worry. I twist the handle and open the door.

What I see inside shocks me.

Boxes lie everywhere. Bry and Knox stand by the wall; their faces are pale with worry. Bry raises her arms in a clear call for comfort. I race over. We share a hug.

"What happened?" I ask.

"Alec is gone. All his stuff is boxed up."

"And I'm evicted," adds Knox.

Bry beaks our hug. "Our apartment is the same deal. Everything is boxed up. We've got an eviction notice, too."

Stepping back, I try to process all this. Not happening.

"Where are we sleeping tonight?" asks Bry.

"I still have my place in the Village," I say. "You guys can crash there, if you like." I press my palms against my eyes. "I can't believe Legend and Diamond did this to us. Poor Alec."

"What about Alec?" asks Knox. His voice has a bit of a growl. I don't blame him. If I were a shifter, I'd be full wolf right now.

"I don't know how to say this, but…" The hairs on the back of my neck stand on end. I'm no expert in my powers, but I can tell when a spell is activated.

"What?" asks Bry.

An electric charge fills the air. *Magic.* I may not be able to cast many spells, but I do know when I've tripped one off.

I set my pointer finger over my lips and mouth the sound, *shh.*

Knox nods. He mouthes some words of his own. *Tracking spells.*

I don't say another thing. Neither does Knox and Bry. We simply walk away and leave the building. Once we're a safe distance away, Bry stops.

"What'll we do about our boxes?" she asks. "There are personal things I want."

"We leave it for now," says Knox. "If they put a listening spell on the apartment, they definitely put spells on our stuff."

Bry gasps. "But those pictures and things are mine."

"Knox is right," I state. "We can get everything later. Sadly, the more personal your stuff, the more likely it is to be bugged."

Knox pulls Bry into his arms. "We can put the boxes in storage for now. We're okay, yeah?"

Bry leans into his shoulder. "Yes, we're safe."

Those words send a jolt of fear through my insides. "We don't know the same thing about Alec."

"No, we don't." Knox narrows his eyes. "We need to talk."

I rub my neck. "I shouldn't have mentioned my place in the Village. They'll cast more surveillance spells there. I have lots of wards set up, but they aren't perfect." I shoot a guilty glance at Bry. She got abducted from my apartment once.

"Az has a safe house in Jersey," offers Knox. "We can go there."

Azizi is Knox's adopted father. He's an old werewolf and tough as nails. Az has also been around for centuries. Knox could say Azizi owns a nuclear fallout shelter that's hidden under the Statue of Liberty and I'd probably believe it.

With that, we do the only thing we can.

Grab a cab to Jersey.

And hope Alec is okay.

ELLE

*T*urns out, Az's safehouse is located under the bleachers at an abandoned speedway.

Yes, that's right.

Safe house.

Bleachers.

Speedway.

Jersey.

Talk about your unexpected turns in life.

Inside, the safe house is an open space of moldy wood. A bunch of beds sits against one wall. The air is musty. Cobwebs dangle from the ceiling.

The cab driver thought we were nuts to get dropped off here. I'm starting to understand why.

Knox flicks on the lights. "Sorry this isn't fancier. It's the only place I'm certain the Le Charms don't know about. There won't be any tracking spells here, that's for sure. And we can find something better ASAP."

"I'm just happy Az has this place," I say.

"And I've never gone camping before," adds Bry. "This'll be an adventure."

"Cool." Knox steps over to a nearby closet. "All the bed stuff is in

here. There should be some canned junk over in the kitchen area."
One by one, Knox hauls large plastic bags of linens from the closet.

Without another word, Knox and Bry set up the beds. Their
movements flow exactly in tandem, like they've done this a thousand
times. I wonder if I'll ever be that way with someone. Which raises a
question.

What's happening with Alec, anyway?

I shake the thought off. We need to make this place livable before
we can discuss what to do about Alec. Since Bry and Knox have the
bedding covered, I move over to the kitchen area. There's an ancient
sink with a rusted faucet. The water runs red for a bit before it goes
clear. *Gross.*

"Maybe we should order pizza," I offer.

Knox nods. "It's an idea at that."

Soon we're all set up and Knox has finished a pizza run. We set up
a makeshift dinner area on the floor and chow down. Once we're all
filled with cheesy goodness, I toss my paper plates and make an
announcement. "I'm sure you're wondering what happened today."

"The thought did cross our minds," says Knox. "But we wanted to
wait until you were ready."

"Thanks for that." I pop open a new can of Diet Coke. "I'm ready
now."

With that, I launch into everything, starting with Cynder
Mercantile. I'd never told Bry or Knox about the place. Sharing
about my parents just sucks. Then I move on to my first visit the
Queen of Hearts when I was fifteen. And that leads up to today's
adventures. I begin with Blackaverre's visit to the school. From
there, I explain how Alec and I got an audience with the Queen of
Hearts, along with a promise of help if we find her Cheshire cat. I
end with Alec disappearing thanks to his parents.

Along the way, Bry and Knox ask questions. Bry is especially
interested in Cynder Mercantile. For his part, Knox sniffs out the
bizarre love history between my stepfamily and Alec's parents. So I
explain that, too. I go through how my mother turned down Legend
Le Charme... the way my stepmother and Diamond blame my Mom
for everything... and how the Le Charmes seem to think the family's
under a curse.

By the time I'm done, I've downed six slices of pizza and a half-gallon of Diet Coke. "After Central Park, Alec hasn't answered any of my calls or texts. I'm worried about him." I scan Knox and Bry's faces. "Has he contacted you?"

"Not a word," says Knox. "Legend and Diamond must be keeping him under wraps. I haven't seen his parents like this since we were little."

I pull my knees against my chest. "What happened then?"

"I'm sure you've noticed how Legend and Diamond love the spotlight," says Knox.

"Hard to miss," cracks Bry.

"One time, they brought Alec on an afternoon talk show," explains Knox. "I think it was the one with the human woman who wears huge red glasses? Anyway, Alec was only nine or so. I came along to keep Alec company because, well, that's what we do. Watch each other's backs."

"You guys are sweet that way." Bry pats Knox's hand. "So what happened next?"

"The talk show hostess asked Alec if he wanted to take over Le Charme someday. He said he didn't. Instead, Alec said he wanted to be free as a wolf."

"A wolf," repeats Bry. "Why would he say that?"

"Alec knew I'd started going on runs with Az. He thought it was cool."

My heart cracks for poor little Alec. What kid wouldn't want to run with wolves when he's nine years old? Hell, I want to do it right now.

"What did Legend and Diamond do?" I ask.

Knox shakes his head. "Took Alec and ran."

I frown. "What do you mean, they ran? What happened to you?"

Knox chuckles. "I got left in a studio in midtown for a few hours. Someone took pity on me and let me borrow a phone to call Az." Knox shakes his head. "I've never seen the guy more angry. Az picked me up and drove right over to the Le Charme building. They wouldn't let either of us in. Alec ghosted me for a year after that."

"Let me get this straight." Bry's brows pull together. "You didn't talk to Alec for a whole year?"

"Nope," answers Knox. "And when we connected again, he never said a word about the whole thing. He just called me and invited me over to play a new game. But I'll tell you what. Alec never made a misstep in front of the press again. He always says that he loves Le Charme and can't wait to run it one day."

A shiver runs up my back. *What kind of parents keep their kid from his best friend for a whole year?* "Do you think they hurt him?"

"Legend and Diamond?" asks Knox. "No. They wouldn't hurt him physically. But I think he was basically in a *time out* until they felt he'd come around."

I nod slowly, thinking through this news. "Alec wouldn't put up with being locked up now."

"No, he wouldn't," says Knox.

My eyes widen as a realization appears. "They must have something on him."

"Like what?" asks Bry.

Knox rakes his hand through his hair. "I think you're onto something. Alec has a good heart. His parents? Not so much, especially when it comes to their company."

Bry scooches closer to me. "I'll tell you one thing. Alec cares about you."

"We're just friends," I say quickly.

Knox taps his nose. "That's not how he smells to me."

A mixture of joy and worry battles it out inside me. I'm happy Alec cares—as friends of course—but I'm still anxious about what's happening to him. I focus on Knox. "You know Alec the best. What should we do?"

"Wait and see," answers Knox. "If I know Alec, he's already working on a plan. We just need to stay alert. Be ready to act when he gives the signal."

I let out a small groan. "I hate waiting."

"There's one thing we can do in the meantime," offers Bry. "And that's search for the Cheshire cat."

"True." I scan the bare room. There are no computers here. Plus, I can't access Gustav and his gang from this distance. Which means there's nothing I can do to find Chesh right this second. It will simply have to wait until we reach a better safe house.

I tear my napkin into little bits and try not to freak out. *Alec, please be all right.*

22. CHAPTER TWENTY-TWO

ALEC

*A*fter the threat to Wilhelm, I've played the dutiful son. *Say the right thing* became my mantra. I even agreed to an outrageous plan for West Lake Prep and the Autumn Masquerade.

Then every night after the penthouse was asleep, I'd pull out my secret stash of gems from their hiding place under an obliging floorboard by my bed. All new stuff. Super powerful.

And the best of these? My midnight diamond. It's a small black stone that holds hundreds of other gems within it. If you stare in the light the right way, you can see rubies, emeralds, and sapphires.

With this much magic inside it, my midnight diamond is arguably the strongest casting stone ever created. No one even knows how to cast a counter-spell to stop it, it's so new. The only trouble? I haven't yet gotten the gem to speak to me. Once we connect, I can start to try out a few castings. For months, this has something I've tinkered with in my spare time.

That's over.

Now I need to figure out how to use the midnight diamond and fast. If I can connect to the gem, I can figure out a way to free Wilhelm and his crew, as well as get myself out of this horrible situation.

And most of all, I want to see Elle again. Being apart from her just makes it all the more clear that, above all else, I want true love in my future.

Things may look bleak, but I won't give up. One way or another, the Le Charme family curse will end with me.

23. CHAPTER TWENTY-THREE

ELLE - TWO WEEKS LATER

ourteen days, twelve hours and thirty minutes.

That's how much time has passed since Alec and I visited the Queen of Hearts. Since then, there's been no word from him. And I'm not the only one, either. Knox hasn't heard from Alec, either.

Bry and I have gotten a new apartment near central park and school. This isn't one of Azizi's safe houses, by the way. Knox actually owns it.

Side note: I never suspected that Knox owned an apartment complex. Then again, I didn't know he had multiple castles in Europe, either. So there you go.

It took a few days of camping at the speedway, but the place finally got magically secured. We moved in last week, and that's when the ugliness happened.

Honestly, it's more than I want to think about right now.

So I won't.

Instead, I focus on the Cheshire cat. I've done everything I can to find that feline. Gustav and his mouse brigade have been searching the city, top to bottom. Doc Eight loaded me up with detection charms. Even Knox and Bry have gotten into the act. They've started what we call Kitty Patrols. the entire pack is on the scent of Chesh.

Still, no sign of the cat. We keep looking, though.

Which brings me to my final bit of news. West Lake Prep. Going there is still mega boring and dangerous. And I should stop attending. After all, the only reason I was there was to see Alec. Maybe that's a little sad, but I'm girl enough to admit this stuff. Unfortunately, Alec keeps to himself these days.

And when I say *keeps to himself*, I mean that Alec doesn't so much as glance in my direction. There are no texts to meet up, either. It's super depressing. I hadn't realized how thoroughly I'd gotten attached to Alec, even as a friend.

That said, I don't believe Alec is ghosting me by choice. I've thought about it a million ways, and the only reason Alec would go into *douchebag mode* like this is because of his parents. They're blackmailing Alec somehow, I know it.

And again, if I could find the Cheshire cat, then I'd be able to shut Alec's parents down. In the meantime, I still go to school regularly. Staring at the back of Alec's head is better than nothing at all. I miss my friend.

And that's all Alec is. My buddy.

Who I obsess about constantly.

And still want to kiss.

Even *I'm* starting to doubt my logic here.

All of which brings me to the present moment—and yet another random school day. Or it was until everyone got called in for a big assembly.

We meet in a massive hall that's divided into thirds by school. The left section is all-natural wood and bench seats. That's for shifters. The center is fancy plush chairs and velvet everything. Magic user central. And the far right is all garish colors and a bunch of mismatched seats. Fairy section, obviously. I sit in the last row of that area. Jacoby is parked a few rows ahead of me. Once we stepped into the hall, Jacoby got dragged over to sit with the Three Seasons, which is fine. I try not to scan the crowd for Alec.

Not looking.

Nope.

So not interested.

I can play it cool.

Oops. I peeked.

Can I help it if Alec has a really distinctive hair color? I spot him chatting it up with two new girls, giving them his brightest smiles. I stare harder.

Alec shivers.

Turns.

And looks in my direction.

Crap, crap, crap.

At this point, I'm not acting on a conscious thought. It's more of a reflex than anything. And that reflex says: *I can not be caught staring at Alec when he's grinning at other girls.* So I focus on Bry and Knox, who are talking to Abe and Hollywood. I give them a friendly wave, like we've been connecting this whole time. Not my best performance. Even so, it seems to do the trick. When I look away again, Alec has turned back toward the front of the assembly hall.

Good.

Our three principals gather before the assembly. It's Babs, the caster principal, who speaks. "We've called you here today to announce some new students in our school."

Goldi, the fairy principal, flits to her side. "We haven't had any new students since classes began this fall."

Winter raises her hand. Goldi immediately calls on her. "Yes, Winter?"

"We have a new girl." She giggles. "Elle."

Ugh. Not this again.

"Oh, yes." Goldi stares at me like I have three heads. "I keep forgetting that Elle's fairy."

Babs steps up. "We could conjure her some fake wings, you know."

"Not a bad idea." Babs points toward me. "Stand up, Elle."

I slump lower in my seat. "I'm good."

"You're new. You should stand."

Across the hall, Bry stands up. "I'm new."

Knox rises beside her. "Same here."

And because shifters are great this way, the entire werewolf section of the school stands. My chest warms with affection. Bry and Knox are the best.

I stand as well. "I'm new, too."

Babs scowls. "Everyone take your seats. You're wasting valuable time from our big event for the assembly. As I was saying, we have two new students. These are true celebrities from the Magicorum world. Please rise, Ivy and Agatha Cynder!"

My stepsisters stand up and my heart sinks. *Oh no.* They're here at my school. I knew from Marchesa's note that she was aware about my life. But sending her daughters to my same school? What the WHAT?

That's when I notice it. Ivy and Agatha are the girls Alec was just chatting up. They sit on either side of him. Babs goes on about how West Lake is so excited to have Ivy and Agatha join us for the Autumn Masquerade. She then invites the girls to say a few words. Ivy is the one who speaks.

"I can't wait to show you all what I can do," says Ivy. She then goes into a lengthy speech about her own awesomeness. Mostly, it involves how she got great grades at a human school without even trying. Not sure how that counts as an achievement, but the West Lake student body seems impressed.

Things get ugly when Ivy discussed all her new friends at West Lake. "I've made some close, intimate relationships in a very short time." Ivy rests her hand on Alec's shoulder. "I can't tell you how wonderful it is to know that you can just talk to people here *any time you want.*" She glares in my direction.

Before, Ivy was monologuing about her own amazingness. Listening to that is not my favorite way to spend the day. Still, I can deal. But pawing Alec's shoulder while describing how she can chat with him any time she wants?

That's just mean.

With every passing second, more of my muscles tighten with an unpleasant emotion. *Jealousy.* It's when Ivy tousles Alec's hair that I make a big decision.

There's really only one thing to do in this type of situation. Shut this nonsense down, fast.

I pull in just a little fairy magic.

Gustav? Are you there?

Seconds later, a small gray mouse hangs out by my shoe. I've known Gustav long enough to read his little expressions. And the way Gustav is glaring at Ivy? He's as ticked off as I am.

I point to Ivy and then to Gustav. The implication is clear. *Go get her.*

Gustav takes off like a little mouse rocket. I lean back on my chair. This will be sweet.

"Again," says Ivy. "It's access to the friends I love that's what's best about this school. Just reach out and touch…" She tweaks Alec's ear and then pauses.

For a long moment, Ivy simply glances around the room. It's the kind of face you make when plunking your bum onto a wet bench in Central Park. There's an unspoken question.

Is that…?

And then comes the answer. "Mouse!" screams Ivy.

Bry shoots me a wink. Then she stands and calls out a single word. "Hunt!"

At this order, the shifters leap from their seats to search for the mouse. The entire assembly hall goes berserk. The wizards race around (mostly trying to avoid the shifters). Meanwhile, the fairies use the opportunity to cause general trouble. I'm talking tripping up casters, summoning rats to befriend the mice, and making the chairs dance.

Fairies really are the worst.

All in all, it takes the principals twenty minutes to get everyone to line up and return to their respective parts of the school.

At the end of the day, I've learned a valuable lesson. When it comes to friends, I'll take quality over quantity any day.

Bryar Rose is simply the best.

24. CHAPTER TWENTY-FOUR

ALEC

*I*vy keeps screeching about the evil rodent on her kneecap. Perfect. That's completely Elle's handiwork. If I didn't love her before, I'm head over heels now.

Principal Babs eyes at me carefully. She's one of many guardians that my parents have hired to watch my every move. It's tedious as well as nerve-wracking. If I swat Ivy's hand from my ear, will Babs report that to my parents? And what would Legend and Diamond do next? I'm under strict orders to make Ivy happy, no matter what. If Diamond and Legend discovered that I refused Ivy anything, would Wilhelm and his crew get hurt?

Not a risk I want to take. At least, not over Ivy touching my ear.

Sure, I keep searching for Chesh, but without magic or technology? My options are limited. In the end, there's only one conclusion: I can't rely on a magical cat to get me out of this situation.

New magic is my key.

Once I get my midnight diamond working, then I'll be able to stop all this nonsense. In fact, I'd like nothing more than to leave this room, grab Elle, and tell her what she means to me.

Yet I can't.

The result is sad but unavoidable. Until I can find the Cheshire cat or activate my diamond, I must play along with my parents.

And today, that means enduring Ivy.

ELLE

*T*he good news is that sending a mouse up Ivy's leg was a really satisfying viewing experience.

The bad news is that I still had to watch Alec be all smiley to Ivy. Not fun.

After the assembly breaks up, Bry finds me in the passageway to the fae section of the school. She grabs my wrist. "Elle, are you all right?"

"No."

Bry lowers her voice. "Were those your stepsisters?"

"Yes."

"Why don't you go home sick today?" She makes little quotation marks with her fingers when she says the word *sick*. "I'll make some excuses for you."

For some reason, I keep speaking in one-word answers. "Thanks."

I march out the front door and cut across Central Park. With each step, my rage fumes hotter. Ivy and Agatha? Really? A small, logical part of my brain reminds me that Alec is probably being blackmailed, but those thoughts are overruled.

Sometimes, a girl just gets to feel angry. For me, that's right now.

I'm half-way across the park when Jacoby materializes beside me. "Don't punch my face," he says with a sly grin.

I stop. "Not once?"

"You're in a snit."

"I hate it when you say that." What is a snit anyway? And who talks like that outside of elves?

"Oh, that's snit talk for certain. Makes it tempting for me to avoid you."

"Act on the temptation, Jacoby. I'm not fit to be near anyone right now."

Jacoby's silver eyes get all wide with sympathy. No one can pull on your heartstrings like an elf. "Elle, I've known you since forever. I saw what happened at the assembly today."

"If you say one word about Ivy…" I ball my hands into fists.

"Wasn't planning on it," says Jacoby. "I just want to be sure you're all right."

Normally, Jacoby is all snarky and pushy. That version of him I can deal with. But this guy is all sympathy and sweetness. Yes, it's probably an act. Even so, it's been weeks since anyone with a y chromosome has shown me any serious attention. Knox doesn't count.

Jacoby steps closer and slowly wraps me in a hug. I should still punch him in the face, but it just isn't in me right now. Being held is just so comforting. Jacoby rubs my back in slow circles. Total bonus.

"You know what you could do to feel better?" he asks.

"Hmm?"

"Attend the Autumn Masquerade."

"I'm not going. *They who will not be named* will certainly be there." Meaning Ivy and Alec. And thankfully, Jacoby knows me well enough to realize that fact.

"Will you allow them to stop you from attending? Everyone will talk."

Jacoby has a point here. If I don't go, it will definitely be noticed.

"There's still time to decide."

"Not really. The masquerade is this weekend."

"Oh." I make some quick calculations. Once again, Jacoby is right. That snuck up on me there.

"Bry and Knox will be there," says Jacoby.

"True."

And did I mention the back rub is nice? It is.

"I would consider it an honor if you would allow me to accompany you. I can take punches to the face or dole them out to others, whatever you prefer."

I open my mouth, ready to tell him *no*. Then an image appears in my mind. It's Alec, grinning up a storm at Ivy. At this rate, he'll definitely be attending the Autumn Masquerade. Maybe Ivy will even go as Alec's date. I refuse to think about the whole *Glass Slipper Ball plus marriage* situation.

Oops, just thought about it.

Barf.

Jacoby is right. I can't *not show*. And if I do attend, walking through the door alone isn't as nice as having Jacoby along. Besides, I've known Jacoby forever. He's a good friend. We'll have a fine time.

That said, I can't deny that it's pretty clear Jacoby might want more than being my buddy.

"You should know," I say. "I'm not much for relationships or anything right now."

"Hey, I'll take what I can get." Jacoby plays with the ends of my hair. That's also very sweet. "I just want to spend time with you."

This may be a bad choice, but screw it. I just released a mouse on my evil stepsister. I'm on a roll. "All right, I'll go."

"Excellent," says Jacoby. "Would you like me to walk you home?"

"I can manage."

"Very well. I'll be in touch."

And in perfect Jacoby style, he vanishes into thin air.

26. CHAPTER TWENTY-SIX

ELLE

No question about it.

Bry and I are under some kind of apartment curse.

It all started when we were evicted from our new place in the Le Charme building. Then we went to the dust bunny haven that was Az's safe house in New Jersey. Now we're in one of Knox's apartments. The spot is free of dust bunnies, which is cool. And the tenant, Jillian, is just away for six months, so she left her stuff. That should be a huge help, too. No need to buy new furniture and schlep it around, right?

Wrong.

Trouble is, Jillian's obsessed with baby dolls. They are every-freaking-where. And those things stare at you. I'm so *not lying*. Bry and I put them in a closet, but then we felt like they were going to break free and kill us in our sleep. Did I mention that Bry and I have very active imaginations? We do.

Long story short, I went to a dollar store and bought a bunch of baby sunglasses. I've since put all the dolls back in their original spots with new eye gear so it doesn't seem like they're staring. It's a little better. I can't wait until my place in the Village is finished being magically cleansed. Not sure how Alec's family got in there, but dang, they did a serious job. I had to call in some favors from Hecuba, a powerful witch who keeps getting her rings stolen.

So after my Ivy encounter today at school, I'm not looking forward to *baby doll central*. But at least Bry will be there, so I focus on that.

I step into the apartment and find Bry in the kitchen. We tend to hang out there as it's the room with the fewest dolls.

"Hey, Bry!" I give her a big hug. "Thanks for standing up for me at today's assembly. You know, literally."

"What else could I do?" She lowers her voice. "Is it just me, or was that doll—" Bry points across the kitchen "—not there yesterday?"

I follow the direction of her point and, sure enough, a new baby doll sits atop the fridge. She's a cute thing with a pink sun hat and a shocking lack of sunglasses. Her beady eyes glare in our direction.

"Um, no." I lower my voice as well. "Do you think Knox moved her?" This place has three bedrooms, which is pretty big for New York. Too bad they're all filled with baby dolls. I've noticed that Bry and Knox don't even snuggle on the couch these days, let alone kiss in the apartment. We always feel like someone is staring at us.

Did I mention I really want my studio back? I do.

"I don't know." Bry's eyes widen. And since most of her face is brown eyes, that's another scary sight, right there. "Did the fridge baby blink? I think it blinked!"

"This is nuts." I whip out my cell and text Knox.

CallMeElle: Hey, did you do this?

I take a snapshot of the doll and attach it. A few seconds pass before Knox replies.

FortMe: Why, does it bug you?

I show Bry my screen. *Knox totally did it.* I take a picture of Bry making a nasty hand gesture and send it back. Knox replies with a bunch of ROTFL memes.

Most of the time, Knox is a chill guy. That said, he does have his moments of downright Alec-ish behavior. Setting up the fridge baby is one such example.

Speaking of the fridge baby, Bry tiptoes over and flips it so it's facing the wall. "Much better," she says.

"How was the rest of your day?" I ask.

"We had more pack activity time."

"Where?"

"Harbor Trampoline Park."

"What?" I make sure my mouth hangs extra-wide for dramatic effect. "That's not even remotely a school activity."

"It is for shifters." Bry starts pulling stuff out and laying on the counter. I count coconut milk, lima beans, and parsley.

Yipes.

Bry grew up with her aunties controlling everything in her life. She never even learned how to cook. Now, my best friend is free from her aunts and experimenting in the kitchen. I don't want to rain on her culinary parade, so I don't stop her. Although it's very tempting to point out that you can always Google recipes instead of, you know, making stuff up. Again, it makes Bry happy so I keep my trap shut. Once the meal is served, I'll choke down a few bites and then order pizza later.

And yes, I get extra slices for Knox.

Bry pulls out some flour, sea salt, and chocolate mints. *Wow. This will be an epic creation.* "How was the rest of your day?" she asks. "I was surprised I got home first."

"I went for a walk in Central Park. Jacoby found me. We chatted."

"That's nice." Bry gets out a big bowl and starts pouring in ingredients at random. "What did you talk about?"

"The Autumn Masquerade. He asked me to be his date."

Bry stops pouring random stuff into her bowl. Little by little, she turns to face me. When our gazes meet again, her eyes are super wide. "And what did you say?"

"I said *yes.*" Bry's giving me her big doe-eyed look, so I keep going. "Alec was chatting up Ivy and Agatha today. They're my stepsisters. Maybe I got a little jealous. When Jacoby asked me to go, it seemed harmless enough. And I know Alec is going through some strange stuff, but it still hurts to be alone."

"Okay. Well." Bry nibbles her thumbnail. *That's never a good sign.*

"What is it?"

"Hmmm."

"Bry."

"You know how Knox was my first real kiss."

Where's going with this? "Sure."

"And we're both founding members of the *Eighteen And Never Been Kissed In Manhattan Club*."

At the time, Elle and I felt we were the only girls on the island who could possibly join. You never know how many girls say they've been kissed when you admit that it's never happened to you.

"Right," says Bry.

"So?" I ask. "Now I'm the only one left." I frown, trying to figure out the deal here. "You know if I had a real kiss, I'd tell you. I mean, Alec gave me a peck on the lips once. That doesn't really count."

"It's like this. Part of the tradition of the Autumn Masquerade is that you share a real kiss with your date at midnight."

I take a half-step backward. "You do? How come no one ever told me this?"

Bry shrugs. "It's on all the posters. Don't the other fairies talk about it? It's all the gossip in the shifter cave."

"Well, that's my problem right there. I don't like other fairies. We don't talk."

"You know how I feel about that," says Bry. Which lead into to an age-old disagreement between us. Bry thinks I'm more witch than fairy. I think the whole *warden of all fae magic thing* seals the deal. Plus, I can't enchant anything if I tried. Not that I've tried a ton, mind you.

"At this point, I'm set in the fairy school. If I had to watch Alec all day long, that would be super tough."

Bry goes back to making her *whatever that is*. "Because you guys are such great friends."

This is another ongoing discussion between us, by the way. Bry feels that it's her role as best friend to point out that I am kidding myself about my feelings for Alec.

I set my fist on my hip. "That's right. Buddies forever."

"Okay, fine." She starts mushing stuff in her bowl. Odd scents waft through the kitchen.

I tap my chin and think this through. "The masquerade ball doesn't have to be a disaster. It's not like I have to kiss anyone."

"You don't." *Mush mush mush.* "But everyone does." *Mush mush mush.* "And folks will notice if you skip out."

An image chills my blood. It's Alec and Ivy, smooching. "If Alec has a date, he'll kiss her." My icy shock quickly heats into fiery rage. "In that case, I'm definitely going. I'll kiss Jacoby's mouth off, too."

Bry shoots me a dry look. "Eew."

"You know what I mean."

"Dinner will be done in a few minutes." Bry lifts up her spoon. Some brown goop with coconut shards drips off the utensil and into the bowl. "Or I can order pizza."

"Pizza would be awesome."

On reflex, my hand goes to my purse. That's where I keep my two little glass slippers and pumpkin carving. It's the only part of my parents I have left. Knowing I just agreed to kiss Jacoby? For some reason, that makes me miss Mom and Dad more than ever.

My thoughts turn to the Queen of Hearts and finding her Cheshire cat. Maybe I should start doing my own nightly prowls around the city. I don't need to sleep, really. Prowl by night and school by day? I could make that work.

Anything to find that cat.

Bry speed-types on her cell. Her tongue sticks out one side of her mouth, which is her classic face for *ordering pizza from an app*. Once she looks up, I launch into my next question.

"Any word from the shifters?" There's no need to explain more. There's only one topic where I'm looking for shifter updates. The Cheshire cat.

True fact: sometimes, it's like I can see Chesh from the corner of my eye. But when I look, there's nothing there.

"Sorry," says Bry. "They're searching but no cat yet. Sorry."

"It's cool," I say. "I appreciate them looking for a feline. It's not a fave wolf hobby or anything."

"I'll keep calling out to Colonel Mallory, too," adds Bry. "He said he'd be stuck in the Faerie lands for a while and out of touch and well, that's turning out to be true." Colonel Mallory is Bry's adopted father as well as a big bad dragon shifter.

"Thanks for trying."

Bry rests her hand on my shoulder. "We'll find Chesh."

"Absolutely." But even as the word leaves my mouth, I know it's a lie.

With every passing day, I get farther away from finding Chesh. Or doing any of the things I really value, for that matter. The animates are lost to me. My parents' store is a ruin. Alec is locked out of my life. And I'm attending a school that I hate with fairies I can't stand.

If I've ever been further from myself, I can't imagine the time.

27. CHAPTER TWENTY-SEVEN

ALEC

I sit on my gaming couch and pretend to watch Real Warlocks of Manhattan. In reality, I'm toying with the midnight diamond in my pocket. In my mind, I reach out to the stone.

Hello?

No reply, but that happens. The great gem caster, Horus Agrippa, once spent a decade reaching out to a stone before it spoke back. And if Horus Agrippa can do it, so can Alec Le Charme.

So while I pretend to watch this show, I keep pouring my mind into the stone and looking for a reply.

Still nothing.

It doesn't help that one of my parents is always nearby and staring. Today, Legend is on duty. He paces the penthouse and makes calls for the Glass Slipper ball. My father's looming presence only reminds me there's so much I still need to do.

Like contact Elle.

Find Chesh.

And, last but not least, rescue Wilhelm and his crew.

Sadly, there's nothing I can do as long as my powers are blocked.

The other day, I grabbed a regular casting stone, just to see what would happen. My parents transported into the room within thirty seconds. Whatever tracking spell they have on me, it's serious stuff. I can't break it without some power of my own.

"I don't care what MNN says," grumbles Legend into his headset. "I promised Oprah an exclusive. MNN is out for an interview with me and Diamond." He pauses. "Then let MNN shoot some stuff at Alec's school. There's a dance or something coming up." He hits a button on his cell and ends the call without saying goodbye. That's classic Legend.

For my part, I pretend to be enraptured by whatever nonsense is happening in this TV show. It's all BS, by the way. For instance, this week's episode features a pair of so-called potion masters, Axe and Baxe. These overly-ripped dudes spend forty minutes mixing up a love serum on the kitchen stove. They use black kettles, empty eyedropper bottles, and something called dragon dust.

What a crock. Potion masters only mix in glass bowls. That way, they can see how their spell is working. In terms of bottles, they only put their creations into glass containers that are hand-blown and magic-ed up not to explode. So a manufactured eyedropper bottle is a big *no no*. And finally, there's no such thing as dragon dust.

Question: Did the Axe and Baxe people even *meet* an actual potion master before they signed up for this show?

Legend plunks onto the couch beside me. The fact that Axe and Baxe are still presenting potion tips doesn't stop my father from interrupting the show. Not that I'm really watching. Even so, it's all part of the stuff I've been realizing lately. Mostly, it's becoming more and more clear how my parents want me to be some kind of *Alec doll* in their plans. Right now, that plan involves talking to Legend at this very moment.

"Good day at school, son?"

I pointedly raise my remote and turn down the sound. "Fine."

"Principal Babs told me all about the assembly. Great way to introduce Ivy and Agatha to the community, eh? Their mother is a powerful potion master."

"Maybe, but neither of her daughters knows the first thing about brewing up a spell. I heard they couldn't boil water. Honestly, I wonder if West Lake Prep is the best place for Ivy and Agatha."

"It's perfect." Legend grins. "I was just on the phone with Giselle, our new publicist. She agrees with me. It will be great for MNN to get some footage of your Autumn Masquerade."

"MNN. As in Magicorum News Network?"

"Brilliant, right?"

"It's a private school event."

Legend has many kinds of laughs. I've categorized them over the years. His current guffaw is a blast of noise that says, *you're totally wrong.*

"I'll talk to the principal," says Legend. "It will be fine."

"Whatever you say." I pick up the remote and crank up the volume again.

"Now wait," warns Legend. "Your mother and I have been talking."

For the record, no conversation with my Legend has ever gone well that includes, *your mother and I have been talking.*

"And?" That's what I ask, although I'm pretty sure where Legend is going with this conversation. MNN will be at the Autumn Masquerade. My father will want to create a viral moment for them.

"We think you should ask Ivy to the gala."

I screw up my mouth, as if seriously considering this idea. "I can't take Ivy."

Legend hops to his feet. "Why not?"

"The media is building up a lot of excitement over the Glass Slipper Ball. Taking Ivy will ruin all the tension."

"Please. All you have to do is walk through the door with her on your arm. You can flirt with other girls or whatever."

"No go. At the senior masquerade, it's tradition for dates to share a kiss—as in a serious kiss—precisely at midnight. If I walk in with Ivy as my date, then where's the drama?"

Obviously, I'd rather have my leg broken in at least three places than take Ivy to the Autumn Masquerade. Some examples why (and these are all from today alone):

One. Excessive grabbing of my thigh at the assembly. Not acceptable.

Two. Calling the cafeteria the *yum-yum room.* Many times.

Three. Referring to her own sister, Agatha, as *that hag.*

Four. Persistently asking me if I hated Elle, or really really REALLY hated Elle.

Legend retakes his seat beside me. "Speaking of Ivy, how did today go?"

"It went well." *And by this I mean, it meant as well as having a hole drilled into my cranium.* Not that I'm giving that detail to my parents. I'm lucky not to be chained up somewhere.

"Did you give her a tour of the school?"

"I did."

"Excellent!" Legend now launches into his classic hiss-laugh. It's a series of low-pitched sounds that are appropriate for an attacking snake. From Legend, it's meant to convey that we are now having *real man talk.* "How much time did you two, you know, *spend together?*"

"Two hours, fourteen minutes, and thirty-seven seconds." *And I loathed all of it.*

"So, you're getting to know each other."

"Absolutely."

"Great. I'll call Giselle now. We need to lock in MNN for Saturday."

As Legend fires up his cell phone again, I grip the midnight diamond more tightly in my pocket. The Autumn Masquerade is just four days away.

I simply must speak to this stone before then.

28. CHAPTER TWENTY-EIGHT

ELLE - SATURDAY NIGHT

THIS is fine.
This IS fine.
This is FINE.

Maybe if I keep saying that, I won't feel like tonight's Autumn Masquerade will go sideways.

Bry and I hang out in my bedroom. As a reward for his snark, we've moved the creepiest dolls into Knox's room. Still, I'm glad mine still all have their mini sunglasses in place. Bry wears a sleek little black dress with matching heels. She looks sophisticated and all-around gorgeous.

Not for the first time, I wish I was in the shifter part of school. They can wear whatever they want tonight. Since it's a masquerade ball, we girl fairies must dress up like someone from history. And it's not like we can choose our person, either. The principal picks for us. I got Laura Ingalls Wilder, author of *Little House on the Prairie*. Not only that, but Principal Goldie specifically warned me not to cook up some kind of sexy prairie dress.

Like I'd do that.

And on top of everything, I was given a fake pair of fairy wings to wear at the event. That's so *not happening*. The prairie dress is drab but fine. Plus, comes with a big droopy hat that will easily hide my looks of loathing during tonight's event. And it could have been worse. One girl I know, Dawn Blossom, needs to show up as a shoe. How is that even a character from history? It's just fairies being mean. Again.

Bry does a final twirl in the mirror before turning to me. "What do you think?"

"You're stunning."

"Thanks. You look, uh…" Bry eyes my floor-length gingham monstrosity. "You know I'm a terrible liar. That's not your best look."

"No complaints here. I could have been forced to dress up like a shoe. That's all I'm saying."

Bry frowns. "How is a shoe even a historical figure?"

"One word, Bry. Fairies."

She nods slowly. "True."

Knox steps into the room. Tonight he looks especially handsome in his new tuxedo. Like all the shifters, Knox also wears a simple black mask. Bry pops on her matching version. Together, Bry and Knox look like a million dollars. They chat about the fastest way to get to the L Center, which is where the Autumn Masquerade is being held. All the while, their phones go berserk.

Bzzz, bzzz…

Meep-meep, meep-meep!

Knox moves on to discussing the weather, and that's when I call it quits.

"Guys," I say. "Your phones are blowing up. Let me guess. Your pack wants you at the L Center."

"Maybe?" asks Bry.

"You have my full permission to take off now. It's not like me and Jacoby aren't alone all the time. Plus, there will be the inevitable *open the door* moment when Jacoby gets here. Lying will most likely be involved. I'd rather not have witnesses."

Knox and Bry share a long look. "All right," says Bry at last. "We'll see you there."

"Have fun." I give Bry a quick hug before walking them both to the front door. They're about to leave when Bry pops her hands over her mouth.

"Oh," she yelps. "I almost forgot." Bry hoofs it back to her room and comes back with a little gingham sack bag. "I got this for you."

"Why?" I ask. Nights like this, I put my credit card and door key in my shoe. Purses can be a pain.

"So you can take your glass slippers and pumpkin with you." Bry jiggles the tiny bag. "Good mojo."

My eyes get all watery, which is fine because I didn't even bother putting on makeup. "Thanks, Bry. You're the best."

She winks. "So are you."

And as she and Knox leave, I come to a big decision.

I am one lucky girl.

Once I'm alone, I have lots of quality time to ponder this evening. Mostly, I worry about the whole *midnight kiss* thing. My thoughts retread a familiar theme. Namely, I'm still eighteen and haven't really kissed anyone. That little peck with Alec but it doesn't count. Not that I don't think about it all the time.

Tonight, I have a chance to change that. Jacoby is attractive in that *I'm an elf and you can't resist me* sort of way. The whole kissing issue is already making me nervous. If I wait until midnight, I'll lose my nerve. Or worse, I'll slobber all over his face or something. And the entire school will be watching, let's not forget that part.

On a side note, how rude is it to have a tradition like this? You'd think adults would be a little more responsible about our emotional development. Then again, all these adults are all Magicorum and a third of those are fairies. So, there's that.

As I pace the doll's den, I come to another big decision. That makes two biggie realizations for me in one evening; it's a record night for this Ellie Belly.

Anyway, here's my plan. I'll keep my eyes open for a private spot to quickly smooch Jacoby. That way, I can get it over with fast and just as importantly, away from the crowd. I'll just grab his face and kiss, end of story.

A knock sounds at the door. Must be Jacoby.

I smile. This is a sign from the universe that my *Stealth Attack Kiss Plan* is obviously amazing. I'm only thinking about my cleverness when I saunter to the front door and swing it open. Jacoby looks devastatingly handsome in a tuxedo. Because, of course, the fairy guys all get to wear tuxes. Life sucks that way. Jacoby takes one look at me and bursts out laughing.

"What..." Jacoby gestures at my dress in a general way "...is that?"

"There's also a hat." I pop that part on. "Get it out of your system."

Jacoby bends over, he's laughing so hard. I step back and make room for him to enter. "Get inside. I don't want my neighbors sharing this humiliation."

"So..." *bwah hah hah* "Sorry." Jacoby strolls inside the apartment while keeping his hands on his stomach. I've seen him do this before; it's his way of trying to calm down.

I close the door behind him. At least, that awfulness is over.

Turning around, I find Jacoby has stopped laughing. That would be good, only now he's walking about in a slow circle and staring at our apartment. And that's when I remember. All the dolls. Jacoby knows Bry and I had to move, but he hasn't actually been inside yet. Even worse, I didn't warn him or anything.

"Hold on there, elf," I warn. "Don't you dare say a thing. Elle and I had to move at the last minute. This is the only place we could find."

Jacoby tries hard to keep a straight face. He sucks at it. "This place is interesting." His mouth twitches with the urge to laugh. "Can we have a Chucky film festival here?"

"Ha, ha. No."

"Oh, I've got it. We don't even have to watch the movie." Jacoby waves his hand. Silver fae dust flies from his fingertips, creating a magical cloud beside each doll. When the mist congeals, each girl now has an evil Chucky boy beside her. And in a matching outfit, no less.

"I hate you right now, Jacoby." Yet I might be smiling a little as I say that.

The many Chuckies blink in my direction. "But we looooove you, Elle," they say in unison.

My eyes narrow. *Jacoby wants to play? I'm game.*

Pulling on my own power, I send out clouds of fairy dust toward the girl dolls. The spell quickly congeals around them. All the girls hop down from their respective shelves and march toward Jacoby. "Take us home with you," they chant.

Jacoby rounds on me. All signs of humor are gone. "Now that," he says slowly "is some impressive magic. Where have you been hiding that power?"

I release the magic so fast, the dolls all topple over in place. "That wasn't a big deal."

"Oh, I disagree. Creating new dolls is easy. But placing movement on a current object? That's a senior-level spell. I used a lot of energy just to get my boys talking. But you? You wrapped magic around existing dolls and fashioned a moving army." He strides closer. That sense of menace and attraction radiates off him in waves. "Who are you, Elle Cynder?"

I scoop my little gingham bag and stomp toward the door. "Someone who's ready for her masquerade ball."

"As you say." Jacoby follows me past the threshold.

As we leave the building, a mega ball of worry settles into my stomach. The night hasn't even begun, and I've already had an *evil doll war* in my apartment. Plus, I maybe exposed my true powers to none other than Jacoby.

Hopefully, that's the end of the drama for this evening.

29. CHAPTER TWENTY-NINE

ALEC

*A*s I step into the ballroom at the L Center, I sport a tuxedo and picture-perfect smile. With any luck, I'm the image of casual. But inside? My heart thuds against my rib cage. The reason is simple. For the first time since visiting the Queen of Hearts, I may actually talk to Elle. Alone.

I scan the place and catalog every detail. Is this my moment? I've spent hours obsessing over tonight, so I run through my mental checklist. Once all my criteria are met, I'll know it's safe to go looking for Elle... Or as safe as it can get. Here's my list:

Packed ballroom? Check.

All the guys dressed identically? Check.

My parents out of the way? Big check. They're chatting up MNN on the other side of the room. That will buy me at least twenty minutes.

Principal Babs occupied? Yet another big check. She's part of the small crowd that's huddled around the video cameras.

So far, so good.

I stroll about the periphery of the room. It's much easier than pushing through a crowd. Along the way, I slip on my sunglasses and stick to the shadows. For the short term, I'm going incognito.

Then I spot her.

Elle.

My breath catches.

She stands on the balcony. Shock and elation churn through my system. It takes every ounce of control in me not to plow through the crowd and rush to her. Instead, I keep to the fringes and slowly circle my way to the balcony entrance. Everyone else is chatting it up in the main chamber. No one's overheated yet from the dance floor and needing a balcony break.

Elle is solo.

This is it. Our moment.

I step out onto the balcony proper. The cool night air brushes against my skin. Before I can say a word, something amazing happens. Elle clasps my face in her hands and brings her mouth to mine.

Our lips meet in a rough kiss.

This is more than I ever hoped for. With gentle movements, I pull Elle's body against me. She fits me perfectly.

Yes.

30. CHAPTER THIRTY

ELLE

*S*tepping out to the balcony was all part of my *sneak attack kissing* plan.

Everyone was saying their hellos and trying to get caught on television. So I slipped away while Jacoby chatted up the Three Seasons. Then I waited on the balcony for him to show. It's a great spot, considering all the shadows and empty space. In fact, the only pieces of furniture are a few tables that sit by the low rail surrounding the space. And nearby, some trees provide extra cover from passers-by.

Perfect.

At first, all I saw was his outline framed on the balcony's threshold. The warm lights from the ballroom framed his outline in a halo of gold. Something about the sight stirred my soul.

Without another thought, I strolled up to Jacoby, cupped his face in my hands, and pulled him into a kiss. The moment our mouths met, an electric sensation charged across my skin.

Which brings me to right now.

My soul feels on fire. Jacoby pulls me closer. Our bodies press together and wow, Jacoby is ripped. I mean, I knew he was built, but that's only because elves aren't normally super bolshie. Feeling him now, it's almost as if Jacoby is as big as...

Like he's the same size as...

I break the kiss.

My heart sinks and soars, both at the same time. Sure enough, I haven't been kissing Jacoby. Someone else is here.

"Alec." The name comes out as barely a whisper.

"Elle."

I bite my lower lip. *How do I explain this?* "I thought you were..."

"Don't say it." Alec's words are a low rumble. "Kiss me again."

It's not even a choice, really.

"Yes."

I press my mouth to his once more. Alec grips me around the waist, twirls me through the air and sets me atop a nearby table. It's the perfect height for me to wrap my legs around his waist, so that's exactly what I do. The press of his firm body against mine is intoxicating. My hands glide against the planes of his chest. It's like I can't touch him enough.

A noise echoes in from the small patch of nearby trees.

"Meow. Excuse me, Meow!"

Alec and I stop kissing. Moving in unison, we turn to look at the nearby treetop. Sure enough, none other than Chesh sits in the branches. "Hello." He grins his over-large smile before leaping off into the night.

I look to Alec. "I hate that cat."

"Me, too."

I slide off the table and hitch my bag over my shoulder. "Let's do this." Alec hoists me up so I stand atop the low railing that separates the balcony from the courtyard beyond. I scan the nearby tree. "I can climb this. You?"

Alec leans forward and nods. "Sure, I hate this tux anyway."

All of a sudden, Jacoby steps out. "There you are, Elle." He looks between me—*I'm still standing on the balcony ledge*—and Alec. "What did I miss?"

"We're off to find a cat," I explain. "It's an early night for me."

Jacoby leans against the doorframe. "Good of you to let me know." He has that *sneaky elf look* in his eyes, though. I'd wonder what he's really up to, but that's not a great use of time right now.

We have a Cheshire cat to catch.

The MNN camera guy pushes out onto the balcony. Rosa Langstrom follows behind, microphone in hand. "Great news, viewers. We've found the elusive Alec Le Charme out here on the balcony. Alec, what do you have to say to our viewers on the Magicorum News Network?"

Oh, crap. Time to get the hell out of here.

Leaping off the ledge, I grab a tree branch and drop to the ground. Alec lands right beside me. The spotlight of the camera cuts through the night as Rosa calls out. "Alec? Where are you going? Viewers, we're here at the Autumn Masquerade where Alec Le Charme has run off with a nondescript girl."

Alec shoots me one his *million-watt* smiles. "You're anything but nondescript."

In the shadows nearby, Chesh clears his throat. "I said, meow." His outline shows in the moonlight as he takes off for Central Park.

I hoist up my skirts and run. Alec keeps pace beside me.

Here we go.

31. CHAPTER THIRTY-ONE

ALEC

*W*hat happens next is a blur. I recall more impressions than anything else.

There's a darkened alley.

A well-lit sidewalk.

Some older gent who jumps out of my way.

All the while, Elle stays at my side.

No matter what, both Elle and I stay focused on the striped tail of the Cheshire cat. Just when I think I'm about to pounce and grab him, the feline leaps out of the way. In the rush of running, I catch more quick moments.

Crossing a busy street.

Without a crossing light.

Cars screech to a halt.

A cabbie yells, *go back to the prairie, you freaks!*

Elle and I end up in Central Park. Again. Chesh scales up a particularly large oak. Elle and I stand by the base, our hands braced on our knees, gasping for breath. We're not alone, either. About fifty white mice encircle the trunk as well. These little ones don't seem winded at all.

I gesture to our tiny friends. "What" *pant pant* "is that?"

"My swarm magic," replies Elle. She sucks in a few deep breaths before going on. "I was sending it out to work on Chesh, but I caught others instead." Her face brightens with a smile. Makes sense that Elle would try to cast while running. I only wish I could have tried as well. On reflex, I check my pocket.

The midnight diamond is still there.

And it remains unreadable.

Familiar voices echo through the darkened park. "Alec? Alec!!!"

I force myself to stand. "That's Legend and Diamond."

Elle pales. "Oh no." She reaches up toward the branches. "Here, kitty kitty."

But I already know what she'll say next.

"Chesh is gone."

I straighten the lapels of my tux. My parents warned me what would come next if I didn't play along. Worse trouble. Who knows when I'll get another chance to tell Elle how I really feel?

Turning, I take Elle's hands in mine. "No matter what happens, know this. You are my choice. Mine. Nothing and no one can ever change that."

A pause hangs in the air. I know Elle cares for me. Will she say it?

Elle opens her mouth. Closes it. Her body trembles. "I'm sorry," she whispers.

"I know you're not there with me yet, Elle. And I understand. When you're ready, I will be here. Believe me."

My parents step out of the shadows. Legend still wears his tuxedo; Diamond sports silver gown. Legend is the first to speak. "We warned you, Alec."

"Your Glass Slipper Ball will now take place next weekend," adds Diamond. My mother rounds on Elle. "You're not invited."

Legend loosens his bow tie. "You can go willingly or not, son. It's your choice."

A line of wizards steps out from the trees. The mice scatter. *Smart move.* I scan the many new faces. All of them are gem casters, same as my parents. Plus, every last one wears a tuxedo or formal dress. That means they were all attending the Autumn Masquerade as well. They must have chased me here. Wizards aren't fans of physical activity, as a rule. They'll be looking for any reason to separate me from my soul.

All of which raises one of my personal battle rules: know when to back off. Now is one of those times. I slap on my most winning smile. "Twenty to one, eh? I'm honored you think me so dangerous."

"Alec," says Diamond.

"I'll go willingly, obviously. On one condition. Elle stays safe."

Legend nods. "She's free to go."

At that moment, Elle presses something onto my palm. I shoot a quick glance at my hand. A small glass slipper rests there. My heart lightens. Elle and I lock gazes while the many wizards surround us. Emotions churn between us.

Longing.

Sorrow.

Worry.

Someone pushes against my back. "Move on."

"No need to be rude," I warn.

Legend steps up. "Hands off my son."

While Legend gets into a staring match with his own wizard, I slip Elle's glass slipper into my pocket and grasp the midnight diamond once more. Pretending to clear my throat, I pop the gem into my mouth, careful to keep it under my tongue.

I've read how *mind vise* spells work. They won't ask me to talk anymore. But they will keep me as far away from gemstones as possible.

Hiding my midnight diamond may be my only chance.

32. CHAPTER THIRTY-TWO

ELLE

*W*as it only a few minutes ago I was sharing the most epic kiss ever?

Why, yes. Yes, it was.

And now, a horde of wizards march Alec away. I pull on my inner fae power. A small cloud of fairy dust hovers over my palm. I send it out to find Gustav. Sure, the mice ran away when the wizards showed. Still, they wouldn't have gone far.

The silver mist flies off my hand and into the nearby grasses. Gustav marches out.

"We lost the cat," says Gustav.

I kneel. This way, I can better chat with Gustav and still keep my voice low. You never know; a rogue wizard may still be lurking nearby.

"I'm not worried about that," I whisper. "I need you to—"

"On it, Elle." Gustav takes off in Alec's direction.

Clever mouse.

Rising, I brush some bits of grass off my skirts. Tonight was a disaster. Even so, I can handle this.

In my heart, the fortress surrounding my emotions grows taller than ever. There's no room for Alec. I must stay inside, alone, and protect my soul.

All the while, I grip my little bag more tightly. If I'm so strong and solo, why did I give Alec one of my glass slippers?

Well, I did. It's done now.

Turning, I scan the park, trying to figure out the fastest route to my new apartment and its creepy doll collection.

That's when I see her.

Marchesa.

She still wears a black dress along with a disgusted look on her face.

"Hello, Elle."

With a flick of her wrist, Marchesa tosses a small potion bottle to the ground. Green smoke balloons into the air. I try to run, but the spell is too fast. Plumes of emerald-colored magic quickly surround me.

And everything in my mind turns to black.

33. CHAPTER THIRTY-THREE

ELLE

*W*hen I wake up, my head's all groggy, like my skull's filled with cotton candy. And not in a good way, either.

Little by little, I become aware of my surroundings. I lay on a moldy mattress. Condensation drips from the cracked ceiling to make patterns on my prairie dress. Some random water bottle sits nearby.

Memories reappear.

That's right. I was dressed up as Laura Ingalls Wilder for the Autumn Masquerade. Alec and I ran after the Cheshire cat. That bit was cool. Then Alec got dragged away by his parents and a bunch of gem casters. Thus began the crappy part of the evening.

The room comes into clearer focus. I'm in a bare basement made from concrete. A short flight of stairs is the only way in or out. A thin beam of light peeps out from under a wooden door.

My heart sinks.

I know where this is. Cynder Mercantile. The basement.

The door swings open. Marchesa stands on the threshold. She steps down the stairs. A figure follows behind her. My eyes widen.

It's a troll.

I learned the hard way how potion masters worked with trolls. So it's not surprising that Marchesa would have one handy. Even so, this guy is especially large and nasty. He has to move sideways just to step down the stairs. Marchesa pauses before me.

"Comfortable?" she asks.

Some questions don't deserve answers. Which is why I ignore Marchesa. Instead of replying, I scooch backward until I'm sitting with my back resting against the wall. Then I spend some quality time picking bits of mold off my skirt.

"Missing this?" Marchesa holds up my small bag.

That gets my attention. I glare at her with all the rage that's inside me. "That's mine."

"I'm aware," says Marchesa smoothly. She makes a great show of opening up the bag, pulling out the glass slipper and holding it up high. Sickly beams of light from the first-floor dance through the tiny item. "I remember when Kokkivo fired these. He always had a talent for capturing light inside glass." Her face creases into a false smile. "Of course, he used your mother's design." She drops the slipper to the floor.

Shock churns through my body. I gasp and scan the floor. *My slipper!* I inspect the nearby ground carefully. The thing got a little chipped, but it looks okay.

"Uh, oh," says Marchesa. She slams her heel down onto the slipper, smashing it into bits. The crunch of glass cuts through my heart.

"You're horrible," I say.

Marchesa's mouth rounds into a sickly smile. She takes out the pumpkin, drops it to the floor and crushes that one as well. "Oops," she says.

I lean against the wall once more. Marchesa just wants to upset me. No way will I give her the satisfaction again. Kicking my legs forward, I fold my arms over my chest.

"You never answered my question," I state. "What do you want?"

Marchesa's eyes flash with anger. *Good.* If my sass ticks her off, then that's what she'll get.

"Diamond has a soft heart," says Marchesa. "She insisted that I not hurt you." My stepmother counts off on her fingers. "No physical attacks. No poisons. No spells."

I smack my lips. "Are you getting to the point any time soon?"

Marchesa's body shivers with rage. I consider this progress. "It took me days, but I figured out how to end you while keeping my promises to Diamond." She opens her arms wide. "Welcome to your tomb. It's warded to the hilt. No one will come to rescue you."

I fake-shiver. "Ooh."

"You'll die of thirst, here with Grunt to guard you."

I focus more closely on my new buddy. Turns out, Grunt is a six-foot-tall troll with a tiny round head and skin that's covered in green lumps. His arms and legs are thick as marble columns. A pair of heavy tusks jut out from his lower lip.

"Guard," says Grunt. And yes, his voice is definitely in the grunt family of noises.

"Don't bother begging for mercy," adds Marchesa. "Grunt won't care."

I mime writing in the air. "No begging. Got it."

"You're so smug. And you think all the world's problems are someone else's fault. All the while, it's you."

There's crap I'll take from evil stepmothers, and it doesn't include a crack like that one. "Ho, there. How is it *my* fault that Mom got cancer and Dad died of a broken heart?" I tap my cheek dramatically. "Could it be perhaps that *you're* the one who won't own her own crap?"

Marchesa raises her fist. "Declan was my true love!"

"You chose to marry someone else. That's on you."

Marchesa's mouth thins to an angry line. "If there's one consolation for me, it's that I've timed your death to the day Alec gets bonded to my Ivy."

It's an effort, but I pretend that statement didn't hurt like hell. "What do you mean?"

"Diamond and Legend moved the Glass Slipper Ball to this Saturday." She points to the plastic bottle at the base of my mattress. "You've enough water to last until then."

"Alec won't be choosing Ivy." I remember his words in Central Park.

When you're ready, I will be here. Believe me.

Marchesa chuckles. "Really? Haven't you heard about Legend's greatest skill?"

A bolt of alarm rolls down my back. Everyone knows the spell Legend created. *The mind vise.* "He wouldn't do that to Alec."

"You've no idea what it's like to lose your one love. Yet. Legend knows." She pounds her fists against her chest. "I know. And soon, you'll join the club." She steps up a few stairs and pauses. "And I haven't forgotten how you escaped last time." She reaches into her pocket, pulls out a silver potion vial and tosses it onto the floor.

Grey smoke fills the basement. The scent of charcoal assaults my lungs. When the haze clears, I'm encased in a small steel cage. I grip the bars. Solid.

"That will block your magic," says Marchesa. "I had it especially designed."

Closing my eyes, I pull on my inner power. Nothing. As a warden, I'm used to a low simmer of magic coursing through me. Now, I just feel empty.

Marchesa grins, and this time the smile shows off her uneven teeth. "That's right. No magic for you. And before you start to feel sorry for yourself, take heart. At least you'll die with your free will intact. No one can say the same for Alec." Marchesa stomps up the staircase and slams the door behind her.

It's just me, Grunt, and semi-darkness.

Worry presses in around me. I've been in some tight spots, sure. But nothing like this.

ALEC

I'm asleep and awake, all at once. Is this magic or reality? Legend's *mind vise* spells can make it seem like both. I float in dark and empty space, my body curled up for warmth. Voices howl in my head.

No hope.

No escape.

Give in.

The voices don't say what I'm supposed to *give in and do*. That's not necessary, though. Legend's spell doesn't require a specific action in order to work. Instead, the pressure on my mind will grow worse until I break. Once I'm shattered, the spell will end. Afterward, I'll look, act, and talk the same. But if Legend ordered it, I'd say the sky is green or leap off a cliff. The voices grow louder.

No hope.

No escape.

Give in.

On reflex, I press my hands against my ears. It doesn't help. Even so, Legend and Diamond probably think the voices are the most painful part of this spell. They aren't. What's worse is that I've lost my parents.

Diamond and Legend may love me, but not enough.

Never enough.

There's only one thing left to do. I focus on the midnight diamond that still rests beneath my tongue. Will it speak to me instead? I can only try.

35. CHAPTER THIRTY-FIVE

ELLE - FOUR DAYS LATER

*M*y mouth is dry. So dry. I roll over, feeling the bars of my cage press into my side. My water bottle sits before me. I've been rationing sips. I can't give in and drink more too quickly.

Grunt sits against the far wall, his hefty legs kicked out before him. He stood for the first two days solid. Impressive.

In fact, it wasn't until the morning of day four that Grunt actually sat down. Other than that, the troll doesn't leave the room for any reason. Every so often, he pulls out a flask of water or a strip of jerky from the leather sack he's got tried to his waist. That's it.

I lick my lips, but that only makes them feel more chapped. "So, how does it work for you guys?"

No reply.

Not that I expect one. Grunt never answers. All he does is stare ahead with his all-black eyes. Still, a one-sided conversation is better than silence. So I go on. "Don't you ever need to hit the bathroom?"

Still nothing.

"Because at some point, you'll have to go." I grab my water bottle with both hands. It helps to string out the drinking process for as long as possible. "You live underground, right? That means you must have to hunt and leave no trail, that kind of thing. I'm guessing that nothing leaves a mark like crapping in a cave. Stuff like that would take thousands of years to go away. Didn't I read something about dinosaur poop getting found in a cavern somewhere? I'm pretty sure I did."

Grunt doesn't even blink.

"Back to my theory," I continue. "If you're sneaking around underground, I'm guessing you must be able to hold it for weeks at a time." I unscrew the plastic cap. "Not that I usually spend quality time contemplating bathroom practices of trolls. Still, I'm sure you understand. There's not much else to do here."

A small pile of shattered glass and wood lays nearby. Straining through the bars, I try to grab a shard of what's left of my glass slipper and wooden pumpkin. They're just out of reach. "Grunt, could you kick me a little of that junk on the floor? Sentimental value, you know." I've only asked the troll this question a hundred and thirty-seven times. You never know. Maybe things will change on attempt number one hundred and thirty-eight.

"What did you say?" I ask.

Grunt doesn't even blink, let alone reply.

"Tell me about your favorite food. I'm pegging you as a chocolate fan."

Still zip.

I'm out of small talk, so I press the bottle to my lips and take a precious sip.

The final drops of water settle onto my tongue. Sweet bliss.

For the first few days here, I waited for Bry, Knox, and a ton of shifters to burst through the walls. Nope. Then I figured at least Blackaverre would pop in with a pity drink. Nothing. Marchesa was right. I'm locked away.

Even so, it's not in me to give up. Closing my eyes, I reach out to my magic once more. I can't access so much as a single silver dust particle.

And time is running out.

36. CHAPTER THIRTY-SIX

ALEC

*T*he darkness stays absolute. I've floated in empty space for so long, it's hard to tell where my arms and legs are sometimes. Shivering, I curl more tightly on myself. All the while, the voices grow louder.

No hope.

No escape.

Obey.

Something new gets added into the mix. Beyond it all, I hear my parents. Diamond says, *our son has been through enough.* Legend counters, *there's no way to stop the process now. Alec breaks or he dies.*

Diamond weeps.

The screech of voices sears through my every nerve ending.

No hope.

No escape.

Obey.

I ball my hands so tightly, my muscles pop from the effort. I'm not giving in. Not dying, either. If only I could sleep, I think I might come up with an answer. There's no rest here, though.

Focusing all my strength, I prepare to reach out to the midnight diamond one last time. A vision appears in my mind. It's Elle at the masquerade.

Kiss me again, I command.

Yes.

I keep the memory of that kiss close as I reach out one more time. The midnight diamond rolls beneath my tongue. I shoot a firm directive at the stone.

Answer me!

All of a sudden, a wave of cool power wraps around my soul. A new voice sounds in my head. It sounds a lot like my own.

Hello, Alec. How can I serve?

It's the stone. *Yes.* I exhale slowly as I reply in my mind.

Keep the voices away. I must sleep.

The stone replies right away.

As you command. Afterward, shall we cast a spell?

I'm already half-asleep when I think my reply.

We'll cast many spells.

Perfect silence encases me as I finally get some rest.

37. CHAPTER THIRTY-SEVEN

ELLE - SATURDAY, THE MORNING OF THE GLASS SLIPPER BALL

I open my eyes a crack. Even that movement hurts. It's as if the insides of my eyelids were covered in sandpaper or something. New beams of light shine out from under the basement door. I've been tracking the days. It's Saturday morning.

Tonight, there's the Glass Slipper Ball.

Squinting, I try to focus on Grunt. The room warps around the troll. Colors merge and slide. Some part of me knows that I'm turning delirious. Marchesa gave me just enough water to last through the Glass Slipper Ball.

That's almost here.

Through the haze in my head, I notice that Grunt's eyes are shut. Is he sleeping at last? I open my mouth, ready to call for him. My throat is too dry.

No sound comes.

My mattress undulates beneath me, like it's made of water. I look up. Gustav sits nearby on his back haunches.

"Don't give up, Elle," he says in his little mouse voice. "We're all here for you."

I force my head to raise an inch. Kokkivo stands nearby, too. So does Harvest. There's Doc Eight as well. Even little Ooks jumps up and down.

If this is a hallucination, at least it's a nice one.

Kokkivo's body erupts in fire. The room becomes consumed with flame, yet no one burns. Grunt stays asleep. Kokkivo focuses his glowing yellow eyes on me.

"You will live," declares Kokkivo.

I force a smile, which is a bad idea. My lips crack and bleed afresh. Kokkivo is sweet, but I've tried to reach out to my magic for days now. Not a chance.

The flames roar higher. Now Mom and Dad step out from the fire. They look just as they did before Mom ever got sick. Dad's all things solid and strong. Mom's simply radiant. Together, my parents kneel by my cage.

"You're a fae warden," says Mom. "And more."

"Nothing of fairy calls to you, does it?" asks Dad.

I want to shake my head. Can't find the energy, though.

"You're both fae and enchanter," adds Mom. "You're the only *you* in all of space and time. No cage can hold you."

With every corner of my being, I want to touch Mom's hand one last time. I try to raise my arm, but it's just too hard.

The flames roar higher once more. When the fire lowers, everyone from Cynder Mercantile is gone. A new figure stands surrounded by low flame. Alec.

"Get up, Elle," he says.

Finally, I find my voice. "Can't. So thirsty."

"What did you say when I asked for your kiss?" he asks. "Yes. Hold to that."

Closing my eyes, I pull on the magic inside me. This time, it's not fae power. It's enchanter energy. Being a fae warden is something that happened to me. But caring for Alec? That's who I am. The enchanter in me connects to the wizard in him.

I focus within my soul. For a long moment, there's nothing. Then, I see it. Loops of red light and power shift inside my deepest being. I pull on those strands. A refreshing surge of magic careens through me.

"Yes, Elle." The flames burn more brightly behind Alec than ever before. "Come back to me. You can do it."

Energy and life move through my limbs. I force myself to roll onto my hands and knees.

In my mind, I command my magic.

Make the cage liquid.

Red tendrils of smoke appear around my hands. Those magical lines move to wrap about the metal structure. For a moment, the entire cage is surrounded in a crimson haze. Then the power soaks into the structure itself. The metal shifts. Undulates. It's no longer solid.

I rise. As I move, my body goes right through the bars. I step out of my prison.

Alec smiles. "It's just as I said. I'm here when you're ready."

Both the fire and Alec vanish. I stand in the basement. No question what I'll do next. I step over to the shards of the glass slipper and pumpkin carving. Reaching out with my enchanter magic, I send new swirls of red power around the broken pieces. One moment, they're in pieces. The next, the slipper and pumpkin are reformed and perfect. Picking them up, I grip one in each hand.

Then I turn to Grunt.

The troll opens his right eye. "Hired to watch you, I was. Saw you in the cage, I did. Now I see you out of the cage. Watch you go. All watching. All that I promised."

I tilt my head. I wasn't expecting him to be kind. "Are all trolls like you?"

"Some good, some not. Part of the Faerie Lands, we are."

"But you told Marchesa you'd watch me. Now you're watching me leave." It may seem nutso to hang out and ask Grunt questions, but if you'd been talking to him non-stop for days with no answer, you'd pause a hot minute, too.

"Trolls twist things to suit them, if you know my meaning."

"What a very Fairy Land thing to do."

Grunt chuckles in a low and rumbly way. "And chocolate is my favorite food."

"Called it."

"Plus, we can hold our pee for weeks."

"Good to know." Honestly? I might miss Grunt a little when this is all over. Assuming I'm still alive and everything.

Turning, I face the basement door. "Here goes."

And I leave.

38. CHAPTER THIRTY-EIGHT

ELLE

*A*top the stairs, I discover my next problem: a line of ten vials, all of them filled with green potions.

"Question for you, Grunt." Turning around, I look for my ex-guard.

No one's there.

Which makes sense. Trolls are shadowcoe, meaning they're experts at vanishing when they wish. Kneeling down, I take a closer look at the tiny bottles. It's a border spell of some kind. This line of glass containers must be magically hiding my position from everyone else. I tilt my head and think things through.

What I know about *potion magic* is next to zero. Maybe I can just walk over the vials, no problem. Or perhaps once I cross the line of vials, their power could singe me into little Cinderella burgers.

I poke at one vial with my finger. It shifts over an inch. Then it tumbles over. Green liquid oozes out onto the floor.

Ick. That smells like old man farts.

Nothing else seems to happen, but it's just too risky to push more. Plus, my jolt of magic is starting to wear off. I'm feeling a little woozy and a lot thirsty. Closing my eyes, I pull on my inner power once more. This time, I lean into my fae ability.

Gustav? Are you there?

My legs turn rubbery beneath me, so I slump down onto the top step. Not sure how long I sit there, but it's enough time that I wonder if I could drink the green fart water and live.

Gustav appears on the other side of the threshold. "Elle? Are you there?"

"Yes," I whisper. "You can't see me because there's a spell."

The wall beside me rumbles. After that, it implodes. A massive white wolf leaps into the basement. It's Bry in her animal form. She gallops over to me.

"Elle!" Wolf-Bry nuzzles her snout into my neck. "We've been so worried."

Wolf-Knox jumps up behind her. "Let's get her to Az. He's a healer."

"No." My voice sounds rusty. "Heal me here. Please. I must go to the Glass Slipper Ball tonight."

Tilting her head, Bry lets out a wolfy whine. "That's not a good idea."

Knox nods. "Bry's right. Alec has changed. You can't go near that ball."

I glare at Wolf-Knox. "If it were Bry at the ball, and you were me, what would you do?" I round on Bry. "And if it were Knox?"

Wolf-Bry nuzzles me again. "I understand. Where do you want to go?"

"My old room is on the second floor. Back right door." I nod toward the line of potions. "Watch out for whatever that is."

Wolf-Knox sniffs. "Border char. It would have killed you, Elle."

I try for a sassy grin. Not sure it works. "I thought there might be a problem."

Wolf-Bry nudges my hands with her snout. "What are you holding?"

Loosening my fists, I show off the tiny glass slipper in my left hand and the pumpkin in my right. "Don't let me forget these," I say.

Then I pass out.

39. CHAPTER THIRTY-NINE

ALEC

a knock sounds at my bedroom door. I'd ask who it is, but that would show independent thought. Right now, my plans rely on my parents believing that the *mind vise* spell worked... and that my midnight diamond still contains enough juice for tonight's Glass Slipper Ball. Protecting me from the *mind vise* really drained the stone.

The question is, how much power remains?

The door swings open a sliver. "It's me. Legend. Mind if I come in?"

So strange. After the *mind vise* spell, both my parents take care to ask my permission for every little thing. Do I want the kitchen light on? Would I mind if they change the channel? Funny how that works out. No free will in terms of my future, but lots of double-checking on TV shows.

With hesitant steps, Legend walks into the room. "So, you look well."

I fix him with a vacant smile. "Thank you."

"The tux still fits. Good. We were worried you lost a little weight."

"Yes." Ever since I came out of the *mind vise*, I find that saying *yes* covers most issues for Legend. I never realized that it was what he'd wanted all along. The same isn't true for Diamond. She chokes up when she sees me.

One Mother Of The Year award, coming right up.

On a side note, there is an extra bonus with this particular tuxedo. It's the same jacket I wore the night of the Autumn Masquerade. The cleaners found my tiny glass slipper in the inside pocket, so they placed it in a bag around the hanger. My parents didn't notice. Now that same slipper sits in my pocket once more.

If this all works out, I'm giving that cleaner a bonus because now? I have the slipper in my right pocket and the midnight diamond in my left. That makes me fully prepared for tonight's ball. Or as ready as I can be.

"So you know the drill?" asks Legend.

We've been through this many times, so I launch right into my answer. "We go to the L Center. Candidates step down the winding staircase. Charles talks. You, Diamond, and Marchesa ask questions. There's a drumroll and I announce the winner."

"And who will that winner be?" asks Legend.

"Ivy Cynder, of course. We will share a dance before the Queen of Hearts bonds us forever."

"That's right." Legend grins. "That doesn't sound too hard, does it?"

"Only one problem. I'll never choose Ivy Cynder. Elle will attend tonight."

Legend pales. "That's impossible."

"I connected to her in a dream this morning. Elle escaped Marchesa. She's on her way, Legend."

Is it one hundred percent sane to have such faith in a dream? Maybe not. But screw sanity. Tonight, I'm getting my girl.

Legend gasps. "No."

"Just kidding." I give my father a playful punch in the arm. "You should see your face."

Legend's mouth quirks with a lopsided grin. "So you're joking."

I force a vacant look into my eyes. "Obviously. I do what you say, Legend. You know that." I lower my voice to a whisper. "No hope. No escape. Obey."

A look of regret might have flashed in Legend's eyes, but it's gone too quickly to be sure. My father leaves the room without saying another word.

Wilhelm appears in the corner. One thing I'll say for my parents. They kept their word about the dwarves. Once I started pretending to be a total and complete worm, they released Wilhelm's crew from the lower caverns. I'm still not happy about it, but I'm glad they're all free, safe, and well.

Wilhelm slings his axe over his shoulder. He glares at the cutting edge with a hungry look. If anything goes wrong tonight, Wilhelm and his crew have my back.

Which means things might get bloody.

40. CHAPTER FORTY

ELLE

I awaken in my old bed. Sunflower wallpaper covers the walls. It's the same pattern I picked out with Mom on my eighth birthday. Hand-carved furniture lines the floor, including a dresser, bed, and side table. One of the animates made this set. Framed pictures hang on the wall, all of them black and white photos of me, Mom, and Dad. My glass slipper and carved pumpkin sit on the windowsill.

Maybe my head is way foggy from sleep, because this must be a dream. When I came back to check Cynder with Alec, the whole building was trashed. Especially my room.

A low and growly voice sounds beside me. "Ah, the patient awakens."

Rolling over, I find a massive gray wolf sitting beside my bed. "Hello, Azizi. Nice to see you again."

"We must cease meeting under such dramatic circumstances."

"True." The last time Azizi and I were together, we were fighting zombie mummies. Long story.

"You seem far better."

On reflex, I lick my lips. My mouth is no longer a chapped mess. I don't even crave a glass of water. "How did you heal m—" I pause, noticing the white bandage tied around Azizi's front leg. "Or don't I want to know?

Azizi chuckles. "I suspect you already realize my methods."

"I've a pretty good idea. You gave me some of your blood?"

"I did."

"Am I a shifter now?"

"No. That wouldn't happen without your permission. I gave you a few drops to drink. That's enough to heal. Becoming a shifter requires were blood in your veins."

Huh. As news goes, this is both fascinating and disgusting. But mostly, it's interesting. "Just a few drops? That's all?"

"I'm a very old shifter."

Which he is. Azizi is also the last warden of shifter magic. So the stronger Knox gets, the more ill Azizi should become. In fact, the last time I saw the old werewolf, there was no missing the way his skin hung loosely on his bones. I hoist myself up to sit and take a closer look.

Azizi looks ripped. His fur is all full and shiny, too.

"Wow," I say. "You look amazing."

"I am."

I press my lips together. Not sure how to ask this next question. "I thought you were… you know…"

"Dying?" asks Azizi.

"That."

"You recharged magic into the world."

I frown. "I thought that hadn't worked. Bry and Knox are super-worried about it."

"They are right to be concerned. Magic isn't returning in a consistent way. I benefit, to be certain. But the effect should be far greater. It's definitely a problem."

A knock sounds at the door. Azizi tilts his head. That's a classic *wolfy-listening routine.* "Bryar Rose and Knox are outside. Should I call them in?"

For a moment, I debate asking Azizi more about magic, but there are bigger things to worry about today.

Like the Glass Slipper Ball.

"Sure." I cup my hand by my mouth. "You guys can come in."

Bry rushes into the room and enfolds me into a huge hug. "Elle, Elle, Elle." Her voice breaks as she speaks.

"I'm fine, Bry." Craning my neck, I look over my shoulder to Knox. "Hello, there."

Knox does one of his classic chin-nod moves. "You look good, yeah."

"Thanks."

Bry releases me from her mega hug. "Are you sure you still want to hit the ball? It starts in an hour."

"I'm up for it."

Azizi does that *dog yawn maneuver* where he shows off a super-long tongue. "If my services are no longer required, I'll depart."

"Sure," I say quickly. "And thanks so much."

"We wardens must stick together," says Azizi. He trots from the room.

I point to where Azizi once sat. "He looks good."

Bry focuses on Knox. "What did I tell you? It's like the return of magic only affected Az."

Knox glances between me and Bry. "You want to do this now? Bry and I don't have anything new to share." He takes a half-step backward. "Plus, both of you need to get all dressy and fast. That's not my department."

Bry steps up to kiss his cheek. "Thanks. We've got it from here."

Knox starts to leave, then stops. "Before I go, I have to ask. How did you glamour your old room?"

I do a double-take. "Glamour?"

"Yes," answers Bry. "When you asked us to take you here, we figured you were delirious."

I raise my hand. "Guilty as charged."

Knox narrows his eyes. "Yet when we took you here, the room changed to what it is now. The place was only magic-ed up to look ruined. But it was all really here."

My breath catches. "You mean everything's fine?"

"Yeah." Knox eyes the room slowly. "You didn't do it?"

"No. I don't know who did." I inspect the room again with new interest. "There were other times I've gotten mystery help. The day I ran away, someone saved a bunch of my nest egg."

"I remember you telling me about that," says Bry. "Marchesa

thought she locked down your Abigail Smythe bank account, but someone had emptied it out for you."

"Maybe it was a mistake?" asks Knox.

"I thought so, too." I keep inspecting the walls. "But it happened again recently. When I came back here with Alec, someone had hidden a copy of the new contract in my parents' safe. That was hidden with a glamour, too."

Elle nods. "It has to be the same person."

I shrug. "It's stayed a mystery for this long, I guess it won't hurt to wait until tomorrow."

"We'll add it to the list," says Bry. "It will be four alphabetized mysteries. A is for *Ah mah gah ... Why isn't magic back in the world?*"

"B is for *Boom*," I add. "As in *boom, someone's helping me and I have no idea who or why.*"

Knox chuckles. He loves it when Bry and I start riffing off each other. "C is for *Crazy*. As in, *I am not crazy enough to hang around here any longer.*"

Bry gives him the side eye. "That's not a mystery."

Knox winks. "Still leaves." He departs and closes the door behind him.

For the first time, I look down at my outfit. Yup, still in the gingham dress. And this thing is rank.

Bry and I have a lot of work to do.

ELLE

a few minutes later, I step into my old bathroom. Everything appears frozen as it was three years ago. I spy my favorite shampoo, a pile of familiar towels jammed in the closet, and even my fluffy white robe. So strange. A chill runs across my skin. It's almost as if my parents will walk through the door any minute.

Something to add to my list of mysteries.

I take a super-quick shower, pull on my robe, and return to my room. All my clothes are still in their closet, which is good. My bust-line had a major growth spurt since fifteen, so none of this stuff fits. My blue gingham dress lies on the bed. I stare at it for a long second.

A figure appears by the ceiling. She's small, blue, and grinning.

It's Blackaverre, all right.

My fairy godmother waves frantically in my direction.

"Yeah, I'm alive. Your troll attack didn't work."

Blackaverre flits above the gingham dress. She mimes waving her wand over the item.

I can't believe this. "You want to give the Cinderella treatment to my gingham dress?"

Blackaverre nods so quickly, her head becomes a blur.

"Let me get this straight," I say. "You lure me to Cynder with a big lie. It's all in the hopes that I'll get squished by a troll. And now you want to fix my dress?"

Blackaverre keeps speed-nodding. *Talk about oblivious.*

Bry knocks on the door. "Elle?"

"Come on in."

"How's it—" begins Bry. She spies Blackaverre and pauses. "Oh. You."

"Just in time," I say to Elle. "My fairy godmother was offering to transform my prairie dress into a ball gown."

Blackaverre points toward my matching ankle-high boots. "Oh," I add. "She'll fix my shoes, too."

"How will that work?" asks Bry. "I thought Blackaverre tried to kill you."

I force a look of pretend surprise. "Wow, Bry. That's totally right." I focus on Blackaverre. "Why should I trust you with my dress and shoes when you just tried to murder me?"

In reply, Blackaverre gestures toward the gingham dress. It's clear what she means here. *Do you want a ball gown or don't you?*

That would be *no*. At least, I don't want a gown from Blackaverre.

In my mind, I gather up my fairy magic. I'll need this for the next part of my chat with Blackaverre.

"How long have you been helping Marchesa?" I ask.

Blackaverre rolls her eyes and spreads her arms out wide.

Bry gasps. "So, all along."

Blackaverre sets her hands against her heart and then points to me. Meaning? *I've been helping you too.*

"I get that," I state. "You're a true *classic* fairy tale life template. Sometimes you cause trouble, other times you cause more trouble."

Blackaverre points to her face. It's a move she does often and it's her way of saying, *that's just me.* Next, she flits around while grinning her face off. This is the equivalent of Blackaverre dancing in the end-zone of her own victory. In this case, Blackaverre is positive she'll be fixing my gown.

Which is so *not happening.*

Power swirls through my veins. Soon silver dust encircles my hands. Meanwhile, Blackaverre flies in a big heart shape. She's now on a self-victory fiesta.

And still totally oblivious.

I angle my palms toward my dresser. Inside my heart, I make a simple request.

Come alive.

Keeping my hands angled, I release my power. Cords of silver energy careen from my palms and land smack onto the furniture in question. The tall box of shelves shivers while the lines of fairy dust whirl around the dresser's exterior. With a burst of light, the silver mist soaks into the wooden exterior. The item shivers with movement. I grin.

Wow. That totally worked.

The dresser comes fully alive. With a wobbling side-to-side movement, the enchanted item marches across the room.

Its goal? Blackaverre.

All the while, Blackaverre zooms around in ever tighter circles. She's like a puppy this way, whirling around until she gets dizzy.

Keep up the spin, honey.

A long creak sounds as the dresser's top drawer opens. Blackaverre still notices zero. A pink knee-sock juts out, tongue-style. The fabric wraps about Blackaverre and pulls her inside. The drawer slams shut with a sharp smack.

"Whoa," says Bry. "You're getting really good with fairy dust."

My chest warms from the praise. "Thanks."

Thunks sound as Blackaverre tries to escape her dresser-prison. The top drawer vibrates especially. "Not sure how long my magic will hold her, though. I can't have Blackaverre running off to warn Marchesa."

"Marchesa may already know. That troll guy is gone."

"Good point." The dresser lurches from side to side. Blackaverre really wants out.

"Then again, why take the risk?" asks Bry. "Knox and I can stay here for a bit until Az can watch her."

A weight of worry slides off my shoulders. "That's a brilliant idea. Thanks."

Bry gestures toward the bed. "What about the dress?"

"Fortunately, I happen to know a fairy who's pretty good with magic."

Bry gives me the side-eye. "Would that be you, perhaps?"

"As a matter of fact, yes."

Closing my eyes, I pull on another round of my inner fairy magic. Tendrils of silver power appear around my palms. I silently command the energy.

Transform.

The cords of energy float off my hands. Soon they hover the gingham dress in a small and glittering cloud. Like sparkling rain, the mist cascades onto the gingham fabric. Even more falls down over the stout black boots.

The silver dust soaks into my dress and shoes. The dress comes alive, taking my full form. It's like I'm invisible and standing inside the garment once again. The dress waves in my direction.

I wave back.

The gingham frock pretends to wash its invisible hands, arms, and pits.

Bry and I share a dry look.

"Is that doing what I think it is?" Bry asks.

"Yeah. It's magically cleaning itself."

"Awesome," says Bry. "I always wondered about that. I mean, Cinderella always wears some seriously nasty rags. Then those get changed into a dress. How can that be sanitary?"

"True. My enchanted dress is a neatnik."

The dress continues to wash its skirt and front. Once done, the dress bends over, rolling its empty arms in a circle. There's no question what the thing plans next.

Hit me at a run.

And that's what it does. The prairie dress speeds my way and slams right into me. My robe gets blasted across the room. The next thing I know, I wear the gingham dress once again.

Next, my boots get into the act. They leap up and click together at the ankles. It's a movement that definitely says, *I'm excited here.* The boots jog in place. With every passing moment, they run at a faster rate. Then they do the same thing as the dress.

Rush me at top speed.

Once the boots hit my ankles, I'm no longer barefoot. All of which leaves me in an enchanted dress and boots. Too bad it's still the prairie stuff.

Fresh bands of silver dust surround me. Like hefty ribbons, they spin about my body, reminding me of so many lines on a candy cane. The magic haze soaks into my dress.

Everything transforms.

My prairie dress morphs into a gorgeous blue gown. Long white gloves cover my arms. The hefty boots transform into glass slippers. My hair now loops up into a sweet updo. Every inch of my skin feels soft and pampered.

Bry claps. "That was amazing!" She steps closer. "Oh, your make-up looks gorgeous, too. What a perfect spell!"

Bry may call this perfect. Still, I'm not ready to declare a magical victory yet. One key question remains. I pat my hips.

"Yes!" I cry. "It's got pockets."

Bry pales. "What do you mean? Are there like fake little pockets that make your hips look huge, or do you have really deep ones where can keep your keys and stuff?"

"Door number two," I reply.

Bry bows in my direction. "What a moment. You're now the true warden of fae magic."

Winking, I head over to my windowsill. Sure enough, my mini glass slipper statuette and craved pumpkin are still there. Lifting the objects, I slip one into each pocket.

Bry claps again. "Yeah! Pockets!"

Closing my eyes, I reach out to my magic once more.

Gustav?

Sure enough, my little gray buddy clambers onto the windowsill. He's not alone. A teacup chihuahua sits beside him. She's a little thing with a huge pink bow atop her head. I'd ask how she got in here, but

Gustav sneaks in and out of places all the time. Dragging along a chihuahua wouldn't be an issue for him.

"Hello, Elle." Gustav whistles. "You look great." He scans the room. "Where's Blackaverre?"

At the mention of her name, Blackaverre goes berserk. The dresser rattles with more force.

"It's like this," I explain. "Blackaverre is wrapped up in a knee-sock inside my dresser drawer. I fixed my dress all by myself."

Gustav goes up on his haunches and checks out the furniture in question. "About time," says the mouse.

Beside Gustav, the chihuahua clears her throat. "Forgive me," says Gustav. "I'd like to introduce you to my girlfriend, Killer."

Bry steps up to our little group. "Did you say her name was Killer?"

"Ruff," says Killer.

Huh. I make a mental note to send some fairy dust her way. Then Killer will be able to chat human style.

Gustav rubs his little front paws together. "So, are we doing the whole Cinderella thing?"

"You know it."

"Yay!" Gustav jumps with joy. "I'll summon my buddies. Want to meet downstairs by the street?"

"Sounds like a plan." I turn to Bry. "Thank you for babysitting Blackaverre."

Bry bobs her brows. "Go kick some ass."

I sashay from my old bedroom. As I near the door, I catch my reflection in one of the black and white photos that hang on my wall. In one, I see my Cinderella get-up. At a quick glance, it seems as if I now stand between my parents.

All of us smile.

ELLE

*S*econds later, I step out the broken front door of Cynder Mercantile. Sure enough, Gustav and five of his buddies wait on the sidewalk. As tourists pause before the house, Gustav and company skitter off to hide under a Starbucks bag. Killer prances around the paper. Clearly, she's protecting her guy.

I understand how she feels.

Soon, a small group of humans surrounds me. A few pull out cell phones. One little girl pulls on her Mom's hand. "Oh, here's another Cinderella!"

Another Cinderella?

My eyes widen as I realize the truth. *Of course.* There will be tons of girls going to the Glass Slipper Ball… or dressing up to celebrate.

I kneel down before the girl. "What's your name?"

"Hannah. Are you really Cinderella?"

"Call me Elle. What did you see with the other Cinderellas?"

"We saw one sponsored by this really awesome TV magician," answers Hannah. "He made the dress change before our eyes."

"Hmm, that's pretty cool."

Hannah lowers her voice. "I think the guy was magic."

"Magic, huh?" I straighten. "Well, I'm already dressed. How about I show you my horse and carriage getting set up?"

"Oh," Hannah frowns. "The magic guy did that, too."

I bob my brows. "Not the way I do it."

Hannah narrows her eyes. "We'll see."

Huh. Tough customer here.

Normally, I can't risk showing my magic in public, let alone in front of humans. But this is no ordinary day. People are faking up Cinderella magic all over the city. A little dose of the real thing won't hurt.

Reaching into my pocket, I pull out my pumpkin and set it onto the sidewalk. Lifting my arms, I twiddle my fingers. "Stand back, folks."

The crowd doesn't move. Welcome to New York.

Inside my soul, I summon a fresh round of fae power. Sure, I just accessed my enchanter abilities for the first time. But that was while I was delirious and in a basement. This is on Second Avenue and for a New York crowd. I'm calling on my strongest ability here.

Girl's gotta put her best foot forward.

Around me, the crowd chatters. I get it. No one expects a big magic show on Second Avenue.

They're in for a surprise.

In my mind's eye, I picture the silver pixie dust that churns throughout my soul. I issue a silent command.

Create.

Threads of silver magic wrap about my hands and arms. The crowd quiets a little bit. I consider that progress. The enchanted mist cascades off my hands to twirl toward my keys for tonight.

I'm talking the tiny pumpkin.

Gustav and his five mouse buddies.

And of course, Killer the chihuahua.

The humans all fall silent. Some pull out their cell phones. More progress.

The colored mist whirls ever faster around the pumpkin, mice, and Killer. The silver dust balloons in shape, masking the transformation of what's beneath.

Now, I'm getting *oohs* and *ahhs* from the crowd.

The dust vanishes, leaving behind a round glass carriage. Gustav and his buddies are now white horses. And Killer is the cutest driver you've ever seen. She wears a white long coat and matching pants. There's still a pink bow atop her white-blonde hair.

The humans break out into applause. Hannah jumps while shouting, "Yeah, yeah, yeah!"

And with that, it's official. I'm so rocking it here.

I take the opportunity to wave to the crowd. I even do the classic Cinderella move, which goes *elbow-elbow, wrist-wrist*. Killer leaps down from her riding bench and opens the carriage door.

"Milady," says Killer. Her tongue hangs out as she pants. "I can talk."

The front horse swings his great head in our direction. "Told you Elle could do it."

I wave at my mouse-buddy-tuned-horse. "You know it, Gustav."

I step into the carriage. Killer closes the door behind me before retaking her driving bench.

"Are we ready?" asks Killer. She still keeps lolling her tongue out one side of her mouth. That will lessen as she gets used to her new powers.

"We're all set," I declare. "Ride on."

The carriage lurches as we take off into traffic. We're not a block down Second Avenue when I realize a frightening fact.

There are a hell of a lot of Cinderellas and glass carriages tooling around New York today. I won't lie here. I did not see this coming. In my defense, I've spent the last week locked in a basement, so that's a mitigating factor.

We get stuck in a line of carriages waiting to drop off their Cinderellas at the L Center. It's not moving quickly, either. After all the excitement on the sidewalk, this is a definite downer.

A figure materializes beside me. Jacoby.

"Hello, Cinderella."

I slump on my glass bench. "Can we do this later? I've had a really dramatic week."

"No, we're definitely doing this now."

I scan the carriage. How hard would it be to open the glass door here and run? Pretty easily, actually. The trouble is that Jacoby would follow me anywhere.

"Fine, Jacoby. Let's talk."

Although I'm pretty sure I'll hate whatever the dark elf has to say.

43. CHAPTER FORTY-THREE

ALEC

*I*t's the night of my Glass Slipper Ball. *Yay.*

The L Center is packed with Cinderellas in their blue gowns. Even more wait outside, trying to get in. Simply put, Diamond is freaking out. The line of glass carriages is blocking half the traffic in Manhattan. The police are not happy.

Claiming I need to check things out backstage, I slip up to the rafters. Sure enough, Gerry sits on a catwalk. Instead of guarding the construction site, Gerry now makes sure the right Cinderella walks down the circular staircase at the proper time. He's even got a laptop for coordinating stuff with the control room.

As I approach, Gerry's wrinkled face creases into a smile. "Alec!"

"Hey, Gerry." I nod toward the laptop. "How's it going with that thing?"

"I'm an old dog, but I think I've learned some new tricks." He cackles, and his wide-mouthed laugh shows how he's missing a new tooth. I make a mental note to check on the Le Charme dental plan.

I pull over a folding chair and set it beside Gerry's. From up here, there's a great view of the L Center studio floor. All the many Cinderellas in the audience transform into a single undulating sheet of blue. It's like an ocean, only one that's partially focused on drowning yours truly.

"Hiding out, eh?" asks Gerry.

"You know it."

Gerry leans back in his chair. "There's been a lot of talk about this Ivy Cynder. I'm supposed to make sure she goes last."

"I've been told the same thing."

"So, is she your choice or what?" Gerry lowers his voice. "Or don't you have a say anymore?"

"I'm good." It's a vague reply, but a true one. Of all people, Gerry doesn't need to get involved in my crazy.

"I know people." Gerry pats down the hair behind his ears. "We can get you out of here now, if you like."

"Thanks, Gerry. But I've got this. Honestly."

Which is a total lie. I don't have enough power in my midnight diamond to do any practice spells. Plus, my plan works best if Elle actually shows up and the Queen of Hearts can work her magic.

All in all, this is far from a certainty.

"There's someone already in your heart," says Gerry. "I'm an old man. I know these things."

"There is," I say. "You're too clever, you know that?"

"Always."

Gerry's laptop blares to life. A voice sounds over the speaker. "Gerry, is Alec with you?"

"That he is, Lady Diamond."

"Tell him to get down here," snaps my mother. "We're starting the show."

Gerry smacks his lips. "I thought we were waiting for all the Cinderellas to arrive."

"Change of plans," says Diamond. "The Cinderellas will keep arriving. Even so, we simply can't wait." My mother raises her voice. "I know you can hear me, Alec. Legend wants you in place now."

My mother is referencing Legend since that's supposed to activate my *mind vise* spell. All it does is make me even more determined to turn things around tonight.

Reaching into my pocket, I grip the midnight diamond in my fist. I have the magic.

Now all I need is the girl.

I march down the metal stairs and onto the main stage. Someone waits for me by the final step.

It's the Queen of Hearts.

"Have you found my cat?" she asks.

We haven't spoken since the day Elle and I visited the queen's castle. Now the Queen of Hearts is tracking me down for news. Sadly, I don't have anything good to tell her.

"Not yet," I reply.

She lifts her chin. "I checked the list of contestants for tonight. Elle's not on it."

"That's true." *And it's not my favorite fact in the universe, either.*

"My hands are tied, Alec. Unless you find the cat, you'll be subject to the curse. And at his rate, I'll stay trapped in a bargain with that windbag forebear of yours."

"Not a pleasant thought for either of us." I shoot her a winning smile. "Any hints where that cat may be?"

"Chesh isn't hiding," states the queen. "You and Elle are." She saunters away. And when I say saunter, I mean *saunter*. Other women walk. The Queen of Hearts does not.

The queen is only a few steps away when she pauses once more. "Another thing. Do not try to out-cast me and escape. If you send any kind of spell my way, I'll take it as an attack, pure and simple." She grins, showing her vampire fangs. "You've a very handsome head. Let's keep it on your shoulders."

With that, the queen vanishes. Our chat covered a lot of important territory, including my prospects for decapitation. Still, certain words echo in my mind.

Chesh isn't hiding. You and Elle are.

Back at the queen's castle, she wanted proof that Elle and I are a couple. The request ended with an almost-kiss. After that, the queen offered us the chance to find Chesh. Later at the masquerade, Elle and I kissed for real.

That was the first time Chesh appeared.

I rock on my heels and think things through. It would only be logical for the Queen of Hearts to seek out true love. That's some of the most powerful magic around, no matter who found the queen's crown. If Elle and I fully love each other, that might be enough to break my curse. And that's whether or not we find any cat.

Reaching into my pocket, I grasp the glass slipper statuette from Elle. She handed me this one week ago. At the time, I knew it was important. This glass slipper came from Cynder Mercantile. In giving it to me, Elle was sharing a little bit of herself.

I never had truly selfless parents. In many ways, Elle is the only home I've ever known. It's different with Elle, though. She's lost so much, and Marchesa just keeps piling on the pain.

Will Elle be able to share her heart before my curse comes to pass?

With each second, that seems more and more unlikely.

ELLE

I sit inside my glass carriage. The line to the L Center inches forward. Nervous energy skitters through my system. The Glass Slipper Ball is being streamed live. Everything starts in just a few minutes.

I can't wait forever here. That said, there's no missing how all the other carriages have paper numbers taped to the back of their vehicles. It reminds me of the New York marathon. Everyone had to register beforehand and get approved to enter.

Obviously, I'm not on any list.

Sure, I could sneak into the L Center itself. But I want more. My goal is to get my butt on that stage and stand beside Alec. This line is for the other Cinderellas who are heading to that same spot.

I simply have to wait. And chat up Jacoby.

Speaking of Jacoby, he folds his arms over his chest. The movement stretches his long-sleeve Henley. "You look lovely," says the dark elf. "That's a rather solid enchantment. I can barely see the gingham monstrosity underneath."

I so don't have time for this. By rights, I should be sitting here alone. If anything, I could approach another Cinderella and try for some intel on how to get backstage. Instead, I'm stuck with Jacoby. I round on him.

"Is there a reason you're here?" I ask.

"Yes. I'm wondering if you need a date for this evening's event."

"No, thank you."

"So you're with Alec now?"

I huff out a breath. "I'm unsure, Jacoby."

"If Alec is your choice, I should be very downhearted." He winks. That's not exactly a *sad face.*

"You look upset," I snark.

"I am, desperately. I even stopped by Cynder to check on your welfare. Blackaverre is still locked up in your dresser, in case you're wondering."

"I appreciate your concern."

"So." Jacoby leans forward. "Who cast that spell on your old bedroom?"

Of all the things I expected Jacoby to say, that wasn't on the list.

"I don't know. In truth, I'm as curious as you are."

"I detected the same magical signature once before," adds Jacoby. "It surrounded the Cynder building right after you left home. Very powerful stuff, too." He lowers his voice to a sneaky whisper. "And I already knew you didn't do it."

"Really." Jacoby always does stuff like this. He loves to tease me into begging him to blab stuff. "Fine. How did you know?"

"The magic was elven."

I'll just add that to the list of things that shock me about this conversation.

"Eleven? Seriously?"

"No question about it. And the power signature was unique. And it appeared twice. First, right after you left Cynder. And second, when your room was revealed. Any ideas about the identity of the casters?"

"I don't think it was multiple people," I say.

"Why?"

"It would make sense that you'd sense the magic three years ago. That would have been when the mystery caster hid my room. Then, you'd detect it again when the room was revealed. Same casting, same person."

"Anything else for me?"

Leaning back on my bench, I think through this news. Who do I know that wields elven magic? There are only four kids at school who are elves. Only one of them will acknowledge my existence, and that's Jacoby. So it can't be a West Lake Prep kid. But could anyone else I know could be behind this?

I shrug. "I got nothing."

"And you're certain about tonight and Alec?"

"I'm positive I don't need a date tonight. Although I do appreciate your asking."

"There's been more to my interest than just tonight. I've been rather frantic this week, just so you know. After you disappeared, I tried to find you."

"Marchesa put me in a prison. I freed myself."

"Clearly," says Jacoby. "To my elven sight, all sorts of magic flows through you now. Undoubtedly, you'd flatten me like a pancake if I tried to keep you from the L Center."

"Undoubtedly."

And that's the double-edged sword that is Jacoby. Just when I think he's all sweet and worried for my safety, he talks about keeping me from the L Center tonight.

"In that case, I'll take my leave." Jacoby's silver gaze turns intense. "Just know this. You're my beautiful and powerful warden. Mine."

All the blood seems to drain from my body. "Warden? How do you know?

"That doesn't matter. What's important is this. Whatever takes place tonight with Alec?" He gestures between us. "This isn't over."

"You can't control me."

"Says the girl with zero idea who I really am."

A silver crown appears atop Jacoby's head.

I blink. Rub my eyes. Blink again. Yes, that's definitely a crown.

"You see, you're not the only one keeping secrets, my Elle."

With that, Jacoby vanishes.

Our conversation keeps spinning through my brain. That really happened. My friend—who as it turns out is eleven royalty—just revealed I'm *his property*.

Mom warned me that an interested elf was worse than a barnacle when it comes to scraping them off.

Why didn't I listen?

45. CHAPTER FORTY-FIVE

ALEC

I wait stage at right. From this spot, the audience and cameras can't see me, yet I can view everything that happens on stage. Basically, my role is to stand here until I'm called to *choose* Ivy Cynder.

No matter what, that isn't happening. I just hope to live through the process. If I'm caught again, there's no way Legend will fail at his next *mind vise*.

Tonight simply must work.

My thoughts roll back to the day Legend walked through his vision for the final L Center. To his credit, the place looks exactly like what he described. There's a winding staircase that loops down to center stage. That's where Charles stands. He still wears his Versailles gear, by the way. The press loves it.

On stage left, the Queen of Hearts sits atop a small throne. She does not look pleased. On the floor before the stage, there's a long table made from glittering gemstones. That's where my parents sit, along with a very happy-looking Marchesa.

The music swells as yet another Cinderella life template steps down the curving staircase. This is contestant twelve. Esther Freeman. She's radiant in the way her ebony skin contrasts with her pale gown. As she walks closer, the back wall plays a video about Esther's life.

"I'm Esther Freeman, and I'm a resident of Lockport, New York. I'm a graduate of City Honors High School and plan to attend the University of Buffalo next fall. My interests include biotechnology and animal rights. I look forward to meeting Alec and sharing a dance."

Once she steps onto the stage proper, Charles approaches her, microphone in hand.

"Welcome to the Glass Slipper Ball," says Charles. He's added a beauty dot to his cheek. It's very seventeenth century. "Why don't you tell us your name once more?"

"Esther Freeman," she replies.

"We've all seen the video of your life," adds Charles. "Why don't you tell us something personal about you? What's your favorite kind of animal?"

"Siberian Husky."

"Oh, that's grand." Charles turns to the gleaming table before the stage itself. "What do our judges say?"

The spotlight swings to focus on Legend, Diamond, and Marchesa.

"What's your favorite part of the Glass Slipper Ball?" asks Legend.

Esther grins. "It could be a great way to pay my college tuition."

The audience laughs. Diamond goes next. "Who do you like better, me or Legend?" My mother smiles, but there's an edge to the question.

"You're both lovely," says Esther.

Next, it's Marchesa's turn. "Are you a member of the Magicorum?"

"Yes, I'm part shifter."

Marchesa's nostrils flare. "A shifter Cinderella?" She doesn't wait for an answer. "Those are all my questions, Charles."

Now, this is supposed to be an entertainment event. Somehow, Marchesa has the idea it's a court case and she's present to cross-examine the witnesses. It's pretty obvious that Marchesa sees every Cinderella contestant as a possible threat to Ivy.

Once again, I wish I could shut this whole situation down. Maybe I could donate this land for a school that educates about the true nature of magic. Humans need some real information. Beyond making my parents feel important, I don't see how this helps anyone.

Too bad I'm stuck here because of my curse.

I can only hope I'll break it.

"Last but not least, let's talk to the Queen of Hearts," says Charles. "What do you have to say to our contestant?"

The camera swings to the Queen of Hearts. She glances over to Esther. "Boo." The audience cheers.

If the queen looked grouchy before, she seems to positively simmer with rage now. How can my parents think it's a great idea to anger someone this powerful?

Oh, right. The audience loves it.

The crowd began cheering right after the word, *boo*. They don't stop until Charles speaks again. "Oh, ho!" Charles cries. "That's Queen of Hearts being saucy once more. It's what we call more… HEARTBURN!"

The orchestra strikes into playing a riff from the song, *Kiss My Queen of Hearts*. It's a new chart-topper from a girl band out of Australia.

Based on how the queen winces, she really hates the music.

And why are we doing this again? In four hours of the Glass Slipper Ball, there isn't so much as a single Le Charme jewel.

Charles turns back toward Esther. "Thanks so much for joining us. We look forward to seeing you at the end of the show, when Alec will choose the lady for his first dance."

The spotlight shifts to the wide area behind my parents' table. Cameras scan the space while Charles keeps talking. "And here we have it. The dance floor for tonight's event. Now let's take a look at the many fine companies who've committed to sponsoring Alec's choice for tonight's Glass Slipper Ball."

Here it goes again.

46. CHAPTER FORTY-SIX

ELLE

*a*t last, I step down from my carriage. A young guy with pimples and a clipboard steps to my side. The name on his Jacket says Kyle.

"Name?" he asks.

"Elle Cynder."

"You're not on the list."

I pull in a little magic. Silver fairy dust surrounds my fingertips. I think my next command.

Add me.

The mist flies from my hand to rest on the clipboard. Then it bounces off into the air.

Oops.

Kyle snort-laughs. "You're not the only one to try magic," he says. "Everything here is warded against cheating. Got another name for me?" He goes on tiptoe to scan the line. "You're the last one here. Give me a name and fast. I really want to go on break, lady."

I narrow my eyes. *Time for plan B.* I scan Kyle from head to toe. Turns out, the guy has a very distinctive tattoo on his neck. To me, that looks like an opportunity for victory.

"Okay," I say. "How about a bet?"

"Bet?"

"Yes, if I can make you scream with delight, you will let me pass."

Kyle gives me a look that says, *you are so full of it*. "Delight," he repeats.

"That's what the Cinderella said."

"Fine. You've got a deal."

I turn to my horses. "Gustav. Do your thing."

There's only one thing that's Gustav loves. It's a particular song. All my horse-mice swing their heads toward Kyle. Moving in unison, they start to sing.

> *I'm the guy they call little Mickey Mouse*
> *Got a sweetie down in the chicken house*
> *Neither fat nor skinny*
> *She's the horse's whinny*
> *She's my little Minnie Mouse!*

This is a tune from the classic black and white cartoon version of Mickey Mouse. And guess who has a tattoo of such a character on his neck? That would be Kyle. The guy goes nuts. In fact Kyle's so pleased, he makes the horses sing the tune all the way through. Twice.

At last, it's time to move on. "You're letting me through, right?"

Kyle smiles his face off. "Absolutely."

"Anything else I need to get inside? I want to step down that curly staircase thing."

Kyle inches closer. "You won't mention my name, will you?"

I wink. "Mention who?"

With that, Kyle loads me up with an ID card and access code. Seems another Cinderella got salmonella and had to stay back. My lucky day. Even better, this adventure is starting to feel more and more like a jewel heist. That's familiar territory.

With my access info in hand, I march into the L Center. In no time, I'm backstage and making my way to the rafters and its swirly staircase. A pack of guards blocks my way. All of them wear Le Charme jackets complete with handy names sewn on the front.

"Stand aside," calls one. "Ivy Cynder coming through."

Sure enough, my stepsister saunters backstage. I pretend to become super fascinated by the far corner. Ivy makes a great show of stepping up to the catwalk... which leads to every Cinderella's grand entrance. Once Ivy's well out of eyesight, I head toward the catwalk myself.

In fact, I'm almost ready to scale my way to the rafters when another guard blocks my path.

"What are you doing back here?" she asks. This guard's name is helpfully written out. *Cora.*

In cases like these, it's important to smile excessively. So that's what I do. "I'm one of the contestants for tonight's show."

"You are?"

I have a certain talent for working my charm. At this point, I turn it up to my highest level ever. "Absolutely."

"But I just heard. We don't have any more videos to play. Where's yours?"

I smack my lips and think. Sometimes, the truth is best. "I don't have one. It's been a hell of a week."

"Well, you'll need a video to make your way down the catwalk." Cora reaches into her pocket. "Here. Use my phone and record one now. I've got a thumb drive you can borrow, too. Just don't tell anyone I let you do it."

I can't believe my luck. "Thanks so much, Cora."

And I sneak off to record my video.

47. CHAPTER FORTY-SEVEN

ALEC

a heavy sense of dread settles inside me. There are no more contestants left—only Ivy Cynder. Once more, I scan the place for Elle.

No sign of her.

I have a bunch of spell options for battling my parents or Charles. But after my chat with the Queen of Hearts? It's clear that to avoid a lifetime with Ivy, I must first take down the Queen of Hearts.

Sadly, the queen made one fact clear. If I cast a spell in her direction, that will be nothing more than a death wish.

That means it's up to me and Elle.

Yet Elle isn't here.

And even if Elle does manage to arrive in time? There's no guarantee she'll be ready to even say the word *love*, let alone show it. And clearly, that's what the Queen of Hearts wants. Not that I blame Elle. She simply isn't ready.

Once again, the music swells. Ivy steps down the winding staircase. She wears the classic Cinderella ensemble, but her smile doesn't reach her eyes. Overall, Ivy seems like more of a plastic facade that covers an underlying simmer of rage.

No question about it. If Ivy and I end up together, it will be a life of pure hatred. As Ivy marches down the crystal staircase, a video plays behind her.

"I'm Ivy Cynder. I'm a Scorpio and an influencer. Not on social media, though. Just in general. I'm from Manhattan and attend the elite West Side Prep high school. For fun, I enjoy kissing Alec Le Charme."

I groan. By tomorrow morning, that *fake kiss* will be all over the tabloids. Won't matter that it's a total lie, either. The press doesn't disprove things that sell subscriptions.

Once Ivy steps onto the stage proper, Charles approaches her,.

"Welcome to the Glass Slipper Ball," says Charles. "Why don't you tell us your name once more?"

"Ivy Cynder," she replies.

"We've all seen the video of your life," adds Charles. "Why don't you tell us something more personal about you? What's your Magicorum power?"

"I'm a level ten potion master."

I do a double-take. When it comes to making potions, there are only ten levels in total. From what I saw in class, Ivy can't even boil an egg. There's no way she's doing level ten work.

"How impressive." Charles turns to the gleaming table before the stage itself. "What do our judges say?"

The spotlight swings to focus on Legend, Diamond, and Marchesa.

"How long have you been dating my son?" asks Legend.

Ivy blushes. "Ten months now. Alec is just the best."

The audience *oohs* and *ahhs*. I fight the urge to howl. Yet another lie to add to the mix. And now that tabloid headline just became a special issue dedicated to Ivy Cynder.

Maybe that's what Ivy wanted all along.

The spotlight swings onto Diamond. "Would I make a great mother-in-law or what?"

"Hey, I already call you Mom," gushes Ivy.

Oh, hell. This is more than a few whopping lies. My parents have teamed up with Ivy and Marchesa in order to create an entire fake dating history with me. Rage corkscrews up my spine. I've been patient, waiting for my chance to be with Elle. But if this keeps up? I'm pulling out my midnight diamond.

I may not survive, but I won't spend the rest of my life stuck in this nightmare.

Next, it's Marchesa's turn. A breathless sort of anticipation hangs in the air. This is more information about my love life than anyone has ever gotten. The crowd is positively riveted.

"What was Alec's first gift to you?" asks Marchesa.

"Oh, that's easy." Ivy flutters her eyelids. "A big old teddy bear."

Unbelievable. If you're making up fake presents, at least pick something from Le Charme jewelers.

Charles gestures to Ivy. "Last but not least, let's talk to the Queen of Hearts. What do you have to say to our sweet Ivy?"

The camera swings to the Queen of Hearts. She glances over to Ivy. "I'll kill you if I get the chance."

Silence follows. There's no cheering while Charles talks about another *heartburn*. The queen could be terrifying while just saying, *pass the salt*. This is her threatening to kill someone. No one is missing the menace here.

Charles turns back to Ivy. "Thanks so much for joining us. Stay right here." Charles turns to the camera. "And now, we've reached the moment you've all been waiting for. Let's bring all the contestants onstage and let Alec choose his dancing partner." He dramatically sets his hand by his ear. "What's that Legend? Did you say something?"

Once more, the spotlight swings to my father. "I say we let Alec choose right now. I think we can all guess what he'll say."

Ivy clasps her hands under her chin. "We were talking about this just last night. In bed." She turns to the camera. "Let's get Alec out here. We all know there are no other contestants than me. Let's end this!"

Unfortunately, Ivy may be right.

I pull the midnight diamond from my pocket. *Ah, well.* If I'm about to be utterly destroyed, I may as well go out in a blaze of magical glory. On reflex, I look for Knox. He's always beside me at these events. But my best friend is nowhere to be found. My parents still have those damned wards up against everyone.

In the end, it's for the best. I wouldn't want Knox to get hurt.

I step out onto the stage. The spotlight swings in my direction.

"And here he is," calls Charles. "The adorable Alec Le Charme!"

The crowd cheers. I raise the midnight diamond in my fist. Ivy is right about one thing.

This all ends. Now.

48. CHAPTER FORTY-EIGHT

ELLE

I march up the backstage stairs. My destination? The rafters. That's the entry point for all Cinderellas to walk down the crystal staircase to the main stage.

And it's my goal now.

Once there, I find an older gentleman in a Le Charme jacket. The name Gerry is stitched on his chest.

"Hello!" I give him my most cheerful wave. "I'm the last contestant."

Gerry smacks his wrinkly old guy lips. "No, you're not."

"Yes, I am," I say brightly. "I even have a thumb drive with my video and everything." I lower my voice to a conspiratorial tone. "Cora says you can upload it right from your laptop."

Some people have zero reaction to fairy charm. Kyle the parking lot guy was one of those. Cora the backstage guard? Total opposite. I could have asked for her grandmother's social security number and she would have handed it over. The question is, what type of guy is Gerry?

From here, there's a good view of the L Center below. A girl stands in the middle of the stage. Even though I can't see her face, there's no mistaking who's down there.

"Is that Ivy Cynder?" I ask.

"Sure is," says Gerry. "She's the last official contestant. Everyone was very serious about that."

I round on Gerry. "You have to let me down there."

"Why?"

"Because I'm the best Cinderella template you've seen today."

"Try again."

I've worked the *sweet and cute* angle. Time for another approach. "My magic could make you do what I want anyway."

Gerry chuckles. "Will you make me coo like a pigeon?"

My skin prickles over into gooseflesh. That whole pigeon episode happened years ago. It was the very day I first met Alec. "How do you know that?"

"Doesn't matter. One last try."

I scan the stage below me once more. Any minute now, they'll force Alec to pledge his life to Ivy. When I next speak, my voice comes out as barely a whisper. "It's Alec."

Gerry rubs the back of his hand against his cheek. There's something both familiar and strange in the gesture. "What about Alec?"

"He's my friend."

"Just that?"

"He's my best friend. Earlier today, I was locked up in a basement by my stepmother." I shake my head. "This may sound strange, but I thought I saw Alec."

"What happened then?"

"Alec is a wizard. My father was an enchanter. I've always felt like my life should be about my fairy side. I've never even tried to access my enchanter powers. But today when I saw Alec? I really tapped into that power for the first time. It helped me escape."

There's an empty chair beside Gerry. I settle into it. "I first met Alec years ago. We were both fifteen. Even then, there was a connection." My voice gets dreamy, just thinking about it. "We're both enchanters. That's why we're meant to be best friends forever." I point to the stage and Ivy. "That's why I can't let Alec make this mistake. Ending up with Ivy will just make him miserable."

Gerry licks his palm. *That's some weird stuff, right there.* "No."

Down below, I notice Alec onstage. There's no mistaking the set of his shoulders or the determined look on his face. Alec has something planned, and it's not good. He raises his fist.

Oh, no.

Stepping around Gerry, I set my thumb drive into the guy's laptop. A pop-up immediately appears onscreen.

Upload to control room?

If there was a *hells, yeah* button, I'd select it. Instead, I click *okay* and step over to the crystal staircase. "I don't care what you say," I call over my shoulder. "I'm going down."

"There's hope for you yet," says Gerry. He may have followed up that statement with a quick *meow*, but I'm too distracted to tell for sure.

Down below, Alec sets his hand in his pocket. It's a movement I've seen a hundred times. Alarm rattles through my nervous system. Alec plans to cast a spell. And considering this situation?

Whatever Alec has planned, it won't end in a *happily ever after.*

49. CHAPTER FORTY-NINE

ALEC

*W*hat happens next only takes a matter of seconds. Even so, each moment sears slowly into my memory. I heard about this phenomenon. Your mind clings to every millisecond when it knows that few remain.

Reaching into my magic, I call out to the midnight diamond.

Get ready.

The stone replies instantly.

What do you wish?

There's only one word for it.

Attack.

Magic churns through me. Every nerve ending I have burns with hidden fire. This is more energy than I've ever felt before, and I had a rather odd encounter with magic and the pyramids.

Dark mist curls around my fingers. I send images to the stone. The dark tendrils of my spell whip out across the audience, wrapping about every Magicorum in the place.

Across the stage, the Queen of Hearts rises. She raises her right hand. A ball of red flame hovers above her palm. She looks between the spell and my face. No question about it. If I finish my spell, her casting is heading straight for my head.

Fine with me.

Closing my eyes, I prepare to send one final command to the midnight diamond.

Get ready to—

A loud whistle sounds from the rafters, interrupting my thoughts. "Hey! Up here."

The audience gasps in shock.

Me? I look up and smile.

50. CHAPTER FIFTY

ELLE

*D*id I just whistle and yell my lungs out on live television?
Why, yes. Yes, I did.

Maybe it wasn't the slickest move in the universe, but it did stop Alec from casting his spell. That's got to count for something. Plus, I have Alec's full attention now. Sure, we're only staring at each other across a busy stage. Even so, connecting with Alec again is like being able to breathe freely after choking for air. I'm alive once more.

Straightening my shoulders, I walk down the windy stairs. After a few yards, the spotlight sets on me. The acoustics are odd up here. I can make out the faint sound of an orchestra playing, but it's tinny and far off.

The massive screen behind me comes to life. An image appears. It's the first frame of the video that I just took backstage. *Thank you, Cora!*

Looking down, I spot Ivy standing beside some old dude in a long coat. Charles Le Charme. He looks ready to spit.

This will be so sweet.

I sidle down the steps while working every ounce of fairy charm mojo I can muster. Behind me, the video plays. Unlike the orchestra, I can hear each word clearly.

"My name is Elle Cynder and I'm a jewel thief. I enjoy eating ice cream with my best friend, playing Magicorum Killers, and murdering zombie-mummies in real life. I want to dance with Alec because he's my best friend and if anyone else goes near him, I'll scratch their eyes out."

A fine creation, if I do say so myself.

Just as my speech ends, I reach the stage proper. That old guy with a massive wig simply stares at me, open-mouthed. Ivy keeps glaring daggers in my direction. This can keep her busy for hours, by the way. Honestly, if there were an Olympic sport for marathon glaring, Ivy would get a gold.

The Queen of Hearts sits nearby. The look on her face is the definition of unreadable. Below the stage, Legend, Diamond, and Marchesa stare up from some kind of *glittery table situation.*

At this point, one fact is clear. I probably should have paid more attention to this aspect of Alec's life. Might be handy to know what's going on here.

Or not.

Only Alec matters, really.

I turn to him and grin. "Hey."

He returns the smile with one of his own. "Elle."

Reaching into my pocket, I take out my glass slipper figurine. Alec pulls one from his tuxedo jacket as well. It's a super-sweet moment.

Friends reunite. At last.

That's when Ivy starts screeching and ruins everything. I'd forgotten how that girl has a serious set of lungs on her.

"She's stealing my boyfriend!" cries Ivy. "Stop her!"

Legend and Diamond stand. Red smoke surrounds their arms.

Uh oh.

I talk to Alec from the side of my mouth. "So we're not going to talk with your parents? I thought for sure we could kill a few minutes that way. At the same time, you and I could also, you know, catch up." *And maybe kiss.*

I pop my hand over my mouth. *Did I say the kissy stuff out loud?*

Alec chuckles. "Let's just say they've both been on a rather short fuse these days."

I exhale. *So I did keep the kissy stuff to myself. Whew.*

Crimson magic rolls out across the massive room. More of

Diamond and Legend's spell takes hold. Clouds of power surround the cameras. Sparks fly as the video equipment fries out.

I side-speak to Alec once more. "Guess they don't want any witnesses."

"Not human ones," says Alec. "There are still close to fifty magic users in the room. My parents will leave them behind."

"Are any of them on our side?"

"Absolutely not."

My skin prickles over with worry. "Glad we cleared that up."

More red mist surrounds the humans in the room. You can tell they're not Magicorum because they try to take camera pics of the spell instead of running in terror. Humans are cute that way.

Red light flares across the studio. When the brightness vanishes, so do all the humans.

Wow. They really don't want any witnesses.

Time to consider a counter plan. I glance over to the Queen of Hearts. Will she help us?

The good news is that the queen is still here. The bad news is that she's painting her nails. I'll take that as a *no* on the *help us* thing.

Without looking up, the queen calls out. "Cast in my direction and you're dead."

Glad she cleared that up.

If only we'd found her Cheshire cat.

A memory appears. Before I walked down those steps to Alec, I'd been chatting up that Gerry guy. For an old dude, Gerry was acting suspiciously cat-like. Licking your palm? That's a total feline give-away. Was Gerry really Chesh in disguise? If so, we can catch that feline pronto and solve a lot of problems.

And by solve problems, I mean that we'll get the Queen of Hearts to stop doing her nails and start helping us to kick butt.

Shielding my eyes from the stage lights, I scan the rafters.

No sign of Gerry. Damn.

Which means we've got no cat.

No help from the Queen of Hearts.

And a lot of angry casters in the room.

51. CHAPTER FIFTY-ONE

ALEC

*I*t's too bad all the cameras are gone, because this is a moment someone should record. Fifty gem casters sit in the audience, all of them in long robes and angry faces. My parents and Marchesa stand behind the judges' table. Charles looms nearby. Part of his wig is askew, which is something I've never witnessed before.

Finally, there's the Queen of Hearts. She's moved on to adding a clear layer to her red nail polish. So there's that.

And against everyone? It's me and Elle. Somehow, that's enough.

Legend steps forward. He stretches his arms wide. "Heed me, son. No hope. No escape. Obey."

"Father. It's time for the game to end. Your *mind vise* didn't work."

Legend's face falls. "That's not possible."

"Let me make it clear." I take Elle's hand. "You don't control me."

"How clever you are!" Legend laughs, but the sound is brittle.

"Listen to me," I state. "I'll make you a bargain. Allow me and Elle to leave, and we won't hurt any of you."

It's only half a lie. Elle has her own magic. I still have my midnight diamond. Who knows what we can do?

Legend snaps his fingers. The fifty gem casters step forward, forming a semicircle behind my parents and Marchesa.

Many times, Wilhelm has materialized out of thin air to stand before me. Now another fifty shadowcoe appear on the show floor.

All of them are trolls.

Even worse, none of them are alone.

Every troll has appeared with a potion master beside them. All wear the black lab coats that mark their specialty.

"There are now more than a hundred and fifty casters against you and Elle. Will you still fight?"

My gaze locks with Elle's. All the determination in the world shows in her eyes.

"We fight," she says.

Moving in unison, Elle and I raise our arms. My midnight diamond lies clasped in my right hand. I reach out to the stone.

Ready?

The stone replies.

Name your demand.

Beside me, Elle pulls in her own power. Silver fairy dust whirls about her arms.

"You've made me very sad," says Legend. He raises his arms. Particles of red light and power whirl about his hands. An electric sense of magic fills the room.

ROWL!

Deep snarls fill the air as a massive white wolf barrels onstage. A huge black wolf thunders along beside the white one. I grin.

It's Bry and Knox in their werewolf forms. Another fifty shifters rush onstage behind them. Their pack. What a sight.

Wolf-Bry looks to Elle. "Told you we'd make it."

"And we brought friends," adds Wolf-Knox.

Another fifty dwarves appear, this time on the floor before the stage. Wilhelm and his crew.

And they're not alone, either.

Every dwarf has brought an animate along with them. I count phoenixes, scarecrows and even a possessed suit of armor. A group of mice scurrying around the floor, along with a single chihuahua. Odd, but that's how things go for me and Elle.

A warm sense of satisfaction swirls inside me. I was happy enough when Elle showed up to help. But now we've an equal number of magical warriors to my parents' army. And I still have my midnight diamond.

Things are looking up.

Legend frowns. "You're about to start a war, son."

Elle and I share another look. When we next speak, it's in unison. "Works for us."

"Then give me the signal, son. Say you'll destroy us, if you have the nerve. If not, pledge your life to Ivy."

Oh, Ivy. I'd forgotten about her. I scan the studio floor. Ivy now stands beside her mother. As my eyes meet hers, she grins and waves.

"We choose war," says Elle.

No question what to do next. Taking in a deep breath, I prepare to state the word that will start everything. "Destr—"

Elle squeezes my hand. "Wait," she breathes.

There's a fierce look on her face that stops me cold. I tilt my head. The look in my eyes speaks a silent question.

What's wrong?

52. CHAPTER FIFTY-TWO

ELLE

I've done a number of extreme things. Stealing gold from a dragon horde, for instance. But what I'm doing now? It's a whole new level of pushing things.

Legend narrows his gaze in my direction. Alec's father just stated that the war wouldn't start until we gave the word.

And I asked for a pause.

Alec moves so we stand face to face. It helps. I can forget the rest of the room, as well as our makeshift army.

By the way, how happy am I that the animates are here? Very happy indeed.

Alec cups my face with his hands. His touch is all things warm and reassuring. "What is it, Elle?"

Even though Alec and I are close, I still feel the many gazes staring in our direction. I focus on Alec. Ever since my conversation with Gerry, a thought has been growing in my mind. I don't think I can face death without setting that realization loose.

In my soul, the little fortress I've built up starts to crack and sway. I plan to tear it down completely.

"I have no illusions," I state. "We may not make it. So I need you to know one thing."

"What?"

"You're not my friend."

Alec tilts his head. "No?"

My inner walls burst. The pain I'd been hoarding falls out and rolls away, leaving me alone and exposed. And now? This man can shatter me with a word. I could lose everything, yet Alec is worth the risk.

"You're far more than that," I reply. "Alec Le Charme, I love you with everything in me. Know this. I choose you as my prince and life partner, no matter what."

"Elle." Alec brushes his thumbs against my cheeks. "You already know my heart is yours."

My soul soars with joy. "In that case, I can face anything."

Alec brushes the softest of kisses against my mouth. "Yes."

With that, Alec and I turn to face Legend's army. Speaking as one, we call out a single word.

"Destroy!"

53. CHAPTER FIFTY-THREE

ALEC

I look to Elle. "I'll take the gem casters."

She nods. "Trolls for me."

Pulling on my inner energy, I unleash the power of my midnight diamond and issue a single command.

Freeze

Thin lines of black smoke whip up from between my fingertips. *Magic.* The cords of power whip out across the studio floor to encircle every gem caster in the place. The mist of my spell encircles each witch or wizard before soaking into their skin. A burst of light surrounds them.

When the brightness vanishes, all the gem casters are stone. I grin. There's nothing like working on a new magical stone and seeing it kick some ass.

Silver fairy dust envelops Elle's hands. "I've been wanting to do this ever since that troll at my parents' office."

Elle's magic spins through the air, reminding me of so many pinwheels. The power encircles each troll in the place. Once the magic vanishes, the trolls all rush off in one direction.

Toward the mice.

I can't help but chuckle. Elle's a swarm fae. She mentioned that her best animals are pigeons and mice. Right now, the trolls are scrambling about on all fours while sticking their noses up in the air. Total mouse behavior. After that, the trolls follow a group of real mice who lead them around in circles. The chihuahua yaps along with the group.

I let out a low whistle. What a spell.

More trolls appear. They must have been hiding for a sneak attack. This time, the animates go to work. The phoenixes burst into flame while the scarecrows and suit of armor take down the trolls in hand-to-hand combat. The sight makes me want to cheer.

There's no time to celebrate, however. The many potion masters raise their vials and smash them to the ground. This time, the vials don't shatter. Instead, each one lets off a stream of sickly green smoke. These are the reverse of potion burst spells, where shattering the vial starts the casting. In these potions, called forevers, these mist canisters will go on spouting spells for all eternity. That is, unless the bottles are destroyed. Not an easy thing to do.

Forevers are a smart choice for these potion masters, I'll give them that. A wall of emerald haze quickly forms around them. It's an excellent protective barrier.

Yet it won't stop Wilhelm and his crew.

Axes raised high, the dwarves let out a battle yell and rush straight for the emerald cloud. The smoke seeks them out, surrounding each dwarf. The dwarves fall to their knees, coughing.

I pull in fresh magic from my stone. Elle summons more fairy dust. The process isn't instant, though. It takes time to gather enough power and then even longer to focus the energy into a specific casting.

Will we get to the dwarves in time?

Turns out, another group is focused on Wilhelm and his crew. Bry, Knox, and their pack rush toward the emerald haze.

The werewolves move in.

The pack pins down the potion masters. Dwarves are tough fighters in any situation, but Wilhelm and his crew see me as their adopted son. They'll fight to the death and I love them for their loyalty. Still coughing, the dwarves rise and march over to the potion masters.

Then they go after the forevers.

Blow after blow rains down on the metallic canisters. The forevers spark and crackle, but they don't break.

Even so, the dwarves don't give up.

Boom! Boom! Boom!

One by one the forevers shatter. As each canister breaks, a dwarf falls over, exhausted. If we live through this, I'm throwing Wilhelm's crew a roast meat celebration that will last three days, minimum.

The green smoke dies down, revealing the only fighters left standing. Now it's down to Diamond, Legend, Marchesa, and Charles... all against me and Elle. Ivy hides behind her mother, which makes her more of a spectator than a warrior.

Diamond shivers. "I can't be part of this."

I do a double-take. My mother's actually showing some heart? It's unexpected but welcome.

"No!" Legend rounds on her. "Le Charme first."

"You're wrong," whispers Diamond. "There are limits."

Charles speeds to Diamond. "I'll escort the lady out of trouble."

"I'm not leaving," says Diamond.

"Perhaps we just stand aside then," offers Charles.

Diamond nods. My mother looks down. Even so, there's no missing the tears dripping from the top of her nose. Charles walks her over to the far wall. Ivy skitters along behind them.

Am I surprised that Charles turned out to be a coward? Not in particular. For centuries, he's been hiding behind his bargain with the Queen of Hearts.

Marchesa strolls up to Elle. A large blue vial lies clutched in the potion master's hand. "How I've looked forward to this moment."

"Same here," says Elle.

My father moves to stand before me as well. "Le Charme first."

My next words feel torn from my soul. "I know."

All this time, Elle and I have been pulling in fresh power for our next spell. There's trouble, though. Elle may be powerful, but she doesn't know how to wield her magic very well yet. And quickly recharging magic is a senior-level skill. Standing beside Elle, I can't help but notice how there's only a paltry amount of fairy dust encircling her fingertips.

I'm not much better off. In my mind, I reach out to the midnight diamond.

Ready?

A rusty voice sounds in my head. The tone is distant and tired.

As I can be.

I've been through this before. My midnight diamond is about empty. Not that I'm shocked. It just took down fifty of the most powerful gem casters in the world.

This time, it's Legend who launches the fight. "Destroy!" he cries.

Elle and I release our spells. Marchesa and Legend do the same. Sickly wisps of silver power wind up from Elle's hands. My stone glows inside my palm. Then it falls dark. I didn't even get a single tendril of magic out of the thing.

Meanwhile, Marchesa tosses her vial to the ground. The glass container shatters. A healthy column of blue smoke heads for Elle. The mist congeals into blue bands that tie up Elle's hands, feet, and neck. Elle topples over, gasping for breath.

A flare of white light erupts from Legend's fist. The brightness vanishes. In its place, Legend now holds a gleaming and spear-like diamond.

My father thrusts the weapon into my chest. Pain erupts from my rib cage. I crumple to my knees. All the while, my focus stays on Elle.

She's choking. I must save her.

As I crawl over to Elle, I'm barely aware of Marchesa and Legend glaring in my direction. Somewhere in the distance, my mother weeps. The weres and animates try to battle closer, but the potion masters throw magical explosions in their path. Bry and Knox's wolf howls echo through the air.

Yet I can't focus on any of that. Elle's skin is turning a pale shade of blue.

I crawl forward. Blood pools on the floor around me. Still, I drag myself to Elle's side. The cords around her neck have turned into a thick sapphire-colored ribbon that perfectly matches the trimming on Elle's gown.

Such a cruel touch from Marchesa.

With ever fiber of my soul, I wish to tear the blue cords from around Elle's neck. I wiggle my fingers under the ribbon, but she's only able to take in the barest of gasps. It won't be enough.

My voice chokes with a sob as I force out a single word. "Sorry."

"No," says Elle through blue lips. "Happy." Nothing but love shines in her bloodshot eyes.

I collapse onto my side and grasp her hand in mine. Elle's skin is so cold. If this is my end, at least it's with Elle.

A voice echoes across the studio.

"Stop!"

Suddenly, the cords fall free from Elle's throat. The diamond spear vanishes from my torso. I pat my chest, finding no wound.

In shock, I scan the studio. Who stopped this, exactly? I quickly spy the speaker.

It's the Queen of Hearts.

54. CHAPTER FIFTY-FOUR

ELLE

I pull in *gasp after gasp* of sweet air. At first, my head feels hazy. As I pull in more breath, my mind clears.

Did that really happen? Did the Queen of Hearts really just yell stop and free both me and Alec?

I reach out and pat Alec's chest. Sure enough, his wound has completely healed over. The only sign of Legend's attack is a hole in Alec's tuxedo jacket.

Speaking of Legend, he turns to the queen. Orbs of red magic and light appear on each of his outstretched palms.

The queen sniffs. "Really?" She snaps her fingers. The spheres of power vanish.

Legend isn't giving up, though. New and larger orbs materialize. The spheres glow bright red and hover just above his hands.

The queen rolls her eyes. "Enough." The queen reaches forward and grips at what looks like empty space.

It isn't.

As the queen pulls her arms back, the veil between this world and the Faerie Lands fade. To my eyes, the Le Center overlaps with a vision of a wide field of white grass. It's surrounded by a line of white trees with crimson leaves.

And there are warriors. Hundreds and hundreds of them. The queen's Vampire Guard.

The queen lowers her arm. The transformation completes. All signs of the L Center vanish. Everyone now stands in the clearing. The queen looms before us.

Is it just me, or does she seem taller now?

The queen waves her hand. "Guards."

The warriors fall out. Every caster and troll gets held down by at least a half dozen of the queen's warriors. Some try to fight or cast counter-spells. Nothing works. Soon our opposing army is now restrained, all except for one.

It's Charles. The Le Charme founder marches up to the queen.

"What's all this?" demands Charles. "We have a bargain."

At this point, something silky purrs by my ankle. Looking down, I find Chesh mewling at my side. I scoop him into my arms. "Your Majesty! Our quest is complete! We've found your cat!"

"We did?" asks Alec. He spies what's in my arms. "We did!"

In arms, Chesh licks his lips. "Gerry says hi."

Alec and I share a dry look. Gerry was totally the Cheshire cat all the time. What a stinker.

"How nice," states the queen. "Bring me my feline and you may claim your reward." She turns to Charles. "I'm sure you noticed what just happened here."

"Yes! You're a liar and oath breaker."

"No," says the queen sweetly. "I just won our bet."

My brows lift. She won the bet? Hoisting Chesh higher in my arms, I march over to the queen. Alec steps along at my side.

This'll be good.

55. CHAPTER FIFTY-FIVE

ALEC

*A*s we close in on the queen, Chesh leaps down from Elle's arms to sit by the queen's feet. For a long moment, Chesh licks his paws before addressing the queen.

"Oh, I was so frightened and lost," says Chesh. "Now I have been found. We should pay these two kind people."

"Agreed," says the queen. "And it's so nice to have you back, Chesh." She looks toward me and Elle. "You have found my cat and may claim your reward. Although you may have noticed I got started a little early."

Charles' face turns four shades of pink. "Reward?"

"I should have thought this was clear," says the queen. "I'm breaking the little curse that hangs over the house of Le Charme. Afterward, Elle and Alec can be together in any way they see fit."

In response, Legend tries to break free from his guards. "Impossible! No one can break the curse!"

The queen shoots Legend a sideways glance. "Quiet, you."

"This simply can not happen," adds Charles. "Ivy and Alec will be bonded tonight. You are magically contracted to perform the spell that will force them to get married."

"Time was, I would be." The queen smiles sweetly, but there's an edge of evil under her grin. "It's like this. Years ago, we made a bargain. You said you and your line could ignore love forever. And as long as you did, I would support you in forcing your offspring into loveless marriages.. and give you a comfortable life in the Faerie Lands."

Now, it's one thing to suspect your forebear traded your happiness for his own comfort. It's another to hear that crime confirmed out loud. No wonder Charles agreed to come back and help with the Le Charme Extravaganza and the Glass Slipper Ball.

"That was our bargain. You're breaking it."

The queen continues. "Now, I have folks come me all the time, begging for favors. So I leave my crown in an open hiding spot. You see, arrangements made with the desperate are hardly a challenge. A queen wants to face off with someone who has a spine."

"That's why you hid the crown," says Charles.

"Obviously," says the queen. "When you recovered my crown from the bottom of the Sienne, I thought you were a challenge worth taking. So I agreed to this bargain. And yes, I figured one of your offspring would surely fall in love. Yet hundreds of years passed with nothing but hateful weddings. It's been rather annoying." She sighs. "When it came to Legend, I thought I came close."

My father stops struggling against his guards. "Rae left me because of this damnable curse."

"No," counters the queen. "She left because you loved Le Charme more than her. But things have changed." The queen gestures toward Elle. "Imagine my joy when someone else finally uncovered my crown. Only true love would break my arrangement with Charles. Asking Elle and Alec to find Chesh was my way of testing the depth of their feeling." She looks to me. "Isn't that right?"

"Yes," I reply. "We didn't need to find the cat." I pull Elle against my side. "We needed to find each other. Fully."

"That's right. And so I have broken the agreement, the curse, whatever you want to call it."

Charles pales. "What about my eternity in the Faerie lands?"

"That will still happen," replies the queen. "Only that forever will take place in my dungeons."

"No!"

"Don't fret. You'll have lots of company." She whistles. "Guards! Take them all to my dungeons!"

One by one, the guards vanish, along with their prisoners. Which makes sense. All the guards are vampires. For shadowcoe, materializing and vanishing is just what they do.

As each so-called enemy blinks out of existence, my heart sinks. "Your Majesty," I say.

"Yes, Alec?"

"About my parents," I begin.

"And my stepfamily," adds Elle.

"As part of your reward, you may decide what to do with them all. Except Charles, of course. He's mine."

"Thank you." Elle and I speak in unison.

The queen scans the clearing and smiles. "Such a nice gathering. We have shifters, animates, dwarves, and my favorite Cinderella and prince."

Chesh's tail flicks slowly behind him. "We should have a proper party."

"Yes," says the queen. "I think we shall."

The Queen of Hearts snaps her fingers. Yet another spell launches into action. Something tells me this will be the best one of all.

56. CHAPTER FIFTY-SIX

ELLE

I curl more closely against Alec's side. The solidity of his form helps to ground me to this moment. Even so, none of this seems real. Minutes ago, Marchesa and Legend almost killed me and Alec.

And now?

The queen raises her arms. Mist and magic appear around her hands. Crimson light streams off her palms. The colored haze takes the form of so many red hearts that float into the air. Soon the sky fills with a shifting canopy of red hearts. The shapes burst in a flare of red light, sending crimson glitter tumbling to the ground.

The queen's spell is cast.

By the time the last of the sparkling magic touches the ground, the space is transformed. We still wait in a clearing of white trees and matching grass. Only now, it's nighttime. Candelabras line the space, casting a gentle glow onto the scene. A full fairy orchestra sits at one end of the clearing. The werewolves are back in their human form. All wear tuxedos and ball gowns. Even the dwarves and animates are in formalwear. My dress is back to perfection. All signs of tears are gone from Alec's jacket.

The queen scans her work and nods. "I do so love a happy ending."

At those words, the orchestra launches into a romantic tune. All eyes turn to me and Alec.

My prince falls to his knee. "Elle Cynder, will you dance with me?"

I smile so hard, my face hurts. And there really is only one answer to this particular question.

57. CHAPTER FIFTY-SEVEN

ALEC

I remain kneeling before my true love. Now, I've seen Elle grin before. Yet all those smiles are nothing compared to the way she now beams with joy.

"Yes," she replies. "I'd love to dance with you."

I pull my woman into my arms. We waltz to the gentle tune. As we dance about, happy faces fall into my range of vision. There's Bry and Knox, as well as the animates, dwarves and shifters. Everyone we love is held in one place, enjoying music and each other's company.

I lock gazes with Elle. At this point, there's only one more thing that could make tonight perfect.

"Yes?" I ask.

And just as she did back when we first entered the palace of the Queen of Hearts, Elle answers with a single word.

"Yes."

Pausing, I pull Elle into my arms and press my mouth against hers.

Pure bliss is mine.

58. CHAPTER FIFTY-EIGHT

ELLE

*O*ver the past week, I've had time to think through all the things I wanted to discuss with Alec. From playing Magicorum Killers and eating Bry's mystery meals to hiding my scary dolls and sitting in class... there were so many things I wanted to share.

I'd been keeping a running list.

There were even some things about my father's powers that I wanted to discuss. After all, gem casters like Alec know plenty of enchanter magic. I planned to ask him to teach me an enchanter casting or two.

But now? All that stuff melts from my mind. The only thing I sense is the way Alec's mouth moves against mine. And the touch of his tongue makes me realize one thing. For years, I've thought about everything I lost and lacked.

Yet, in this moment, what Alec and I have found is now enough for me.

No, it's more than that.

It's everything.

EPILOGUE

JACOBY - ONE MONTH LATER

I loathe visiting my family's castle in the Faerie Lands. The place is drafty and full of ghosts.

Not metaphorical ones, mind you, such as the types who slam doors or go *boo* in the night. I'm talking real spirits with opinions that they insist on sharing. Overall, I find it's best to do my business here and return to Earth as quickly as possible.

To that end, I step in my newest throne room. This was my late brother Frey's seat. As I cross the threshold, one thing becomes obvious.

The decor here is horrible.

Frey had an unhealthy interest in bull themes. Therefore, horns adorn the walls while a mosaic of charging bulls covers the floor. And the throne itself is coated in a rather putrid brown hide. I'm assuming that's a bull skin, but with my family, you never know.

My animate servant, Doc Eight, stomps in behind me. He was originally a suit of armor, so his steps are always noisy. "What a grim day, your Highness."

"It should be grim," I reply.

And it certainly was when my older brothers Abner, Barnaby, Cramley, Damascus, and Edwin died.

I inspect a set of horns stuck onto a nearby wall. Frey really did have the worst taste. And it concerned more than bulls, too. Frey had

CHRISTINA BAUER

a nasty habit of attempting to murder us brothers. Rude. The royal family has enough trouble with outsiders and assassinations.

"So not as grim this time?" asks Doc.

"Correct."

Doc shakes his head. Since he's an enchanted suit of armor, the movement involves a lot of squeaking noises. "I can't believe it," he says in his deep and echoing voice. "You're now fourth in line for the royal throne of dark elves." My parents were killed off years ago. Now it's a rotating line of brothers.

"Don't remind me," I state. "My family has a dismal record when it comes to life span. Now only Gorgan, Harold, and ..." I snap my fingers, trying to remember the name.

"Prince Ignatius."

"Right. Now only Gorgan, Harold, and Ignatius stand in line before me." I step closer to the very pungent throne. "Ah, well. Best to get it over with."

Now that Frey is dead, I must officially take over his seat. The process involves actually reclining on Frey's throne while saying a spell. After that, I shall return to Earth before I'm poisoned, shredded, or otherwise destroyed.

I take my throne and pull on my inner power. The room darkens. An electric sense of magic crackles in the air. "I, Prince Jacoby of the Dark Elves, do hereby acknowledge my new place in the line of accession."

"Is that all?" asks Doc. He knows there's a long version of this particular speech. To begin with, I have about twelve separate names and titles that I could add into the mix. Frey's not worth it, though.

"We're doing the short version today," I reply. "And thus endeth the spell." The room lightens. All sense of power fades from the air.

Time to return to Earth.

Speaking of the human realm, I still need to find a powerful wife to help keep me alive. Elle remains my top choice. She's a warden, nice to look at, and not yet wed to that Alec fellow. And, most importantly, I really don't care if she lives or dies.

That's the ticket to staying alive in the Faerie Lands: pleasant detachment.

Emotional entanglements are only a horrid waste of good energy. Other elves see your affection as weakness. And they're right. In short order, those feelings will be used to murder you in any number of ways.

Mother always said that she'd rather drink poison than fall in love. Both cause your death, yet only poison allows you to set the time and place.

A wise woman, my mother.

Knocks sound at the chamber door. I hadn't realized Doc had closed us in. It's a wise choice, though. No point being seen by relatives. Or anyone, really.

"Shall I check the door, my Prince?"

"Please do."

Every reception chamber has a hidden peephole for the outer hall. Doc marches right over to the one for this space. He really is extraordinarily efficient. I couldn't ask for more in a servant. Doc even pretends to be my boss when we are hiding out on earth. That isn't easy, once you know who I really am.

Doc removes an obliging bull horn from the wall. A small hole sits in the plaster. Doc looks through. "You have a group outside who wishes to speak with you."

"Assassins?"

"Not exactly."

Stepping down from my throne, I use the peep hole myself. A rather ragtag group waits in the outer hall. It's Marchesa, Agatha, Ivy, Diamond, and Legend. I'd heard they'd been pardoned from Queen of Hearts dungeon. So long as they are in the Faerie Lands, they may remain free.

I roll my eyes. Elle and Alec are really too soft-hearted, pardoning them all like that. Ah, well. If Elle becomes my bride, I'll have to educate her on the uses of sympathy. As in, there are none.

I reset the bull horn into its spot in the wall.

Doc tilts his metal helm. It's his silent way of asking. *Do you wish to see them?*

I'm about to say, *never*, but then I sense it.

A pulse of power.

In fact, it's the very magical signature I detected in Elle's bedroom. It's elvish and of unknown origin. I retake my stinky throne.

"Allow them in," I command.

The pack of supplicants spills into the room. Legend seems the self-appointed leader.

"We heard you'd returned to the Faerie Lands," says Legend. "We wished to see you."

It's an effort not to roll my eyes again. "Obviously."

Marchesa steps forward. "I hope you won't resent how we treated you back on Earth. We'd no idea who you really were."

Legend continues. "Imagine our surprise when we're released from the queen's dungeons, thinking we don't have a friend in the Faerie Lands. Then we discover who you really are!"

I sigh. "Is there a request you wish to make?" *Because this is taking way too long.*

"We want our lives back," says Legend. "Marchesa and I want to return to Earth and our rule over Le Charme Jewelers. Marchesa and her daughters desire their station restored at Cynder Mercantile. And we all need gold to support ourselves."

"And what do you offer in return?"

Marchesa steps forward. She pulls a small container from the folds of her cloak. "I can offer you this: the Coffer of Wonders. It could be aligned to the dark elves and give you whatever you need that day."

Interesting. "Show me."

Marchesa opens the box. There's a small pouf of smoke, followed by a scrap of paper flying out of the container. I pluck the tiny document from the air. "This provides the address for Kokkivo."

"Yes," confirms Marchesa. "No doubt, the coffer wishes us to bring the phoenix back to Cynder Mercantile."

"Does the coffer do such things often?"

"Absolutely," answers Marchesa. "The coffer offers excellent advice."

"And sometimes, it even provides a nice luncheon," adds Legend. "Isn't that right?"

"So delicious," confirms Marchesa.

I crumple the paper and drop it to the floor. "That's rather limited, isn't it? More bossy than actual help."

Legend lifts his chin. "We can offer you other things."

"Name it."

Legend bows low. "You'd have a promise of our eternal loyalty."

I laugh. "Not acceptable."

Once more, that pulse of power moves through the room. This time, the source is easily discerned.

Agatha.

Stepping down from my throne, I cross the floor and approach the girl. Like always, she wears a boxy dress, large hat, and wide sunglasses. I stop before her.

"Remove the hat and glasses, please."

Agatha does nothing. It isn't a *freezing of motion* that comes from fear. No, this girl's got some fight in her. Clearly, Agatha doesn't like being ordered around. The waves of elven power turn even more intense. I scan the other faces nearby. They can't detect a thing.

Who is this girl?

Stepping closer, I take care to gentle my voice. "Please."

Agatha removes both her glasses and hat. She has an aristocratic face with wise emerald eyes. Long waves of brown hair cascade down her back. I reach forward and slide some strands behind her ear. The feel of her skin sends a pleasant jolt through my chest. And my touch reveals something even more exciting.

No question about it. The tips of her ears point upwards. Agatha is an elf.

"I want them safe and taken care of," she whispers. I scan the room. No one heard her words.

Again, I wonder. *Who is this girl?*

I retake my throne. "I have reconsidered. Elle and Alec aren't married yet. For my own reasons, I do wish to break up that relationship. Am I right in assuming we share that goal?"

"Oh, yes," gushes Legend. "That's exactly what we *all* wish!"

While Legend speaks, Diamond takes a pointed step away from the group. It's a small movement that speaks volumes. Alec's mother may be a problem for this particular scheme. Something to consider later on.

"What is your plan?" asks Marchesa. "What can we do to help?"

"You can stay here in the Faerie Lands and stay out of my way. But I do need your consent that I take one of your daughters back with me to the human realm. Consider it a sign of your support."

"Of course," says Marchesa. "You have my agreement. My daughters are yours."

A small grin rounds my mouth. Marchesa should never agree so quickly to anything with a resident of the Faerie Lands. I speak a single word. "Excellent."

"You'll take Ivy with you, of course." Marchesa pushes her eldest daughter forward. "If you wish to break up Elle and Alec, Ivy is the one to do it."

"I'll take Agatha," I state.

"What?" Marchesa gasps. "You must take Ivy."

"I must do whatever I want. You already promised both your daughters to me. " I crook my finger toward Agatha.

A smile quirks the girl's mouth as she steps closer. "You have a request for me?"

A request. She even talks like a royal.

"Yes," I state. "How do you fancy working in an Earth store with me and Doc Eight?" I tap my chin. "On second thought, don't bother answering. You're going with me. Now."

With the blink of an eye, I cast a spell to transport me, Doc, and Agatha back to the human realm.

I haven't been this intrigued in years.

—*The End*—

The adventure continues in BANDITS AND BALL GOWNS (Magicorum #5)!

ALSO BY CHRISTINA BAUER

BANDITS AND BALL GOWNS

The story of Elle, Alec, Jacoby, and Agatha continues in BANDITS AND BALL GOWNS (Magicorum #5)!

ANGELBOUND

Check out ANGELBOUND, the kick-ass paranormal romance with more than 1 million copies sold!

DIMENSION DRIFT

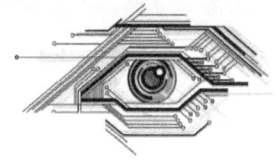

A kick-ass heroine + a swoon-worthy prince + an all-girl heist = the DIMENSION DRIFT series!

BEHOLDER

Medieval mages ... Slow-burn love ... And heart-pounding action! Check out the BEHOLDER series!

PIXIELAND DIARIES

PIXIELAND DIARIES tells the story of sassy pixie Calla and 'her' elf prince, Dare.

DESCRIPTION - BANDITS AND BALLGOWNS

One Prince Finds True Love ... *And Risks It All*

*E*lle Cynder has fallen hard for Alec, the 'prince' of Le Charme Jewelers. Time for some *happily* in their *ever after*, right?

Not so much.

While the new couple shares joyful moments--and sizzling kisses--serious trouble is brewing. Elle's evil stepmother, Marchesa, schemes with none other than Alec's twisted father, Legend. Their plan? Destroy Elle and Alec, along with everything the young lovers hold dear, including Bry, Knox, and Wilhelm.

Another Royal Freezes His Heart ... *But For How Long?*

As a prince of the dark fae, Jacoby focuses on one goal: avoid assassination. Marrying Elle would certainly aid in that cause, considering how she's both a Cinderella life template and a powerful fae warden. Even better, Jacoby doesn't truly love Elle. In court life, deep romantic attachments only mean certain death.

Then Jacoby notices Elle's youngest stepsister, Agatha.

For the first time in his life, Jacoby's cold heart warms with true affection. The elven prince struggles to ignore his feelings, but it might be a losing battle. And what would the prince's newfound emotions mean for Elle and Alec? Could Jacoby really stand by and watch another's true love be destroyed?

Buckle up for a wild ride as Cinderella's time-honored story gets some all-new twists.

~

Order BANDITS AND BALL GOWNS (Magicorum #5)!

SAMPLE CHAPTER - BANDITS AND BALLGOWNS

ELLE - MANHATTAN

"*E*lle, Elle, we want Elle!"

Loud voices wrench me out of deep sleep. Jamming my pillow over my head, I try muffling the noise. *No go.* More ear-splitting yells come through, loud and clear.

"Elle, Elle, we want Elle!"

What a coincidence. I want to punch you all in the throat for waking me up.

No question who's breaking my personal sound barrier. Enchanted humans are marching outside my apartment building. *Again.* All while screaming my name. *Again.*

"Come out, Elle! We want you!"

It isn't clear what they'd *do* with me if they ever *got* me. I can't imagine it's anything good.

None of this is a surprise, by the way. For weeks, these supernatural stalkers have been drawn to me like subway rats to a dropped Egg McMuffin. It's because I'm Magicorum, meaning I'm one of the lucky folks whose future is locked into a *fairy tale life template*. In my case, that's Cinderella.

The chanting starts up once more. "Elle, Elle, we want our Cindereeeeeeeeeella!"

Sadly, whatever's happening here is related to the dark side of my fairy tale life template. Being Cinderella isn't just ball gowns and glass slippers. There's a reason it's called the *Grimm's Fairy Tales*, not the *Chipper Funtime Stories*. When magic gets into the mix, stuff turns ugly. Humans become enchanted. Shouting is involved. I eventually lose a shoe. You get the idea.

Not that I worry about it too much. I take my Cinderella-ness, kick it in the ass and call it a bitch. *Boom.*

Case in point. You may wonder how someone like me—meaning an eighteen-year old with a crappy life template—can afford my own apartment in Manhattan. Short answer: To make ends meet, I un-steal jewelry and run the occasional con. Don't judge. Fairy tale life templates are the pits.

"Elle! Get out here Eeeeeeeeeeeeelle!"

Wow, they're really yappy this morning. That gets me curious. Rolling over, I peep through my window and scan the sidewalk below. Since my apartment is twenty stories up, I have the perfect view. Today, about thirty humans mill around the concrete. In most ways, they're typical New Yorkers. I count adults of all ages, sizes and nationalities. What makes this group unique is how their eyes all glow with a magical orange light. It's a look that says, *guess what? I'm totally possessed.* At least, that's how it appears to *moi*. Other humans can't detect anything strange about my stalkers. They're unable to even hear the chanting fiesta.

Suddenly, azure light flares beneath my bedroom door. A heavy charge fills the air, along with the faintest hint of ozone. *That would be a spell.* And based on the particular shade of sparkly blue which peeps across my carpet? Someone just magically transported them-selves into the hallway outside my bedroom.

Unlike the stalkers, this is a good thing. Being Magicorum means more than getting dragged into a fairy tale future. We also wield the power of either witches, fae or shifters. In my case, I'm a fairy. And with my knowledge of the supernatural, I know exactly who just transported into my hallway: Alec Le Charme, expert warlock, prince of a jewelry empire, and (as of six weeks ago) my boyfriend. Cue angelic choir.

Gentle knocks sound. "Elle? It's Alec." His voice has the low rasp of a sleepy guy. So cute. "Time to study your enchanted humans again."

Joy bubbles up inside me. "Come on in."

The door swings open. Today, Alec's the definition of charming with his sleepy eyes, muscular frame, low hanging jeans and white T-shirt. Alec is also barefoot, which absolutely kills me. I'm such a sucker for *hot guy feet.*

Alec pauses on the threshold. "What's today's variety?" No question what he means here. Alec is obsessed with my PJ collection.

I gesture across my torso. "Dancing yetis."

He shakes his head. "Where do you find these?"

I bob my brows. "I have my ways."

The world seems to collapse until it's just me and Alec. An electric sense of awareness pulses between us. Since Alec is my first kiss, he insists that we take things slowly in the romance department. That said, if Alec gets anywhere near me right now, I'm tackling him, linebacker-style.

Alec shoots me a sly grin. He absolutely knows what I'm thinking. "Are you open for dinner this evening, by any chance?"

"Let me check." I look around the room as if my schedule's written on the walls. "Why, yes. I happen to be available. My roomie is off on an adventure."

"What a coincidence," says Alec. "My roommate is away as well." Alec lives with Knox, who's dating my own roomie, Bry. Both are gone on a secret quest that's led by none other than the Magicorum's most famous dragon shifter, a fae named Colonel Mallory the Magnificent. Also joining them is a mysterious fairy, the Queen of Hearts.

And did I mention that their mission is a total mystery? *It is.* I don't even know when Bry and company will return. Major bummer.

Across the room, Alec plunks onto his favorite chair. "I brought my notebook." To accent this point, Alec waves the leather volume I gave him weeks ago. The cover reads, *Operation Bag The Baddie.*

Here's what we've figured out so far. Someone's enchanting humans to march underneath my window. Since I'm a Cinderella life template, the driving force behind this ugliness *should* be my evil stepfamily. But Marchesa, Ivy and Agatha are all in exile. That's why Alec and I are on the hunt for the real culprits. By tracking *what* happens and *when* with my stalkers, we figure a clue is bound to show up eventually.

Alec holds up his pen. "Let's start with messages. How many signs are the humans holding? What do the words actually say?"

Leaning my forehead against the glass pane, I make some quick calculations. "Thirty-three humans are traipsing around down there. Sixteen carry signs. All say the same thing. *Pick a new prince, Elle!"*

Six weeks ago, Alec and I started dating at the world-famous Glass Slipper Ball. For some reason, my human stalkers want me to find a new boyfriend.

Meh. They can stick it.

Alec scribbles on the sheet before him. "That makes two-hundred and forty-seven times that sign has appeared in the last six weeks. It's your most popular message."

"Whoever's casting this spell, they want you gone."

"I'd like to see them try and get rid of me." Alec's eyes light up with fire and determination. Waves of power and magic roll off him, filling the room with his presence.

Tackling is definitely becoming an attractive option again.

Stay focused, Elle.

I look down at the sidewalk once more. A different face appears in the mix of enchanted humans. This new woman stands out for two reasons. First, she's dressed up as a sheriff from the Old West. That doesn't happen often, even in New York. Second, her eyes are regular blue instead of glowing orange.

In my personal stalker history, that's never happened before. Enchanted humans are their own bubble of strangeness. No one without orange eyes gets anywhere near them. Yet this sheriff stands right in the middle of the pack.

Could it be a clue?

I scooch closer to the windowpane and try for a better look. But when I check again, the mysterious woman is gone.

Alec snaps his notebook shut. "Sadly, I have to run."

"More Le Charme fun?"

Alec rolls his eyes. "Welcome to my new life of suck."

Here's what that means. My family isn't the only one in exile. Alec's parents, Diamond and Legend, also got chucked off into the Faerie Lands. *Good riddance.* Since then, Alec has become the new CEO of Le Charme. It's as much fun as it sounds.

"Good luck with that," I state. "Go meet the people. Sign the things. Crush the lesser jewelry guys. Woot."

"And so I shall. But not until I'm certain you've safely arrived at West Lake Prep. These enchanted humans worry me." Alec offers me his hand. "May I transport you to school, Milady?"

What a man. Alec runs a multinational company while finishing off his high school degree online. In other words, he's a super-busy guy. That's why it means the world to me how—even with so much happening—Alec still wants to transport my butt around.

With that realization, warmth and love radiate through my soul. My affection swells so high, I totally give up on my *not-tackling plan.* Crossing the room, I wrap my arms around Alec's neck. His skin feels warm and smooth under my touch. As our bodies press together, excitement swirls within me. Going on tiptoe, I press my mouth to Alec's. His lips are soft and firm; our connection sends a slow burn through my core.

I smile into our kiss. "I'll take you up on that transport spell."

"Can you be ready in twenty?"

"You know it."

"Good."

Alec steps away, reaches into his pocket and pulls out a huge sapphire. Magical gems are how wizards like Alec enact their spells. Using that stone, my boyfriend will transport back to his own apartment. Alec lifts his fist. As he begins his spell, blue light shines between his fingers. Tiny points of sapphire-colored brightness rise from his hand and then multiply. Soon it looks as if Alec is surrounded by a column of miniature shooting stars.

Alec's pillar of brightness flares with more power. A moment later, Alec is gone.

But I know he'll return. Alec gave his word.

NEW APPENDIX OF AWESOME GOODIES

ON ASH MAIDEN, AKA THE ORIGINAL CINDERELLA

When I was nine years old, I got my hands on a copy of Grimm's Fairy Tales from the 1890's. It had a pretty red embossed cover; it had lovely woodcut illustrations; it had gruesome stories that were freaking terrifying.

I loved it instantly.

Thanks to this wonderfully nasty book, I got to know the original fairy tales in all their pre-Disney horror. Few of the stories had happy endings. Snow White, for example, was a dumbass who kept taking obviously-dangerous gifts from her stepmother until a pair of shoes danced her to death. The moral? *Use your brain, twirp.* There won't always be a huntsman around to save your pretty face.

Ash Maiden was one of the few tales that ended well, but for one simple reason: Ash Maiden (what was later Disney-fied into Cinderella) worked her tuchus off... And not in the *sweeping the floors with happy rodents* way that we think about today. Yeah, you read that right. Ash Maiden's main challenge in life was NOT boring chores, her mean step-mother, or ugly step-sisters. Bizarre, huh?

Here's the shocker (to me anyway): in the original story, Ash Maiden's big problem was that she lost her mother and had grief work to do. And no, I am not kidding.

Don't get me wrong; our lovely lady worked hard. She was forced to sleep in the ashes and given a not-so-clever nickname. But Ash Maiden didn't weep every day because she had chores to finish or teasing to endure. She cried because she missed her Mom. It was mourning that drove Ash Maiden to plant a seed in her mother's memory. Every day, she'd find time to be alone and cry, her teardrops falling on the tiny seed until, bit by bit, it grew into a massive tree.

SIDE NOTE: This is something I love about the original Grimm's fairy tales. No easy answers. People had to empty lakes with thimbles, stay trapped in animal-form for centuries, or cry on a seed until it grew into a huge goddamn tree. Got problems? Shut up and grab a thimble, bitch.

Back to the story. For those of you who've lost a loved one, you know what Ash Maiden was going through at this point: the valley of the shadow of death, one tear at a time. And Ash Maiden's ball gown? Fell out of *that freaking tree*, along with her famous shoes. In *that tree* perched a bird that led her to her Prince. There was no fairy godmother, no quick fix. It was this young girl's unflinching bravery in facing her sorrow that brought about positive change in her life... and that thought inspired me.

Once I began writing my first book, ANGELBOUND, I decided it would include action, adventure, and romance. However, I wanted all of that to be secondary to the central story of someone coming to terms with their relationship with their mother. In this case, a mother who was in some ways 'dead' (I can't say more without spoilers). That theme continues with SLIPPERS AND THIEVES as well.

From a storytelling standpoint, this was a huge risk for me as a writer. Many YA stories are about the heroine realizing they have some kind of power they never expected or earned, like the immunity to paranormal mind-reading, magical abilities and so on. To me, that's symbolic of one kind core YA experience: that of changing from a child into a woman. The idea is that suddenly (and without any effort on your part) you have sexual power. This is something you may never have seen coming, and it can be a trial to deal with it. That is very different from heading out on a quest to come to terms with something, like what Ash Maiden did.

The latter kind of story captured my imagination, and I've been off off and running ever since.

$\mathcal{T}$HE THREE WORST FAIRY TALES IN THE HISTORY OF EVER, IMHO

Three. Princess and the Frog

In this story, the princess is a witch-with-a-b who chucks a defenseless amphibian against a wall. Not okay. She's then *rewarded* for this violent behavior (I'm making finger quotes while typing *rewarded*) by getting a prince. Eew, eew, eew.

Two. Princess and the Pea

Here the so-called princess is identified by her ability to whine about bedding. Acting like a high-maintenance guest should not be equated with royalty. That's just being a douchebag.

One. Goldilocks

This is another tale that I place in the category of *high-maintenance behavior mistaken as cool*. Breaking and entering is against the law, end of story. If one is in need of support, then it's appropriate to wait *outside the home* for the family to return before helping yourself to their shit.

THREE SUPER-COOL FAIRY TALES THAT I ADORE

Three. Athena

This one is more of a myth than a fairy tale, but this is my list, so *nyah*. Athena is the Greco-Roman goddess of war. Even though she is the only deity (other than Zeus) who can wield the infamous thunderbolt, she normally uses clever ruses to defeat her opponents instead. That's class.

Two. Isis

The Isis myth was a top story in northern Africa for more than 40,000 years. Its lessons even informed ancient Egypt, a culture that survived 3000 years (that's more than ten times longer than the US, for those who are counting.) The tale is all about doing the right thing over materialism. YES! I write about Isis in more detail here.

Three. Cinderella

This is my all-time favorite story and I adore the Grimm's Fairy Tale version. In the original, Cinderella gets her own ass to the ball. No fairy godmothers involved. I adore this take on the character and definitely was inspired by that approach when writing my own Cinderella book.

Yay, Elle!

MY CINDERELLA PLAYLIST

*H*ere's what I listened to while writing SLIPPERS AND THIEVES!

One. The Wallflowers – One Headlight

First of all, how cute is Bob Dylan's son, AKA the lead singer of the Wallflowers? So cute. In fact, Jakob Dylan is an inspiration for another character of mine, Rhodes, who's both a dragon shifter and a guitar player (in the Angelbound Offspring series).

But I digress.

This particular tune has a line that goes: "me and Cinderella, we put it all together." Every time I'd hear this song in years past, I'd think, *damn! One day I got to write me a version of Cinderella*. And now, it's here! Yay!

Two. Elastica – Connection

To me, this song is all about the in-your-face feeling when you really connect with another person. In particular, this tune inspired me while writing the scene where Alec Le Charme first sees Elle Cynder. BOOM!!!!

Three. Lady Gaga – Paparazzi

This one was another inspiration for Alec Le Charme. As a celebrity, Alec's life involves a lot of dealing with press and fans. As this song hints, being in the public eye can attract some real kooks! As lyrics go, *Paparazzi* is right up there with Sting's *Every Breath You Take* as a true stalker anthem.

Four. Destiny's Child – Survivor

This song may be on virtually every book playlist that I create. It's just the best anthem for chicks kicking ass while still keeping their dignity and kindness. I want my characters to be strong, not douchebags. It's easy to cross the line and this tune helps me stay on track.

So there you have it – my playlist for SLIPPERS AND THIEVES!

ON MY AUNT SANDY

*A*ll my books are dedicated to my aunt Sandy and uncle Henry. Their story is something I kept in my heart until I saw headlines about the downfall of Bill Cosby. For whatever reason, that made me ready to discuss a major (there's no other word for it) catastrophe of my life.

Here goes.

My dear aunt Sandy, the woman who inspired me to write (she was a poet), was murdered by my uncle Henry when I was 22. This was three months after uncle Henry shared that his new doctor okayed him to go cold turkey on what he called his seizure meds. After he shot Sandy, Henry killed himself.

I cried every day for a year after they both died. Seven years went by before I saw a day pass without my actively mourning them. I still feel hollowed out by the experience.

Back to Bill Cosby. Many folks have fond memories of him. His work with *Fat Albert* and the *Cosby Show* were important and ground breaking. Even so, he did terrible things that mean he should definitely rot in jail. How do you reconcile them?

If my experience is any guide, then you don't reconcile, not really. It's no longer okay to idolize someone with that level of fault. But you can't ignore the good, either. For me, my aunt and uncle's attention to me and my writing saved my life in a truly horrible time (a catastrophe story for another day). Although the change in meds may have driven Henry off the rails---and may provide some reasons for his actions---that's still conjecture on my part. The guy could also have been a major asshole all the way around. Chances are, it was a combination of ending meds and toxic masculinity.

Over the years, I've come to cherish the good in my uncle and recognize the bad. It isn't fair to idolize Henry as I used to. Even so, I can't lump him in with thoroughly evil people. The man still dedicated himself to helping a chubby pre-teen girl gain some self esteem. In terms of my aunt Sandy, she stays on her pedestal for all eternity, end of story.

I suppose that's why I like my good folks awesome and my big bads super-evil. Real life is tricky. It's nice to take a break from reality, and nowhere is better for that than in a book. Plus, if I can share my fantasy break with someone else? Bonus.

To sum up, I guess that's my biggest lesson for when superbad shit happens: focus on turning it into a positive. I write every day thanks to my aunt and uncle. It's how I cope. Share. Reconcile. And the mourning doesn't end, but it somehow has ended up creating joy.

All in all, that's a very good thing indeed.

STANDARD APPENDIX OF STUFF THAT'S STILL PRETTY COOL

IF YOU ENJOYED THIS BOOK...

...Please consider leaving a review, even if it's just a line or two. Every bit truly helps, especially for those of us who don't *write by the numbers,* if you know what I mean.

Plus I have it on good authority that every time you review an indie author, somewhere an angel gets a mocha latte. For reals.

And angels need their caffeine, too.

ACKNOWLEDGMENTS

If you're reading my freaking acknowledgements, chances are, I should thank you for something. So, for the record: you are awesome, dear reader.

That said, huge and heartfelt thanks must go out to my husband and son for their rock-solid support. Being an author means a lot of early mornings, late nights, long weekends, and never-ending patience. You two are the best guys in the universe, period.

After that, I must thank the extensive network of reviewers, friends and colleagues who helped me build my writing chops in general. Gracias.

Finally, deep affection goes out to my late, much loved, and dearly missed Aunt Sandy and Uncle Henry. You saw the writer in me, always. Thank you, first and last.

COLLECTED WORKS

Fairy Tales of the Magicorum
Modern fairy tales with sass, action, and romance
1. Wolves and Roses
2. Moonlight and Midtown
3. Shifters and Glyphs
4. Slippers and Thieves
5. Bandits and Ball Gowns
6. Fairies and Frosting

Angelbound Origins
About a quasi (part demon and part human) girl who loves kicking butt in Purgatory's Arena
1. Angelbound
2. Scala
3. Acca
4. Thrax
5. The Dark Lands
6. The Brutal Time
7. Armageddon
8. Quasi Redux
9. Clockwork Igni

Angelbound Offspring

The next generation takes on Heaven, Hell, and everything in between
1. Maxon
2. Portia
3. Zinnia
4. Rhodes
5. Kaps
6. Mack
7. Huntress

Angelbound Lincoln

The Angelbound experience as told by Prince Lincoln
1. Duty Bound
2. Lincoln
3. Trickster
4. Baculum
5. Angelfire

Pixieland Diaries

Sassy pixie Calla loves elf prince Dare. Too bad he hasn't noticed her. Yet.
1. Pixieland Diaries
2. Calla
3. Dare
4. Winter Prince
5. Ley Queen

Dimension Drift

Dystopian adventures with science, snark, and hot aliens
1. Scythe
2. Umbra
3. Alien Minds
4. ECHO Academy
*This is a completed series.

Beholder

Where a medieval farm girl discovers necromancy and true love
1. Cursed

This is a completed series.

ABOUT CHRISTINA BAUER

Christina Bauer thinks that fantasy books are like bacon: they just make life better. All of which is why she writes romance novels that feature demons, dragons, wizards, witches, elves, elementals, and a bunch of random stuff that she brainstorms while riding the Boston T. Oh, and she includes lots of humor and kick-ass chicks, too. Christina lives in Newton, MA with her husband, son, and semi-insane golden retriever, Ruby.

Stalk Christina on Social Media

Blog:

http://monsterhousebooks.com/blog/category/christina

Facebook:
https://www.facebook.com/authorBauer/

Instagram:
https://www.instagram.com/christina_cb_bauer/

Twitter:
@CB_Bauer

VLOG:
https://tinyurl.com/Vlogbauer

Web site:
www.bauersbooks.com

COMPLIMENTARY BOOK

Get a FREE novella when you sign up for Christina's newsletter:
https://tinyurl.com/bauersbooks

BEVERLY HILLS VAMPIRE

A NOVELLA BY
CHRISTINA BAUER

AUTHOR'S NOTE

Welcome to the end of the book! If you've read this far, then maybe you're interested in some extra background on this story. Here goes!

I loved the Cinderella myth growing up. LOVED. As in, I pretty much played Barbie Cinderella non-stop. And when you replay something a million times, you start to notice where the gaps are. Here are some of the questions that (seriously) haunted me from my youth:

When Cinderella's parents die, how does her stepfamily make a living? Her father was a merchant. If he stopped doing his thing, how did the bills get paid?

Who was the stepmother? In this I mean, how did the stepfather meet her? I didn't picture her as another merchant, so it must have been that she was part of the same social set. If so, wouldn't the stepmother know Cinderella's birth mother?

Why didn't Cinderella DO SOMETHING about her crappy situation? She could make clothes for mice and clean houses, so she clearly had marketable skills.

Plus, what was up with the fairy godmother? Nice to show up for the ball, but what about when her parents died? It seems like the godmotherly to have done would be to at least send a card. Showing up the night before the ball with fashion tips is a little thin.

And finally, why does the Prince have to be so wimpy? He's about to become king one day and yet allows himself get bossed into this *ball-for-a-bride* deal. Every country has problems. What are the ones facing his realm? How will going to kick ass and take names ... with his new partner at his side?

Those are a lot of questions to answer, and I couldn't fit them all into one book. Hence why there's another Elle and Alec story, BANDITS AND BALL GOWNS.

There's more I wanted to do with this story than fill in some missing world building. If I've done my job right, this tale is about finding your authentic self and facing some real-world problems. I like my romantic partners to team up and take problems down. In that department, there's a lot more to come from Elle and Alec!

ANOTHER-NOTHER AUTHOR'S NOTE

This marks the second edition of SLIPPERS AND THIEVES. Huzzah! Here's what's changed:

1. I fixed a ton of type-os

2. I changed the cover to a picture of Marchesa (I'm redoing all the covers in this series... wait until you see what comes next with the revised one for BANDITS AND BALL GOWNS!)

3. I added an extra appendix of goodies, WOOT WOOT!

That's it. Hope you enjoyed the book!

~